DIRTY SOUTH

ALSO BY ACE ATKINS

Dark End of the Street

Leavin' Trunk Blues

Crossroad Blues

ACE ATKINS

DIRTY SOUTH

WILLIAM MORROW *wm* *An Imprint of* Harper Collins*Publishers*

Grateful acknowledgment is made to reprint the following lyrics from:
"It's Too Late Brother," written by Al Duncan. © Al Duncan Music Company (BMI). Administered by Bug. All Rights Reserved. Used by permission.
"Grown Man," written by D. Carter and B. Thomas. © 2000 Money Mack Music. All Rights Reserved.

HarperCollins books may be purchased for educational, business, or sales promotional use. For information please write: Special Markets Department, HarperCollins Publishers Inc., 10 East 53rd Street, New York, NY 10022.

FIRST EDITION

Printed on acid-free paper

Library of Congress Cataloging-in-Publication Data
Atkins, Ace.
Dirty South / Ace Atkins.—1st ed.
p. cm.
ISBN 0-06-000462-2
1. Delta (Miss. : Region)—Fiction. 2. New Orleans (La.)—Fiction. 3. Blues musicians—Fiction. 4. Musicologists—Fiction. 5. Mississippi—Fiction. I. Title.
PS3601.T487D57 2003
813'.54—dc21 2003053982

---

04 05 06 07 08 WBC/RRD 10 9 8 7 6 5 4 3 2 1

For my mom and sister,

"Ain't nothin' like family."

Ain't no needa go no further, brother.
Ain't no needa go no further, man.
Tole you packin' .45
You had better quit that jive.

LITTLE WALTER (B. LOUISIANA, 1930)

⚜

I ride DL into the CL,
gun right in my grip.
I slip a clip in every rip,
cause hatas likely to trip.

LIL WAYNE (B. LOUISIANA, 1981)

Acknowledgments

Thank you: Master P, Joseph L. Porter, BET's *106th and Park,* Dashiell Hammett, Lil Wayne, Polk Salad Annie, John D. MacDonald, Mystikal, Blind Willie's, *XXL,* Louis Armstrong, the late, great Hummingbird Grill, and the Pirate's Alley Faulkner Society.

Special thanks to Keith Wehmeier, Debbi Eisenstadt, Tim Green, Jere Hoar, Laura Lippman, Ted O'Brien, Keith Spera, Tom Piazza, Kline Sack, and Randy Wayne White.

Carolyn, thank you for always being a friend to Nick, understanding the cooler parts of Southern culture, and making sure everything is the best it can be. And a big thanks to RP in NYC for being a terrific friend and reader and for taking care of his people.

An extra special thank you to Van Humber Robertson for saving a story from disaster.

None of this would be possible without Angela—my muse, fellow barbecue connoisseur, and best friend.

DIRTY SOUTH

Prologue

I SPED ALONG HIGHWAY 61, darting from one small town in the Mississippi Delta to the next with nothing but my old army duffel bag and CDs of blues singers I spent my life researching. Two weeks on the road from New Orleans and still nothing to show for it. I drove back to Clarksdale on a spring afternoon where heat broke in gassy waves from the pavement to find my old buddy JoJo. He was waiting for me when I arrived, a sack lunch filled with cold fried chicken sandwiches and potato salad. Loretta waved to us from the porch of their old farmhouse. Large and brown, she squinted into the white-hot sun, knowing I had to get back to New Orleans by Friday and that only JoJo could help me.

"This man doesn't like white people," JoJo said, unwrapping our sandwiches and rolling down the side window to my 1970 Bronco. He was a black man in his late sixties, white hair, short mustache. Wisdom around the eyes.

"No, sir."

"You think bringin' along a black man will help?"

"Yes, sir."

"You think 'cause he know me from the day might help, too."

"Yes, sir."

"He's eighty years old," JoJo said. "He may think I'm Jesus or Harvey the goddamn rabbit."

"There is a possibility of that," I said.

Hot breeze. Black birds cawed and screamed at stop signs at crossroads hanging in the pine and oak. Mimosa trees surrounded barns faded to a dull red and trailers lay on piles of concrete blocks. Gas stations out of the 1930s turned to Quickie Marts with long humming coolers filled with frozen candy bars and Cokes. Soft white bread. Stale peanuts.

"He was a good guitar player," JoJo said. "Sonny Boy liked him. Sonny Boy said he made him sound real fine."

"How long has he been in Marks?"

"Bronco says he heard he'd been in Marks since '72."

"What's he do?"

"Carve the faces of dead people."

We rolled along Highway 6 talking about old times at the bar JoJo used to own in New Orleans. It was a beautiful little place before it burned. A little cove on Conti Street with brick walls and a long mahogany bar dented and scarred from elbows and cold Dixie bottles. Loretta sang there every Friday and Saturday. During the week, she cooked. She made soul jambalaya and a mean batch of gumbo. JoJo and Loretta took care of me then. They were still my family.

We passed over a small metal bridge running over a creek and by a junkyard filled with hundreds of rusting cars. The creek had flooded into the ditch where the cars sat in stagnant water, reaching over their hoods and suffocating them in the green muck.

We talked about Robert Johnson and Lee Marvin. Bessie Smith and Earl Long.

JoJo told me about his corn crop coming up and a new John Deere tractor he bought and how he did not miss the bar he'd run for as long as I'd been alive.

"It's still there."

"Fuck it," he said.

We rolled into Marks at sundown. A broken-down collection of gas stations and abandoned buildings stood around an old church and a graveyard. I had to slow down to miss a couple of wandering dogs, skinny and coated in mange. I put on some Robert Johnson and I told JoJo about Johnson coming to a juke joint in Marks in the thirties. He played guitar for Son House and Willie Brown with his new skills he'd acquired from a man named Ike Zinnerman in Hazlehurst. Son House said Johnson had sold his soul to the devil to get those skills.

We found an old black man on his porch, eating purple-hulled peas and cornbread and listening to Z. Z. Hill. JoJo got out of the truck with me and we asked him about where we could find a man who called himself Tip-Top. JoJo said his real name was Bob and that he liked to carve dead people.

The man pointed down the hill where some dogs gathered to eat a rooster that had been killed. At the end of the road, the sun was a dropping orange orb that looked as if, if you kept following the road for a mile, you could touch it. Walk into its big burning fire.

"How's Maggie?" JoJo asked as we headed up the hill.

"Good."

"This one gonna last?"

"Maybe."

I parked on a gravel road and walked with a couple dogs trailing me. JoJo walked by my side whistling a little Muddy Waters song. The porch had been screened in, the front door hanging loose by its hinges. Wood shavings littered the buckled floor. Two pinewood coffins. New and fresh smelling. The sound of a television inside. Canned TV laughter.

"What's he watchin'?"

We heard the familiar *Love Boat* theme song.

"Always liked that woman who ran the cruise," JoJo said.

"Julie McCoy."

"Yeah, she looked like a nice lady."

"She liked the cocaine," I said.

JoJo nodded. He wasn't thrilled about Julie's coke problems.

The door opened after a knock. An old black man strapping himself into a pair of overalls eyed us. He fixed up the strap on his shoulder. His left eye twitched. "You the man lookin' for me?"

"You Tip-Top?" JoJo asked.

He nodded.

"This man don't want to do you no harm," JoJo said. "Wants to know about you and Sonny Boy."

Tip-Top looked at JoJo. "I know you," he said.

"I know." JoJo walked off the porch and began to play fetch with a few of the dogs. I asked the man if he would mind sitting on the porch and letting me record him for a project I was working on about Sonny Boy. I told him I was a professor at Tulane University and was working with the University of Mississippi about the great harp player.

"Sonny Boy was a motherfucker who stole my whiskey and my women and once took a piss in my boot. I spent half my life tryin' to forget about the Goat. Now you leave me be. Got work to do."

He slammed his door and I heard the canned laughter of *Love Boat*.

JoJo kept playing with the dogs. He kept his eyes on one in particular, rubbing the dog's head. She was of questionable breeding, somewhere a German shepherd in the mix, with long drooping ears and a curved tail.

"Look at her," he said. "She ain't no more than a pup. Smart. Look at her watchin' me."

JoJo walked back to the truck and grabbed some chicken from the sandwich he hadn't finished. He fed the dog. "I don't like people who don't take care of their dogs. Show they're evil. I know you tryin' to find this man 'cause he got some stories about Sonny Boy. But he evil if he let a fine dog like this get all skin and bones."

I heard a screen door slam behind the old shotgun house. I followed a dusty trail behind it and saw Tip-Top working a planer on top of a casket. A life-size dummy—some kind of stuffed black suit with a face made out of wood—watched from a lounge chair nearby.

I walked over to Tip-Top, moving my hand to the back of the dummy's head. I wanted to do Señor Wences or even the Parkay margarine ad. "Friend of Charlie McCarthy?"

"Don't know no Charlie."

"Listen, man," I said. "Give me twenty minutes. Heard you were with Sonny Boy at his last gig in Tutwiler. Something happened with a bottle of gin."

"He threw it at me."

"Will you tell me about it?"

"Why do you want to know these things?"

"I write about the blues."

He kept planing. A steady *thump, thump.*

"The world don't make no sense," he said. "The blues is dead."

"I don't think so."

Thump, thump.

"JoJo brought some whiskey," I said.

He stopped planing.

Thirty minutes later, he was drunk, had told the story, and JoJo had bought the dog from him for five dollars. JoJo liked to joke but didn't joke with Tip-Top. When he was through making the deal, he found some rope to put around the dog's neck and waited for me by the old truck that my friends called the Gray Ghost.

"We was in this church," Tip-Top said. "Down where he buried now. And it was still a church then. And he sat in there all night askin' God to let him die. He walked outside in this thunderstorm. I was too drunk to move and he kept cursin' God."

I wrote down some notes. Asked a few more questions. It was the story I needed to finish the piece.

"They pay you for doin' this?"

"Yes."

"Don't seem like an honest living."

"It's not," I said. "Thanks."

JoJo loaded up the new dog in the truck and she curled into a seat behind us, yawning. "We need to get her some water down the road."

"What you gonna call her?" I asked.

"Don't matter to me," JoJo said. "It's your dog."

"No way."

"You need a dog," he said. "Every man needs a dog."

"Where's she gonna piss in New Orleans?"

"There are a few trees," JoJo said, watching the yellow lines of the blacktop heading back to Clarksdale. "Can't you stay till Monday?"

"Got to head on back."

We passed through a couple of small towns and stopped at a Texaco station for Annie's water. We decided on Annie because of the old song "Work with Me, Annie." But I told JoJo it was more like the song "Polk Salad Annie." This dog was straight Delta mutt, could probably eat a cottonmouth and make the alligators seem tame.

When we reached the crossroads at 49 and 61, I looked over at the big metal sculpture someone had erected to the history of the blues. Metal guitars and road signs. I knew there wasn't any real crossroads and it was a nice gimmick to bring folks in. But it made me think about something Tip-Top had said.

"Is blues dead?"

JoJo thought about that as we headed down 49 and passed by the old Hopson plantation where JoJo had worked as a child. The old commissary was now some kind of bar. The sharecroppers' shacks motel rooms to give tourists a feel for the old days.

The sun was gone. It was night. Only the headlights of the truck and Annie's panting to keep us company.

"About the best I can say is it's different," he said. "Ain't the same. Doesn't mean the same."

I saw his old profile in the dim light as we rounded onto the footbridge and country road to take us home.

1

SIRENS AIN'T NOTHIN' *but ghosts. They reach out every damn night, red and blue, white spotlight flashin' 'cross your eyes as you sleep on that concrete floor patterned in blood and dirt. You covered in a torn yellow blanket that once hid your dead mamma for weeks. In its touch, you see a bit of her cold ear and the edge of that face you tried not to imagine while you kept goin' to school, cuttin' her las' ten dollars in a hundred ways at Rob's Party Store down on Claiborne. You remember? Don't you?*

Back then, you hold your own in the Calliope yard, the ole CP-3, and find your only friends are a mean-ass pit bull you call Henry and a little rottweiler with short legs you name Midget. Your mamma stay alive to you for weeks underneath that blanket. Through it all, she stay like she is 'cause that room don't have no heat and it's February, like it is now, and her own family live on the other side of the project.

Y'all know Calliope—its own little galaxy in New Orleans. Findin' your people on the other side is like shootin' over to the moon. They long ago forgot about her. Don't know you. Your daddy ain't nothin' but a word and the only future you see come from a box of Bally shoes you traded for two of your mamma's rocks out in the yard. Henry and Midget backin' you up like thugs in the rope-and-barbed-wire collars you made for them. A hundred windows covered in aluminum foil watchin' you like eyes stand on the grassless ground.

You take those shoes down to some fancy-ass shoppin' mall by the Quarter. The dollar you spend on a streetcar is the last green you have. Ten minutes later, that worn box of shoes you was gonna return for a hundred dollars—like that man said—is dumped out on the street along with your ole mongrel ass. But you don't cry.

Why would you?

Don't take that streetcar. You walk. All damned day. It's a day from Calliope.

It's dark when you get back. You remember. You thinkin' about it all tonight with the sirens and the spotlights and them ghostful sounds.

It was Friday and Calliope was workin' plenty down the cross streets. Strawberries' heads bobbin' in white men's Lexuses and Hondas. Boys you once knew jacked up as hell, wide-eyed and watchin' for drugheads to slow down and make that deal. Shit made out of flour and toilet water.

Room a hotbox when you crawl up the fire escape. Television on, playin' BET and Aaliyah. She on a sailboat but dead. Like your mamma. You can smell Mamma now and you want to shake her awake, have her find people she know but you don't, to get somethin' to eat. Your belly all swole up after four days without food. You hungry and you know you need it. It hurt to even swallow.

Knock on the door. Ole man who you seen your mamma kneel before on the stairwell is smilin' at you with a wrench in his hand. He tell you he hooked you up, but then he see your mamma, nothin' but a hidden hump, and you duck under his arm as he walk back and puke on hisself.

Five days out of juvie, you back with a forty-year-old woman callin' herself your grandmamma. You only know her as a woman your mamma would see and turn the other way to spit. Your grandmamma don't like you. Make you run around like you work for her, makin' corner deals by the Stronger Hope Church. Bringin' her weed pipe to her with copies of Jet *and* Star. *But you got a place on a small couch next to your twelve-year-old uncle who has fits and drools on himself when he don't take his pills.*

They got food, too. Cold Popeyes and cans of green things you ain't never tasted. You gain a little weight, start pocketin' bus money she give you to go to school, and buy a dictionary, even though you don't know most of the words in it. You want to be like the silver mask on the bus signs. Diabolical. He don't have no eyes or a body, just a silver face. God? You'd heard about him comin' from the Calliope and how he makin' rhymes from all the words he know.

Sometime when you on the corner, hearin' your own beat and bounce in your head, rhymin' for fifty cents for some hustler to smile, you see Dio's face on a passin' bus. He comin' back. He'll hear you.

One night you find a white girl and you rob her with a knife you made from an oak tree splinter. Don't feel bad. She's pretty fucked up and lookin' for some more shit to fill her head. You scare her good and she runs away. With that money, you start it all.

Thirty-two damned dollars. Water into wine, what Teddy always say.

You buy a minimixer with a dual cassette made for a kid and a beat tape. You got a microphone about the size of your finger. But it's all you need to make your own.

It's all you do. Sleep on Grandmamma's couch, run her business, run her drugs a bit, and make them tapes. You sell them. They cost you a dollar at Rob's; you sell 'em for three. Pretty soon—we talkin' weeks, man—you known. Calliope ain't no galaxy; it's a planet. It's your planet. You grabbin' your toy and hittin' Friday- and Saturday-night block parties and you eatin'.

Then—don't know how—Teddy Paris finds you at that Claiborne corner with your dogs. Kids swallow his Bentley and mirror rims. You don't. You hang, till he call you over and offer you a ride. At first you don't, everybody workin' you. Everybody a freak.

The kids tell you it's about your tapes.

You go.

You ride. Ninth Ward Records.

You keep ridin'.

Four months later, you livin' Lakefront.

You got a half-built house with iron gates and three girls who clean your underwear and wash you in the shower. Henry and Midget wearin' Gucci and eatin' filets.

Ain't nothin' but rhymes and ambition.

Ambition feel somethin' like that heat in the room when they took your mamma away.

It's all what you believe. You can believe anything.

Least that's what you tell yourself as you slip that gun in your mouth, listenin' to the sounds of the Calliope around you. It's old beats, old music that you never wanted to hear again. It's shoes and cold gray skin and swollen bellies and a shakin' uncle whose eyes disappear into his head.

But you back.

They say you $500,000 less a man.

It all look good, you told yourself that day back in December when that white man came to you. It all look good on paper when they tell you about this trust fund you had and all the money Teddy and Malcolm keepin' from you.

You saw it all until they worked you. Then everythin' disappeared. That office on the Circle sat empty. Them business cards that felt like platinum, all to disconnected phones.

Teddy didn't talk to you.

Everythin' was gone.

Tonight, you hear the bus make its stop outside and you pull the gun from your mouth, gag a little. You bend back that foil in the window. Just a bit.

You got to smile, huggin' arms round your body, metallic taste of your gold teeth in your mouth. It's your face out there. All thuggin' and mean-lipped on the side of the bus. Platinum and diamonds. Do-rag cocked on your head.

You like that until you hear that Raven pop in your hand and feel your legs give out and a hot, sticky mess spread across your belly and leg.

It was all there.

Now you ruin.

You ruined as hell.

You are fifteen.

2

WITHIN THE FIRST TWENTY-FOUR HOURS I'd known Teddy Paris, he'd stolen my Jeep, bruised my ribs in the ensuing fight, almost gotten me cut from the Saints, and become one of the best friends I'd ever known. I often wondered why he found it so funny to break into my Wrangler while we were at training camp that summer and disappear in it with a few buddies to blow their rookie paychecks on stereo equipment at a mall in Metairie.

I thought he was making a point because I was white and from Alabama and he hadn't known I'd lived in New Orleans since I was eighteen. But I later learned, while we bonded over our mutual love for Johnnie Taylor ballads and a nice shot I'd given him in the jaw, that Teddy chose me, out of the dozens of players, because he thought I could take a joke.

Teddy and I had been friends even after our short-lived careers in the NFL ended, mine trailing into getting a doctorate and becoming a roots music field researcher, and his into a multimillion-dollar rap music partnership with his brother, Malcolm. His professional path came in a dream—he'll tell you complete with a sound track—after opening five failed nightclubs and a pet photography studio.

Teddy was always into something.

I'd been back from the Delta for only two weeks and already missed JoJo, Loretta, and a woman I'd been seeing for the last few months in Oxford. It was early on Friday, about 10 A.M., and I'd just turned in my students' grades for spring semester and was looking forward to heading back to Mississippi.

The day was crisp and blue with a warm white sun peeking through a few thin clouds. The air seemed clean, even for New Orleans, tinged with the tangy brackish smell of the Mississippi. Muddy Waters's *Folk Singer* album with Willie Dixon slapping and plunking his big stand-up bass in stripped-down perfection played on an old cassette player.

I needed to finish up this job and pack, I thought as I pulled out the old water pump from my Bronco. I inspected its rusted blades and wiped the blackened oil and grime from my hands onto my jeans and prized Evel Knievel T-shirt. I thought about Maggie and her farm. And her legs and smile.

Polk Salad Annie trotted by, sniffed my leg, and then rummaged for a bone she'd hidden in a pile of old milk crates that held my CDs and field tapes. She chomped the bone, found a nice spot on an old pillow she'd grown to love, and then started to sniff the air.

My five-dollar dog.

I was already planning out the day's drive when Teddy walked through the gaping mouth of my garage and called my name. I knew the voice and told him to hold on.

I heard the familiar click of his Stacey Adams shoes nearing on the concrete floor. "My woman so mean she shot me in the ass and run off with my dog," Teddy sang, his voice booming in the small cavern. "Why you listen to that sad ole music?"

"The blues ain't nothing but a botheration on your mind," I said, speaking low.

"No wonder it makes me depressed."

"What? You want me to 'Shake That Ass'?" I asked, naming one of his New Orleans competitor's top-ten hits. Asses, champagne, and platinum usually dominated his preferred style of music. Dirty South rap. I shook my butt a little while continuing to work under the hood of the truck before turning back around.

"Travers, you got to remember, I seen you dance," Teddy said, straightening out the folds in his tent-sized black double-breasted suit. Teddy was 300 pounds plus with a deep insulated voice from all the fat around his neck. His words seemed to come from inside a well. "Ain't pretty."

As I leaned back into my thirty-year-old truck, I noticed his newest electric blue Bentley parked outside. Chrome rims shining like mirrors into the sun. I'd heard the inside was lined with blue rabbit fur. Real rabbits died for that.

One of those new Hummer SUVs painted gold with black trim pulled in behind the Bentley, shaking with electronic bass. Teddy's brother, Malcolm, walked across Julia.

I grunted as I fit a pipe plug into the heater hose outlet of the new water pump. Malcolm wandered into the garage, decked out in hard dark denim, a tight stocking cap on his head and a platinum cross ticking across his chest. "What up?"

"Hey, brother," I said, reaching back from the hood and giving him the pound. I liked Malcolm. Always streetwise and hard. Sometimes in and out of trouble but always himself.

"Came by to see if you want to have lunch at Commander's," Teddy said.

"I'd settle for fried chicken and greens at Dunbar's."

"Travers, you are the blackest white man I know."

I cleaned my hands with a gasoline-soaked rag and ran my fingers over the sleeves of his suit. "Nice."

Malcolm laughed.

You would've thought I was a leper, the way Teddy yanked his arm away. "Get yo' greasy-ass monkey hands off me."

Malcolm crossed his arms across his ghetto denim, a scowl on his face. "Teddy don't want no one messin' with his pimpin' clothes."

"Nick—" Teddy began.

Annie ambled on over and made a slow growling sound. I scratched her antenna ears. She smelled his crotch and trotted away.

"What in the hell is that?" Teddy asked.

"A hint," I said. "She says arf."

"Look like a goddamn hyena to me."

"So?" I asked, cleaning grease and oil off the timing cover. I reached for a putty knife resting on my battery. Teddy strolled in front of my workbench and admired my calendar featuring Miss March 1991. Annie found her bone.

Sweat ringed around Teddy's neck and he kept patting his brow with a soiled handkerchief. Malcolm lit a cigarette from a pack of Newports and leaned against my brick wall. He kept his eyes on his brother and shook his head slowly. His beard was neatly trimmed, his thick meaty hands cupped over the cigarette as he watched us.

"Y'all never asked me to lunch before."

"Sure we have," Teddy said.

"When you wanted to borrow $3,000 to start your own line of haircare products."

"Macadamia-nut oil. It would have worked."

"Well?" I scraped away at the old sealant around the timing cover. I studied the crap caked over the cover after decades of use. At least the truck was running even after I ran it into a north Mississippi ditch last fall.

"You ever listen to the CDs I send you?" Teddy asked.

"Nope."

"You know ALIAS, right? You ain't that livin' in 1957 that you ain't seen him. BET, MTV, cover of *XXL*."

"I don't watch TV except cartoons. But, yeah, I know ALIAS. So what?"

"He got caught in some shit," Teddy said. His voice shook and he wiped the sweat from the back of his neck. "Need some help."

"I can't rap," I said. "But I can break-dance a little."

"Not that kind of help," Teddy said.

"Aw, man. Kind of wanted some of those Hammer pants. Need a long crotch."

"Kind of help you give to them blues players," he said, ignoring me. "Them jobs you do that JoJo always talkin' 'bout."

"Royalty recovery?"

Malcolm spoke up in a cloud of smoke: "Finding people."

I began to remove the screws from the old pump and looked at Malcolm. I still remembered when he was a nappy-haired kid who shagged balls at training camp for our kickers. Now he was a hardened man. I noticed a bulge in the right side of his denim coat.

"Who do you need found?"

"A man who conned my boy out of 500 grand," Teddy said. "Goddamn, it's hot in here."

"Sorry, man," I said. "Sounds like you need more help than me."

"You the best I got."

"We'll talk."

"There ain't time."

"Why?"

Malcolm looked at his brother and put a hand on his shoulder before walking back to his Hummer with an exaggerated limp.

"Some Angola-hard punk gave me twenty-four, brother," Teddy said. "I only got twenty-one hours of my life left."

3

AFTER TEDDY DROPPED THE NEWS, we decided there wasn't a hell of a lot of time for soul food at Dunbar's. So when we watched Malcolm head back out to the studio, I pulled on my walking boots and a clean T-shirt, closed down the garage, and we rolled down Freret and headed up to Claiborne in Teddy's electric-blue Bentley. I cracked the window, lit a Marlboro, and sank into the rabbit fur while he leaned back into the driver's seat and steered with two fingers. A sad smile crossed his face as we moved from the million-dollar mansions off St. Charles to candy-colored shotguns and onto a street populated with pawnshops, check-cashing businesses, and EZ credit signs. Neon and billboards. Broken bottles lay in gullies and yellowed newspapers twirled across vacant lots.

The air felt warm against my face, heavy bass vibrating my back and legs, when we rolled low under the giant oaks that shrouded the corners around the Magnolia projects. The trees' roots were exposed, rotted, and dry near portions of the housing projects that had been plowed under. Their tenants now living in Section 8 housing in New Orleans East.

I felt the rabbit fur on the armrest and looked into the backseat, where Teddy had a small flat-screen television and DVD player. A copy of *Goodfellas* had been tossed on the backseat along with a sack of ranch-flavored Doritos.

"Why don't you sell your car?"

"It's a hell of a ride but ain't no way close to 700 grand, brother," he said.

"Your house?" I asked. "That mansion down by the lake with your dollar-sign-shaped pool? What about a loan on that?"

"Ain't time," he said. And very low he said, "And I got three of them mortgage things already."

"Oh, man."

"What about J.J.?" I asked, dropping the name of our teammate who had just won two Super Bowls. "He's got more money than God or George Lucas. You try and call him? He'd float you a favor."

"J.J. and I ain't that tight no more."

"What happened?" I asked.

"I owe him $80,000."

"Jesus."

"Don't you go blasphemin' in this car."

"Why?" I asked. "You pay to have it baptized?"

We stopped at the corner of Claiborne, where on a mammoth billboard two hands were held together in prayer. Someone had spray-painted the words WHY ME? over the address of the church. Across the wide commercial street, I saw another billboard of Britney Spears. She was selling Pepsi. Britney hadn't been touched.

"You're deep in debt and can't get a loan from anyone else," I said. "Who is this Cash guy? Just kiss and make up."

He didn't even look over at me as he accelerated toward the Calliope housing projects. "Yeah, yeah, yeah. Crack a joke. See, Cash is a real humane individual." Teddy licked his lips and wiped his face for the thousandth time. "Heard he once stuck a set of jumper cables in a man's ass for spillin' wine on his Italian leather coat. Up his ass, man. That's fucked up."

"Did the man turn over?"

Teddy shook his head. "Listen, I came to Cash 'bout two months back so we could get the money for ALIAS's CD. Had to get some promotional dollars."

"For what?"

"Advertisin'. This video we shootin' tonight."

"Call it off."

"Too late," he said. "Everyone's been paid. See, we were all in some trouble and then Cash and me was tryin' to put together this movie? I had this idea about New Orleans bein' underwater and only the folks in the ghetto survived. You know like we were livin' in this underwater world with boats made out of Bentleys and shit . . ."

"So he loaned you $700,000?"

"Half a mil," he said. "He added another two for interest and his hard-earned time."

Teddy shook his head as he drove, hot wind blowing through the car. The asphalt more cracked on this side of Uptown. We passed a Popeye's fried chicken, a McDonald's, some bulletproof gas stations. Barbershops. Bail bonds.

"Tell me about Cash," I said. "Maybe I can reason with him."

"You got a better chance of gettin' a gorilla to sing you 'Happy Birthday,' " Teddy said. "This ape raised in Calliope like my man ALIAS. But he don't have no heart like the kid. He's an animal. Bald head. Got all his teeth capped in platinum and diamonds. Stole everythin' he have. Even his beats. Got his sound from this badass DJ 'bout five years back. Now Cash eatin' steaks and lobster, screwin' *Penthouse* pets and that boy coachin' damn high-school football."

"How'd he steal his sound?"

"The bounce, man," Teddy said. He turned up the music. That constant driving rhythm I'd heard played all over New Orleans shook the car. The drums keeping the rap elevated as if the music was made of rubber-reflecting words.

"Why don't you just run?" I asked. "Get out of town till you can raise the money?"

"I got family here," Teddy said. "Besides, a Paris don't ever run. You know that."

"That's bullshit," I said. "Quit your posturing before you do get killed."

"Ain't no bullshit," he said. "I leave and then he fuck with a member of my family? Man, I couldn't live with myself."

"Can't you just sign over something to him? Just give him your house. You can stay with me."

"I appreciate it, brother," he said. "I really do. But there is only one thing this mad nigga want and he ain't getting it."

I looked at Teddy—out of breath, sweating like hell—as he turned into the housing projects. Two men on the corner with hard eyes and wearing heavy army coats watched us turn. Teddy lowered the stereo. The heat whooshed through the car, just making the silence between us more intense.

Teddy gritted his teeth as he passed the men. "ALIAS my boy and I ain't neva losin' that boy. Not again."

I watched him. "I want y'all to meet," he said.

4

"YOU GONNA VALET this thing in Calliope?" I asked. "Or are you trying to collect insurance?"

"You don't know who I am," Teddy said. "Respect everything around here."

"Even for a Ninth Warder?"

"For Teddy Paris."

"What the hell does that mean?"

He kissed a ruby pinkie ring on his fattened little finger and gave me a wink. "You'll see."

Calliope soon swallowed us into endless rows of four-story colorless brick buildings seeming to sag with exhaustion. Fire escapes lined each building in V patterns; some hung loose like broken limbs. In a commons that reminded me of a prison yard, Dumpsters spilled trash onto the wide dirt ground. Along the walls of project houses, signs read NO DOG FIGHTING.

We slowed and rolled into the commons.

As Teddy shut off his engine and coasted to a stop, dozens of black children wrapped their arms around the car. I could hear them laughing and breathing and giggling. Making faces with their eyes pressed against the glass. Teddy got out and ripped out a massive roll of ten-dollar bills, palming them off to more than a dozen kids.

Stay in school; get yo' mamma right; no way, you been back twice.

I smiled as the kids formed a tight circle around the car, the chirp of Teddy's alarm locking them out.

We walked along a buckled path and by a brick wall where someone had painted the huge face of a rapper named Diabolical. I'd read he'd been killed in some gang shit last year and now he'd taken on some kind of martyr status in the projects. The slanted warped image of his face in bright colors surrounded by painted candles reminded me of a Russian icon.

Teddy nodded to his face, "That's the one I lost."

We found ALIAS among a loose group of teen boys and two girls tossing quarters along a concrete staircase stained with rust. Teddy pointed out the kid, and as he saw Teddy's wobbling figure coming toward him, he picked up the collection of cash and sat back down.

He didn't look up. Teddy took off his coat and sweat stains spread under his arms and across his back in a big *X*. ALIAS muttered something and the kids broke away.

He was a tall kid. Lanky and slow-moving in red basketball shorts that slipped past his knees. He wore a white FUBU baseball jersey with his sleeves rolled up and sneakers made of black fabric and gel. He sported an awkward mustache that only a fifteen-year-old could appreciate.

He still didn't look at us, counting the money.

"How you feelin'?" Teddy asked.

"Sore," ALIAS said, pulling up his shirt and showing a white and red puckered scar on his side. "Still don't know who jumped me."

The kid shook his head and pocketed the money, watching the uneven open earth and the slabs of projects that stacked farther north like dirty caves. He leaned forward, a piece of platinum jewelry slipping from his shirt. The Superman symbol inscribed in diamonds.

"Happens out here in the yard." Teddy leaned down and made the kid look at his face. "Didn't want you to come back here where that kind of shit happen. But you fucked up, kid. That's a lot of money to lose. Put me in a hell of a tight."

The kid nodded. "Yeah, I heard about that shit. I'm sorry, man."

Teddy opened his big arms wide and the kid fell into his clutch. Teddy swallowing him into his sweaty silk shirt, patting him on his back.

In the yard, a shirtless man clutching a long bottle staggered toward Teddy's child security. "Teddy," I said, nudging him.

"Get back, motherfucker," Teddy yelled and rolled off to the yard.

I sat down next to the kid. He pulled the money back out, probably about twenty in cash, and I watched him recount it.

"Teddy told me what happened."

He looked at me. One eye had yellow flecks in the iris and he had a very pink scar that slashed from the bridge of his nose and ran into one eyebrow. His teeth were gold.

"You want to tell me what happened?"

"What you gonna do about it?"

I watched Teddy's fat butt jangle in his $2,000 suit as he ran off the man. The children laughed while the crazy shirtless man darted across the grass and mud field like an aimless dog.

"I helped a woman who got sent to prison for forty years because people lied," I said. "She got stuck. No one believed a word she said. Thought she was crazy."

He looked at me. Then back at the money.

"If you don't help," I said, "your boy Cash is gonna mess Teddy up bad."

"What the fuck you know about Cash?" ALIAS asked. "He ain't my boy."

"What did the man who shot you look like?"

"I don't know."

"Are you crazy?"

"Fuck no."

"What did he look like?"

"White."

"Terrific."

Teddy looked down at us, sweating and out of breath. "Y'all ready to go? I ain't got the energy to run that motherfucker off again. What you poor-mouthin' for, kid? I said let's go."

"What'd you do with my dogs?"

"I got 'em."

"You ain't got the right."

"Sure I do. That was a ton of money. Had to make you think about the shit you done."

"That was my money."

"Yeah, I heard Cash was fillin' your head up. Wants you to roll with those Angola ballers when I'm dead. Right?"

I got up from the stoop. Looked at the time. Noon. I should've been on the road by now. Eatin' chicken-fried steak in Vaiden, Mississippi. Headed into Maggie's heavy iron bed. Her Texas show boots by the door.

"You see this man?" Teddy said, pointing at me. "See him? He don't look like much. All that gray hair and don't shave his face and tries to be funny all the time. Which of course he ain't. But he gonna help find them fuckers. He ain't like the police."

"Why wouldn't they help?" I asked. He did bring it up.

" 'Signal 7,' " ALIAS said.

Two teenage girls in halter tops, lollipops in splayed fingers, strolled by ALIAS and smiled. Both with bright red lips. Bare feet dusty from the broken concrete around Calliope.

ALIAS smiled back.

"What's 'Signal 7'?"

" 'The popo ain't got answers,' " ALIAS began in a slow, deliberate rap. Enunciating words to me the way you would to a retarded person or a very smart monkey. " 'Ain't nothin' but lies. Put that Glock in their face and see if they read our minds.' "

"The 'popo' didn't like that too much?" I asked.

Teddy nodded his head.

"Guess not," I said.

We followed ALIAS into a small room with three filthy windows crowded with dead plants and covered in comic strips. A haggard woman, oddly old in a way I couldn't quite place, had her feet up in a ratty recliner chair. She flipped through channels on a television that flickered so much it made me dizzy.

No one spoke to her. ALIAS disappeared down a short hall and returned with a leather duffel bag with the Timberland logo.

"That's it?" Teddy asked.

ALIAS said, "You locked me out of my own home."

"Did I?" Teddy asked, leading the way as we passed the silent old woman living in her TV.

When we got back to his Bentley, the commons was bare of the children. A low bank of dark clouds rolled toward the river and there was the slight smell of rain in the distance mixed with the loose dust of scattering feet.

ALIAS held his bag. No expression.

Teddy circled his ride, searching for scratches or dents.

He shook his head. We both scanned the four clusters of housing projects surrounding us. No one. Loose popping of dried clotheslines stretching from metal crosses.

He pressed the release on the locks. The alarm chirped and I looked back at the long row of clouds. The silence was almost electric as I waited for him to take me home.

We rolled away in the Bentley, his car smelling of leather and new wood and some kind of lime perfume he sprayed on the rabbit fur. When we drove away, I watched three teenagers being hustled into the back of a black Suburban by about ten DEA officers. An old woman in pink house slippers yelled at them and kept throwing rocks at their back as they all loaded into the car.

5

"HOW DID YOU MEET this man?" I asked ALIAS, while we waited for a streetcar to move on St. Charles Avenue heading uptown to Lee Circle. Rain splattered the hood of my truck and wooden shop signs in the Warehouse District shook in the wind. Teddy had left me with the kid at my place and had gone back to the studio to make calls for last-minute loans. I told him I'd do my best but wished he'd just leave town.

ALIAS wasn't listening to me. He'd busied himself by flipping through some blues CDs in my toolbox as we headed to the office where he'd had most of his business meetings. "Who the fuck is Super Chikan?"

"A guy I once got drunk with in Clarksdale. Can make his guitar talk like a chicken."

"Man, that's country-ass."

More and more abandoned brick warehouses sported new rental and sale signs for the district. One showed a mural on an old cotton warehouse advertising white couples playing tennis, swimming, and drinking foaming coffees.

"How did you meet this guy?" I asked again.

"Through this woman I knew," ALIAS said. He'd moved from the blues CDs to a cardboard box holding articles on Guitar Slim. I watched in the rearview as he scanned the articles and moved his lips.

"Who was she?"

"She came up to me when we was at Atlanta Nites," he said. "Don't remember her name. But man, she was fine."

"That doesn't help much."

"She just gave me his card and was sayin' that he worked with Mystikal and shit."

"Where did you first meet him?"

"At my lake house. Dude just knock on the door like we old friends. Knew my name. Started to talkin' to me right off about my Bentley. Knew all about my ride."

"Who else was there?"

"That fine-ass woman."

"You know anything else about her?"

"She smelled real nice."

"Stinky ones don't get much work."

I downshifted, rain against my windshield, and saw a parking spot by the Circle Bar. The bar made me think of cigarettes and Dixies and Jack Daniel's and me about five years ago.

Robert E. Lee stood tall on his pillar at Lee Circle, where streetcars made wide turns around its grassy mound and headed uptown.

I reached across ALIAS and into my dash for a pack of Bazooka.

I offered him a piece.

"What's that shit?"

"Gum. You chew it. Brings enjoyment."

"Man, that shit looks old as hell."

"I will have you know that Bazooka is the finest damned gum ever known to man. All other bubble gum tastes like rubber paste. And they have comics inside. Brilliant."

He looked at me and flashed a gold grin.

"What did he look like?" I asked.

"Kind of bald but kept his hair real tight. Like shaved so no one would notice. White."

"You said that."

"Well, he kind of dark for a white dude. Nose kind of big."

"I'd ask how he dressed but it doesn't matter," I said. "Anything different about him? Moles? A tattoo?"

"Naw, man. He did have this weird shit about his ears," he said, and rubbed the cartilage in his ears. "Like he got shit stuck up in it."

"You mean like cauliflower ear?"

"Yeah, sumshit like that."

We stopped at this three-story tan brick building on the Circle and got out. Most of the windows were open and we could hear a construction crew with their drills and hammers blaring Tejano music from small radios while they worked. We walked right into the first floor. It was gutted and open with exposed metal support beams. Even with the air flushing through the open space, it smelled of hot wood and oil from their tools and lifts.

No one was on the floor.

"Where were they?" I asked.

"Second floor."

Upstairs, we found the office. Two Mexican workers were inside cleaning up a mess left by Sheetrock hangers. They swept the floor in their hard hats, T-shirts bulging with cigarette packs. They didn't even look up at us as we walked over the stained plywood floor. I watched ALIAS taking it all in.

"Tell me what you remember."

"They had a secretary. Every time I come in, she'd make me sit there awhile and read magazines till Mr. Thompson was ready."

"Did Mr. Thompson have a first name?"

"Jim. He acted like we was friends."

"How'd you get here?"

"Drove."

"By yourself?"

He nodded.

"Anyone know about this besides you?"

"Naw."

He walked over to a window where you could see the statue of Lee on his pillar. A streetcar lapped him. Clanking bell. Gears changing. You could only see the back of Lee.

"What'd they promise you, kid?"

"ALIAS."

"What's your real name?"

"Tavarius."

"I like that better."

"Whatever."

I smiled.

"I got a business card they gave me."

I shook my head. "Won't do any good. Were any of these construction crews here when you came in?"

"No."

"Didn't see anyone else in this building except Mr. Thompson and this secretary? Who was she?"

"I don't know. She was just always runnin' around and answering phones and interruptin' his meeting with calls from Britney Spears and shit," he said, dropping his head.

"So how did it work?" I found a huge paint bucket to sit on and nodded to its mate by the window. He seemed pretty embarrassed. He prided himself on being smart and quick-witted. It was his job. He was a rapper.

Basically, this guy said he represented a ton of celebrities and boasted a long list of phony clients that included everyone from B. B. King to the Nevilles. He even had eight-by-ten photos of clients hanging above the secretary's desk both times ALIAS visited the office. Once for the hook. The second was the yank.

He told ALIAS long stories about his clients losing millions to their record companies—a common and unfortunately all-too-often-true tale of the recording business—and that he wanted to protect him. He said his group—ATU, or Artists Trust Union—would handle the major balance of ALIAS's earnings that up until that point had been kept in a trust fund because he was a minor. The guy spun wild tales about potential earnings and even hooked ALIAS real good about being able to invest in a private island in the Caribbean. This all sounded like complete 101 con horseshit to me, but then again, I'm not fifteen years old. He exploited every facet of ALIAS's teenage dreams and paranoid fantasies about Teddy and Malcolm ripping him off.

But the true genius in the plan was that this guy really had to do little work. ALIAS had to break into Teddy's office and get the bank account numbers for the ALIAS money market account. Mr. Thompson—bless his heart—acted as his legal guardian (with just a little maneuvering or forgery) and siphoned every bit of cash from the fund that was earmarked for the kid when he turned twenty-one.

I told him that I'd start with the owners of the building and look for any short-team leases he probably did not sign. I asked ALIAS more about the woman from the club and the secretary. The club girl was hot. The secretary had a big butt.

"Why an island?" I asked. "Where did that come from?"

"Shit," he said as we climbed back in the Gray Ghost. The smell of a warm rain mixed with exhaust and heat from the asphalt.

"You sure no one else could've seen them?"

He shook his head.

"No one ever came with you? Took a phone call? Vouched for these folks?"

"No one," he said. He turned the bill of his Saints cap backward and slumped into his passenger seat.

"I'll have to talk to your friends," I said, spitting the Bazooka out the window. The gum had lost its taste and I reached for a fresh piece.

"Do what you got to, man," he said. "My friends got heart."

He pounded his chest two times and raised his chin into the wind cutting from the road.

6

WHEN JOJO OPENED HIS BUSINESS back in 1965, he hired one of the best bartenders in the Quarter. Felix Wright transcended just pouring Jack into a shot glass or popping the top off a Dixie. He performed. He'd have a cold beer rolled down to you from five feet like in an old Western. He kept a file of New Orleans facts in his head, things about Jean Lafitte or Andrew Jackson. Louis Armstrong or Sidney Bechet. Some of it was probably bullshit. But Felix made you feel welcome. Made you feel like you owned a little bit of JoJo's, too, while he'd tell you about the night he'd seen Steve McQueen shooting *The Cincinnati Kid.*

I'd dropped ALIAS back at the Ninth Ward studio and picked up Polk Salad Annie from home. I'd finally taught her to hop up in the Gray Ghost with me. We parked down by the old bar so I could find Felix. Someone had rebuilt the place after the fire last year and turned it into a martini bar where everyone wears all black and compares what they do for a living.

I turned my head as I passed. The blue neon and velvet drapes were enough. I missed the old blues posters in the window and those tall doors fashioned for a Creole restaurant more than a 150 years ago.

I had to find Felix and I knew where to look.

It wasn't pretty. The top bartender in the Quarter had taken a job at Kra-zee Daiquiris down on Bourbon Street. It was the kind of place where you had the option of pouring your drink into a pair of plastic breasts or a long green penis.

Kra-zee's pumped with that song "Mambo No. 5" and had Polaroid photos of *Girls Gone Wild* on the walls. The bar was long but thin, maybe six feet from door to counter, just stools lined up under a fake grass canopy like the place was in the middle of the South Pacific. I knew the building used to house a bar that had been around since the early 1800s, serving presidents and pirates in its time. But the new owner wanted to update. Bring in some new tourist dollars in the form of to-go cups.

Felix wore a Mardi Gras Indian headdress on his bald black dome. Strong forearms and quick in his step behind the bar. He was frowning, but his face brightened when I took a seat.

He gripped my hand very hard as he slid down a couple of daiquiris to two women at the end of the bar. Maybe more like plunked them down; apparently the plastic penis doesn't slide in the same way as JoJo's glasses.

"How you been?"

"Workin'."

"You all right?"

"Fine," he said. He didn't look me in the eye. Hadn't since I'd walked in.

"JoJo wanted me to tell you hello."

He didn't respond.

"He's finally got the farm running again. Bought twenty-five head of cattle."

"Good for him."

He looked at me and then flashed his eyes away. He poured me a margarita made out of blueberries. I was thankful for the regular to-go cup with just the logo of the bar. I asked for a small glass of water for Annie. He poured it and didn't comment on a dog being in the bar. Just normal. Crazy Nick and his friends.

"You seen Sun?"

"No."

"Oz? Hippie Tom?"

He shook his head. "JoJo's Bar is closed," he said. "Ain't you heard?"

I nodded and looked at my hands. A couple of men in pink tank tops and cutoff shorts sauntered into the bar and asked for some margaritas. They began to dance to "Mambo No. 5." More followed. Drunk at one in the afternoon. I lit a cigarette and waited for Felix to finish.

Felix poured the margaritas with a little panache. He wiped down the cheap Formica bar as if it were still the worn mahogany of JoJo's. He took drink orders, sometimes three at a time, and worked the stirring machines as if pouring a perfect shot or finding the right head of foam on a Dixie. I kind of respected that. A professional to the last.

"I need to find Curtis," I said.

"Peckerwood Curtis?" he asked, laughing.

"Is he out?"

"Yeah, got out a few months back. Went back to Stella, too."

"Sorry to hear that."

He nodded. I took a small sip of the blueberry margarita and pushed it away.

"You seen him around?"

"Puttin' in some floors at some new bar on Decatur," he said. "You know that place that used to be a coffeehouse where them vampire people hung out?"

"Thanks." I got up to leave and shook his hand again.

There was a long mirror behind the daiquiri machines framed in some dripping red chili pepper lights. I watched us—even as I continued to talk—and noticed the fine line of gray on the back of Felix's normally smooth head. To me, he'd always been ageless, between forty and seventy. I'd never asked. Watching our reflections, I was jarred with a memory of when I was nine and at Disney World with my parents. It was the Haunted House, the end of the ride, and there was a trick mirror when you didn't see who was sitting with you, only the ghosts who'd stowed away.

"You tell Loretta hello," he said. "Would you do that?"

I told him I would.

7

THE FRENCH QUARTER is a shiftless little town. People gain and lose jobs the way some change underwear. You may be working as a bouncer at a club on Decatur one week and the next you find yourself as cook at a four-star restaurant on Bienville. Addresses don't mean much. Most people just crash, always looking for the cheapest housing where you won't be too worried about getting jacked every night. I needed to find a buddy of mine named Curtis Lee. Curtis, as I learned from Felix, had been out of Angola for at least six months and had gone straight. Again. Either it was religion or AA; Curtis always found the latest salvation. After one short stint in the Jefferson Parish Jail—this for pissing on the sheriff's boots during Mardi Gras—he told me he wanted to become a monk and spent months at JoJo's reading prayer books.

I parked at Decatur and Esplanade behind the French Market, smelling the strands of garlic, dried red pepper, and fish on ice sold there as I hooked Annie onto a leather leash. We walked down Decatur underneath a metal overhang and past a couple of Italian delis and a store that sold Christmas ornaments all year. Cajun Santa. An alligator Rudolph.

I heard hard hammering and the buzz of a saw. The air inside the open door smelled of sawdust and burned wood. On his knees by a miter saw, I saw Curtis, all wiry and mullet-haired, smoking a cigarette and cutting down a tongue-and-groove board.

He smiled up at me, the cigarette pinched between his front teeth. He shut off the saw and stood, shaking the shavings from his coveralls and bending the bill of his Styrofoam hat. The hat asked: GETTIN' ANY?

I shook his hand. He was playing some Journey on an Emerson cassette player that was held together with duct tape.

"Travers, I heard you was up in Mississippi."

"I just got back," I said. "Finished up the project."

"What was it?" He said *wuzzit* in that redneck drawl. New Orleans was a long way from Curtis's north Louisiana home.

"Researching the early days of Sonny Boy Williamson. Found an old partner of his who was the only man I ever met that could take a leak and walk at the same time."

"How'd he stop from pissin' on himself?" Curtis asked.

"He didn't."

He walked over to a cooler and cracked open the top of a Bud Light. He asked me if I wanted to join him and I said I was cool. I knew it was going to be a very long night.

The hammering in the other room stopped. A large-framed white woman wearing a jogging bra that could've comfortably held a third-world country came in and grabbed the beer from his hand. She swigged it, looked at me, and blew out her breath, foam still on her chin.

"Hello, Stella."

"Eat me, Nick."

"I'll take a rain check."

She turned back to her husband. "Soon as you finish with the professor, let's get rollin'. You wanted to lay 300 feet today. I'm already growin' mold."

Annie started to growl low at her.

"That your mutt?" she asked.

"Yep."

"Figured you for the mutt, Travers," she said. "He's just your style."

"Her name is Annie."

She laughed, making snorting piglike grunts in her nose. "Hope you're happy together."

Curtis cracked open a beer for himself and watched his wife's big ass waddle away. "Man, she still makes me hard."

"Oh, boy."

"So what can I do for you, brother? Those red maple floors of yours cracking up?"

"Nope. Need some advice on working a con."

He nodded outside and spoke a little louder for his wife's benefit. "Let me finish this cigarette outside. All right?"

Outside, he leaned against a metal support pole and watched a couple of Hare Krishnas banging the shit out of a tambourine. "Hey," he yelled. "Hey."

One of the Krishnas, orange robe and standard bald head, turned around.

"Y'all fuck off."

They started singing and banging some more but turned the other way.

"Goddamned assholes," he said. "Jesus will turn those fuckers into an orange quilt."

"About the con."

"Yeah, what's up? I didn't want to talk about it in front of Stella. She'd keep my nuts in her purse if she knew you had something for me."

"Need some direction. I'm working a job for an old buddy of mine. He has this kid he works with—he's in the music business and they make rap records—and this kid got taken for a huge one."

"What they use?"

I told him about the offices at Lee Circle and this guy named Thompson and the way they worked on the kid's paranoia about his trust fund.

"Man, that's some good shit."

"Sound like anyone you know?"

He shrugged. "Not really. You say he had fucked-up ears?"

I nodded.

"I know people with fucked-up noses and necks and faces. Maybe even some peckers. But no ear things. Wow, man. How much was it?"

"A lot."

"What's that mean?"

"Means I don't want to say."

"That's cool," he said, taking a sip of beer, starting on what would be one of the first of about one hundred today. He had small hands and yellow teeth. I knew he'd been busted last year for trying to work a handkerchief game on a couple of Lithuanians. When he made the switch and they found the bag full of cut-up newspapers, they tried to stuff him into a mail drop. Apparently the slot was thinner than Curtis and there had been chafing.

"I can ask around," he said. "Could use a little help, though."

I knew it'd come to this. Curtis liked to be paid and I didn't blame him. He had Stella to feed.

"How much?"

"Five hundred."

"Shit, no."

"You said it was a ton of money."

"I said it was a lot. What the hell do you think I keep in my bank account?"

"Two?"

"A hundred if this pans out. I don't know if I'll be paid back for this shit."

"Done," Curtis said, lighting up his second cigarette. Stella began to yell for him to get back inside. Her voice made nails on a chalkboard seem like chanting monks.

"Goddamn," he said. "She's on this new kind of diet from TV. Something that all the stars are onto. Like those little girls on that coffee-shop show in New York. You know where all the girls got tight little asses?"

"*Friends.*"

"Yeah, whatever. Anyway, we was watching the other night and she says she wanted her ass to look just like that Courtney Love."

I didn't correct him.

"I told her I like that booty," he said. "I like 'em full and healthy."

Stella screamed: "Hurry up."

Curtis's shoulders shrank a bit. "Maybe it would make her more quiet."

"You're a lucky man, brother."

He winked. "I'll call."

"I need this fast," I said. "Today."

I held his gaze and he slowly nodded, understanding. Some of the biggest fuckups I've ever known always come through in a pinch. Maybe they do because they've been in similar situations.

"What's up?"

"My friend borrowed money from the wrong folks."

"Greaseballs?"

"Nope," I said. "A mucho bad motherfucker."

"Man," he said. "At least with the greaseballs you knew where the shit was flyin'. This city has turned to shit ever since the Mafia turned into a bunch of pussies."

He wrote my cell-phone number on his hand.

8

I STOPPED AT THE MARKET and bought a large Sno-Kone in a cup, black cherry, and sat on the back loading dock trying to figure out what to do next. I had to wait for Curtis, since ALIAS hadn't given me anything to work with. I shared a little of the cone with Annie while a farmer in overalls unloaded crates of strawberries. She worked her tongue over the ice neatly as her tail wagged a lot. I scratched her chest and kept watching the man unload the crates.

"Dem dogs are nasty, no?" he asked in a deep Cajun accent.

"No," I said, smiling. "Dogs' mouths are cleaner than a human's."

"No human I know lick their backside like that," he said.

"Annie doesn't lick her ass," I said, digging my spoon into the ice. "Very much."

The old Cajun shook his head and disappeared with a dolly full of strawberries. I turned back to Annie.

"You want to stay with me?"

Annie wagged her tail, the twisted muttlike loop knocking against my arm. I thought about where she'd been in the Delta, days before. Starving out by a dusty road where she would've probably died under a truck tire.

I called Teddy from my cell and asked him about the DJ he'd mentioned. The guy who'd been sold out by Cash.

"Lorenzo Woods?"

"Where does he coach?"

Teddy told me. I laid the rest of the Sno-Kone on the ground for my new friend. Annie scarfed it up and pawed at the Styrofoam when it was gone.

"What you wastin' your time with him?" Teddy asked, his voice broken by static. "He doesn't know shit."

"He knows Cash."

"Yeah," he said. "They was tight."

"And now he doesn't like him."

"Yeah."

"JFK is on Wisner, right?"

THE SCHOOL'S security guard stopped us as soon as we hit the front door. He had a big belly and a small gun and snorted when he talked as if announcing a sermon on where dogs are welcome. Apparently school wasn't one of them.

"That's racism."

"A dog ain't no race."

"It's a species."

"That ain't no race, and it needs to be outside."

He put his hands on his hips.

"Will you call Coach Woods?"

"Why would Coach Woods want to see some dog?"

"She's the best placekicker in the southern parishes."

He squinted his eyes up and shook his head, turning his back to us.

"Wait till you go pro, Annie," I said. "They'll all be sorry."

Coach Woods found us a little while later on this old practice field where Annie and I were playing with a tennis ball she'd found. He was about forty and black. Wore a crewneck T that said KENNEDY D-LINE. LIKE A ROCK.

"You lookin' for me?" He kept his hair short and it had started to turn gray at the temples. Annie trotted over with the tennis ball and dropped it against my leg. I took the slobbery ball, tossed it about thirty yards, and she took off for it.

"Heard you used to be DJ Capone."

He just watched me.

"Heard that Cash stole your beats."

Woods walked closer. "What you sellin', man?"

"I'm a friend of Teddy Paris. Said maybe you could help me figure out Cash a little bit."

"Teddy?" he said, smiling.

He squinted into the sun behind my head as Annie looped back and dropped the ball by my foot. Out in the field, the team still kept the old-school goalposts that were shaped like an *H*. They reminded me of a field with high grass in south Alabama where my dad coached. He used to have to cut the grass himself. Sometimes he'd make me weed the field as he slipped back into his office to drink some Beam on ice.

"You know Cash?"

I shook my head and dropped to a knee to slow Annie down a bit. She was still too skinny to be a healthy dog.

"He give you that scar on your face?"

"Got that myself."

"Figured as much," he said. "What business you got with Cash?"

"Teddy and Cash are fighting over money and recording this boy out of Calliope."

"ALIAS," he said. "Yeah, I know all about that."

"I'm looking out for the kid's interests."

"Cash will kill you if you get in the way."

"Maybe," I said. "But would he really kill Teddy?"

"Teddy owe him money?"

"How'd you guess?"

"Teddy owes everybody money."

"You want to take a walk?"

I hooked up Annie to her leash and we began to walk around a rubberized track that circled the football field. We kept looping around the field and I still felt like I needed to be weeding all these years later. I thought about ALIAS at fifteen, wondered how long he'd been out of school.

"You're Nick Travers, aren't you?"

"Yeah," I said and shook his hand.

"I seen you play many times, man. Y'all had the best defense those years. You and that man from Mississippi, linebacker?"

"Ulysses Davis."

"The Black Knight."

"Yeah, I'll tell him that somebody remembers him," I said. "He'll like that."

"Y'all stay in touch?"

I nodded.

"Tell me about what happened with you and Cash."

"I grew up in Calliope," he said. "Proud of that. Most of my kids come from there or Magnolia. I got out by workin' block parties. Hustlin' for any money I could make. I invented bounce, man. You know bounce?"

"It's the Dirty South sound."

"Damn right," he said. "That's me."

"Cash took it."

"Took my beats, put his lame-ass raps over it, and threatened all the record stores in Uptown. Made 'em sell his record or he'd fuck their ass up."

"Man, that's good marketing."

"That ape don't play," he said. He patted Annie on her head and reached down to pull some high grass from some broken asphalt inside the track. "When I confronted the man, he just walk away. We was at a block party at the Y when I let him know he was a thief. Didn't even answer me. But that motherfucker sure broke into my apartment one night. Tied up me and my girl. Made her watch while he beat my ass."

I changed the leash into the other hand. Woods put his hands into his coaching shorts and pulled out a whistle. He twirled it into his fingers. "Stuck a knife into my mouth. Cut my tongue."

He shook his head. "Made me go back to school, though. I played ball in high school but I wasn't like y'all. Didn't have the speed. No real size. Got my degree from Xavier on my twenty-sixth birthday, man. Now I teach computer skills to these kids."

Annie kept pulling on the leash, not sure why it was slowing her down. Her tongue lolling out, antenna ears askew.

"Someone took ALIAS," I said. "They conned him. Made him think he was represented by some big agency. Does Cash have the connection or the smarts to make that work?"

"Man's smart. But he don't have the patience for something like that. He wants the kid. Wants Teddy to look bad. But see, Cash doesn't work that way, conning somebody. If he wanted something done, he'd head right to it. He'll lie, steal, and cheat. But he'll do it face-to-face. Con games and playin' ain't the man's style."

"You answered my question."

"What kind of dog is that anyway?" he asked.

"A Delta dog," I said. "The finest breeding outside Memphis."

"Got some pit in her?"

"Maybe."

"What else?"

"Boxer. Shepherd. Wookie."

"Man," he said, laughing. "Listen. You think you could come by practice sometime this fall? Kids 'bout to get out of school now. Tryin' to make 'em show up to workouts this summer and all. Ain't workin' that great. All kinds of distractions. Girls. Drugs. Money. Man, when I was a kid, football was everything. Now they just into ballin'."

"I guess when you hit the big time, you don't even need school."

"ALIAS will have to come down hard one day," he said. "You ever want to help out, let me know."

"Sure, man," I said. "I work at Tulane. They know how to find me."

I stopped walking at the gate to the parking lot. Annie needed some water and to be fed. I needed to make a few calls. "Who would want to cheat this kid?" I asked.

Woods stretched out his fist and gave me the pound. Hard black clouds rolled in from the east, a few small trees planted around the field started to shake. I heard thunder crack. The rain was back.

"A millionaire kid with a Calliope education?" he asked. "I'd look at everybody who breathes in this city."

"Will Cash come for me?"

"If you're in between him and the boy, you better bet on it."

9

CASH STAYED UPTOWN *in this purple mansion with yellow shutters just off the streetcar line where white people played tennis and parked their cars behind thick iron fences. You'd heard that his neighbors don't like him none. Not 'cause he's black and rich but 'cause he throws parties about every night, rips apart some old-as-hell house breakin' the law, and threatens folks with sawed-off shotguns. He even made some white lawyer get on his knees and kiss his buck-naked ass after the man told Cash to cut his lawn. In a lot of ways, you got to respect that.*

At 3, it's dark as hell from that storm rollin' in off the Gulf, and you see all his boys sittin' in rockin' chairs on this wide porch like gunfighters from old movies. Drinkin' Cristal and forties and listenin' to the music comin' from open windows. Thin curtains ruffle like ghosts. The thunder breaks above your head, and fat little salty drops that you imagine come from around Mexico slap you in the eyes as you walk to the porch. You don't pay them niggas no mind. Cash called you. This his invite and you welcome as hell. It's payday and you got to smile.

This fat ole oak's roots has cracked open the sidewalk like ripped skin and you almost trip while opening up the gate to Cash's place. The floors inside are wood and bleached and buffed smooth. Cash has lined the walls in blue and red neon, his gold records behind a long glass case lit up with little lights. The rest of the house is dark and smells like the inside of this old shoebox where your grandmamma used to keep her needles. The floor tilts slightly to the left, and in the dark, the thunder coming again, you follow the slant to that back room where you find Cash.

He ain't wearin' no shirt and he's sweating with the windows open and playing poker with three women and some young white dude. Cash smiles a silver mouth. The red tattoo on his big chest muscles seems to beat when he flex up. The white dude don't look right, sweat rings under his shirt, his tie hangin' loose.

Two of the women are black. One's white. One of the black girls is naked as hell and her fat old titties lay over a pile of money that Cash has been tossin' to her.

"How 'bout a hundred for them li'l ole panties," he say when you walk in.

The girl shake her head and ask for a thousand.

"Girl, that trap ain't worth fifty," Cash say, and laugh, taking a sip of champagne in a jelly jar and grabbing some potato chips. The music is all around you and low. Some raps and sounds you ain't never heard and you recognize the voice as Dio's and you wonder about that.

Cash introduces you to the white dude. Some man from L.A. who's workin' on distribution, and the man about shits on himself when he hears your name. He palms you off a card and smiles a little too wide to be real.

You and Cash wander out back, past a couple women in bikinis playin' with his pit bull, Jimmy, that he uses in all his videos. They rubbin' the dog's stomach and cuttin' his toenails.

Y'all walk into a maze of bushes, some ole hedges cut higher than you and Cash are tall and you wander through the cuts and turns as he tell you about some Greek man and a freak that had the head of a bull.

"Yeah, boy," he say. "I like that history shit. You know what the Civil War is?"

You nod. But you don't.

"Nigga, don't lie. You know some peckerwood white folks used to keep us

like hogs, right, and there was a big war 'cause of it. Don't be all ignorant. Learn to read."

You look at him. He is open and easy and you see all the holes and cracks that run from his face to his heart. The sky opens and begins to rain but Cash is drunk and shoeless and you don't give two shits. He unzips his pants, whips out his dick, and starts pissin' on the shrubs.

"Reason I'm sayin' that," he says, while you look away so he don't think you a sissy. You notice the yellow Christmas lights clicking and burning off some balcony on his purple house. "Reason why is 'cause the man who was the peckerwood president of the Confederacy or some shit died in my house. My house, nigga. Ain't that a trip? Wonder what that boy would think with the Red Hat crew all up in it?"

You nod and mumble you understand as you twist again into the hedge. When you look back up, the house is gone. Cash stumbles on and pulls the black do-rag from his bald head to wipe his armpits. He hands you a champagne bottle and it's warm as piss. You don't drink and he don't notice.

"You made up your mind?" Cash asks.

You fold your arms inside each other. "I want three records. Want $500,000 up front."

"That ain't the way it work, kid."

"Don't try and jack me, Cash," you say. You put some force behind his name. "You get that back in six months. And I want the house too. Want you to buy it outright from Teddy."

"Thought you said it was yours."

"You know what's up. Don't try to pull my dick."

You want to be free of Teddy and Malcolm and that white dude Travers. You didn't make Teddy's play. Ain't no reason to try and save his ass.

"You one hit, kid. 'Signal 7' ain't comin' round again."

You bite the inside of your cheek and don't take your eyes away.

"It's better than bein' dead," he says.

"I ain't afraid of you," you say. "I can handle myself."

You feel like you can't breathe, like you in the green stomach of some dragon. The walls gettin' close.

"You don't need to be," he says. He smiles, his teeth chrome. "Not of me."

And he let that threat hang there and you know what he's talkin' about and suddenly a bunch of birds rush from under a stone. All the talk is making you feel light in the head. Kind of like smokin' that first blunt.

You turn and try to find the street. Then Cash pats you on the head. You push his hand away but he's two feet ahead of you.

Cash smiles and disappears. The scars on his back scorched and hard and seem to you like iron strips.

10

I TRIED FOR FORTY-FIVE MINUTES to talk to a human at this super-conglomerate bank in the CDB about Teddy's account. I held Teddy on the cell for most of the wait to get someone to release the information on the transfer. But after being shuffled around to, no lie, eight people, I was finally told by a vice-president returning from a very late lunch that this was now a police matter, and Teddy's accounts were confidential, even to him.

The woman wore white makeup, making her almost look like a spooky clown with her dyed black hair, and her face cracked with the stress when she forced a smile on me. I just winked at her and pushed out onto Carondelet where I'd left Annie in the truck with the windows rolled down. I thought about letting her shit in their lobby but decided to take the higher road. Besides, even with all the account information in the world, I didn't think I'd be able to decipher it. I'd need an accountant to work out the details.

Since it was a police matter and there was someone investigating, I knew I could get access to them through my old roommate at Tulane who was now a detective in homicide. I called Jay from the cell, got voice mail, and heard him give out his beeper number. I beeped him and five minutes later, as I was already headed down Canal toward Broad Street and police headquarters, he called back. A second afternoon shower hit my windshield and I turned on the wipers. Toward the end of Canal I could still see the sun shining.

"Detective Medeaux? I have information on the Fatty Arbuckle case of 1921."

"Is that right?" he asked, a slight edge in his voice. "Oh yeah, I remember. Asphyxiation by farting."

"I have some beans and rice that need to be questioned," I said. My arm was hanging out the truck window and I had on sunglasses looking into the late-afternoon sun. It was almost four.

"You sure? I heard it was *carne asada*."

"You ever work a homicide like that?"

"No, but when I was on patrol in the First District, I once saw a homeless dude humping a burrito."

"Hey, it's Nick."

"No shit."

"Listen, man. I need a big favor. You remember Teddy Paris?"

I told him the whole story in about thirty seconds. I asked him to make a call and put me in touch with whoever was in white-collar crime and was pushing the paper on the ALIAS con.

"Guy named Hiney."

"Really."

"Don't make fun of him. He's really sensitive about his name. Tries to pronounce it Hi-nay, like he's fucking French or something."

"What's his deal?"

"He's our Bunco guy, bra," Jay said in his thick Irish Channel way. "Works all the hotel cons. Real pro, even if he is kind of a dick."

"You'll call?"

"When you want to come down?"

"I'll be there in two minutes."

"I'll try," he said. "If this Cash guy really wants Teddy bad, we can send someone over. Or why doesn't he just hide out awhile?"

"Good questions," I said. "But Teddy won't have it. Says it's all about rules he laid down."

"That's bullshit," he said.

"Well, if something happens to Teddy, you won't have to look far."

I hung up. Five minutes later, I walked the steps to the gray concrete building down by the parish jail. The cell phone rang and Jay said to give my name to the officer at the front desk. "The Hiney is waiting for you."

"Thought it was Hi-nay?"

"Fuck him. He's an ass any way you say it."

A FEW minutes later, Detective Hiney walked in—short dress sleeves and clipped black mustache—and asked me what I knew about these black shitbags in the Ninth Ward. I presumed he meant Teddy and Malcolm. Then the conversation with this guy somehow veered away from the theft of the $500,000 and into his theories on race. I drank a cold Barq's root beer and watched his eye twitch.

He'd actually divided the blacks of New Orleans into different tribes, and according to him—as I was unaware he'd received a degree in sociology or history—most blacks were the same as they'd been in Africa.

I felt I'd wasted the drive over to Broad Street to his little cop office that he'd had decorated with Norman Rockwell prints and awards he'd received at law enforcement conventions.

"How do you know Medeaux?" he asked.

"He was my roommate in college."

"He said you played ball. I don't remember you, but some guys said they kicked you off the Saints. Heard you choked your coach on *Monday Night Football*."

I shrugged. "My hands slipped."

He watched my eyes as if he couldn't tell if I was joking and gave a half grunt to stay on the safe side either way. I saw a tattoo of an anchor on his hairy forearm when he leaned forward and ran a stubby finger along some notes he'd made.

"Five hundred thousand," he said, giving a low whistle. "What the hell is a fifteen-year-old gonna do with that kind of money but lose it?"

"He didn't lose it."

"He lost it," he said. "Maybe it didn't fall out of his pockets. Let's just say if this kid had a second brain, it would be awful lonely."

I nodded again, finished the Barq's, and threw it into a trash can. I watched his face as he spoke. He had to be in his midforties but his skin was worn and sallow. Crumbs caught in his mustache and his breath smelled of wintergreen gum. He kept chewing as he leaned back in his seat and studied me.

"Who in New Orleans has the balls to follow through with that act at Lee Circle?" I asked. "These guys were good."

"From what you told me, they were all right," he said. "So you wanna know how many con men in New Orleans would work that game. Maybe fifty? A hundred? Bra, I been workin' Bunco since '83. I know a lot of these people. But you got to realize if you hit some kid up for that much, you're gonna retire. How many scores you think people make like that?"

"Who have you talked to?"

He stayed silent for a few moments, waiting for the impact his words would bring. "I asked Medeaux why he has a buddy who'd be mixed up with these shitbirds," the detective said, smiling slightly. "He told me that you played on the Saints with this Teddy Paris guy. Said Paris and his brother Malcolm are hot shit in the record business. So is that it? Money? They payin' you a bunch to listen to their horseshit?"

I leaned back and let him keep on rolling. The windowsill behind him was caked in dirt and broken concrete. Sunlight had yet to come close to the hulking gray building on Broad Street. Only rain. I waited.

"Just some personal advice," he said. "Medeaux said you're smart. But let me ask you a question: If you're so smart, why didn't you check out the people you're working for?"

He tossed a manila file at my hands, stood, and stretched, his bones creaking like old wood, and walked away. "I need some more coffee. I need a smoke and maybe take a dump. Why don't you read a little bit, Professor."

He walked to the door, his shoes making ugly thumping sounds. Before he closed the door to his office, he peeked back in. "I know what you think of me. I know how you liberals are. But after you're done reading, why don't you think about what made me this way?"

He left. There was silence in the room. Rusted file cabinets and sun-faded posters of crime prevention lined the walls.

I flicked open the file.

It was an investigation into the disappearance of a twenty-year-old named Calvin Jacobs. By the second page, I knew the man had been abducted last January at an Uptown club called Atlanta Nites. I knew that he was better known as Diabolical or "Dio" and he was a rapper employed by Ninth Ward Records. By the twentieth page, scanning through the depositions and detective notes, I knew that Malcolm Paris was the main suspect but they couldn't find a body. Never really a crime.

One unnamed source said: "Malcolm was bragging that he got enough Dio's shit on tape to last for years after that motherfucker was gone. Just like Tupac, he's worth more dead than alive."

I read back through.

A couple had spotted Malcolm's Bentley at the club two hours before the abduction by two men in a black van. Teddy had been walking out with Dio when the men appeared and threatened them with their guns.

I read the file again.

The file ended. Dio's body was never found.

Hiney walked back in and lifted up the blinds in his little office. He was eating a Zagnut bar and had chocolate in his teeth when he smiled at me. "Why don't you ask me why I don't like Malcolm Paris?"

"Because he's black."

"You don't understand, do you?" he said. "You work this job for two days and tell me what you see out there. Tell me what it's all about from the inside of your office at Tulane."

I didn't say anything.

"I'm having to get a fucking subpoena this week because Malcolm Paris is the only shitbird involved in this thing with the kid who won't let me look at his bank records."

11

I RAN ANNIE BACK by the warehouse, ate half of a muffuletta I'd bought at Central on Tuesday, and made a pot of coffee on my stove. A pile of pictures Maggie had sent me a few weeks back lay splayed on the table. Shots of me on her painted horse Tony and a couple of her son catching the football we'd been tossing around her old white farmhouse. One shot had been tucked neatly in the pile, a photo of us down at this catfish restaurant in Taylor, where you ate on plank wood tables and listened to bluegrass. She'd had a few glasses of white wine and was resting her head on my shoulder when a friend of hers had grabbed her Canon. Maggie showing she had her guard down. Black hair and green eyes. Bright white smile. Maggie.

Shit.

I called her. It was almost five, about the time I should've been getting into Oxford. Tomorrow I was supposed to help JoJo repair his aging barn.

As the phone rang, I reached underneath the sink and pulled out a Glock 9mm where I'd rested it on a hidden ledge. I was down on my knees peering up into my hiding place by the rusted pipes when she answered.

"Where are you?"

"New Orleans."

"Nick?"

"I'm sorry," I said. "I got held up."

I explained Teddy's situation, leaving out the worrisome details.

"Well, I'd already gotten the horses into the trailer and was waiting like a dumb-ass for you to roll down the road," she said. "Why do you do things like this?"

"He needed help in a bad way."

"I knew you'd do this to me."

"Maggie, I swear to you, it's not that," I said. "I swear."

"Well, tomorrow's your birthday," she said. "You can fuck it up any way you want."

I'd forgotten.

"I'll be there tomorrow," I said. "I promise."

I heard her son Dylan talking to her in the background. She said something short to him and then said to me, "I've got to go."

Dial tone.

Annie barked.

I poured out some dog food and scratched her ears. "You like me. Right?"

I PARKED beneath the expressway leading up to the Greater New Orleans Bridge about thirty minutes later. Above what felt like a concrete cave with a ceiling of twisting on-ramps, cars and trucks made roaring sounds. I passed by thick columns spray-painted with graffiti and elevation markers and smelled the exhaust. Crime-scene tape marked the set. The light had faded into that summer afternoon golden glow and softened all the asphalt and concrete. The sun touched everything as it grew weak and I sat watching it fade for a few minutes, aware that I was just getting started with my day.

I saw Teddy talking to a skinny black man wearing a Metairie Zephyrs baseball hat backward and a satin Yankees jacket. The man watched a video monitor and pointed to a loose group of dancers surrounding

ALIAS. The kid was breathing hard and soaked with sweat in a circle of 1960s American cars with low-rider shocks to make them jump up. About forty women in bikinis, all hard-bodied and sweating, and about fifty or so thugs stood ready to go wild when ALIAS pointed to them. They were at his command and every few minutes he'd flash a gold smile and point to the center of the group just to hear them scream.

During the break, I yelled for Teddy, who gave me the one-minute gesture. Thumping bounce rap music thudded from some speakers near ALIAS and he started into a rolling rap about Reebok sneakers, FUBU shoes, and a whole lotta Cristal was gonna make it real smooth. He bragged about a Mercedes-Benz and two Escalades and how the women who kept his company just couldn't behave.

He had a roughened, musical voice and worked his tricky lyrics and rhymes as if he were juggling words and verses in midair.

I didn't know rap but I knew he was good.

"Hey, dog," Teddy yelled. He wore rimless sunglasses tinted a deep red and a toothpick hung out of his mouth. The rap music was loud and shaking and the red, green, and yellow cars bucked like wild horses, the bikini girls popped their asses, and the posse just shouted and waved black-and-gold bandannas over their heads.

We walked to a far corner of the expressway cavern, behind one of the huge columns, where we were somewhat shielded from the music.

"I know about the cops and Malcolm," I said.

He was silent.

"You could've just dropped a word, man," I said. "I like to know these things."

Teddy was six feet six and 300 pounds and loomed over me while I talked. Not a lot of people made me feel so small.

"The cops wanted Malcolm 'cause it was easy," Teddy said, finally speaking.

The rain from earlier dripped down in dirty beads from underneath the expressway and dropped onto Teddy's sunglasses. He wiped his face and looked over my shoulder.

"Why won't he let them see his bank account?"

The music stopped and I heard the director yelling at one of the women to put her bikini top back on. While Teddy and I watched, a young white man in loose khakis and a plaid untucked shirt came by.

"I need to talk to Malcolm," I said.

Teddy nodded and said, "Later."

The man offered his hand to me and I shook it.

"This your friend Nick?" the man asked. He was in his late twenties. Easy smile on his face. Relaxed handshake. His eyes kind of unfocused, slow and lazy in his movements. He looked like he'd just woken up and stifled a yawn with his fist.

"This my dog Trey," Teddy said. "Take care of my financial things. Keep the Ninth Ward show runnin' hard."

"Y'all work together?" I asked.

"Trey Brill," he said. He had that carefully disheveled hair that was supposed to make you look like you'd just crawled out of bed. He was kind of tan and had a slight blondish stubble on his face. He kept his sunglasses on Croakies around his neck.

"Thought I was your one and only token," I said.

"I like to diversify."

"Hey, man," I said to Trey. "I need to talk to you for a few minutes."

"You can come by the office tomorrow."

I looked at Teddy.

"They ain't no tomorrow," Teddy said to Trey. "I'll explain later. I need you to do this."

Trey looked confused. "I don't understand."

"I told you about Nick looking into what happened with ALIAS?"

"Yeah."

"Give him what he needs."

"What do you do, Nick?"

"Pick up my paycheck at the end of the week," I said. I hated that question.

Trey gave that relaxed smile. "You're a teacher or something?"

"At Tulane."

"Teddy, I'm sorry, but I really don't understand."

"Take care of Nick," he said. "I ain't got time."

"I've got to head back to my office," Trey said.

"I'll meet you there."

Trey looked back at Teddy, but Teddy had already disappeared under the concrete caves.

12

FIFTEEN MINUTES LATER, I rode the elevator up to the thirty-second floor of a nameless CBD building made of steel and mirrors. A black leather sofa and a small coffee table covered in back issues of the *Robb Report* sat inside the glass door to BRILL & ASSOCIATES, SPORTS AND ENTERTAINMENT MANAGEMENT. A wooden humidor of cigars and a cutter waited for anyone who needed to indulge. The magazines featured articles on test drives of the latest Ferraris and new Caribbean resorts with nights that started in the $3,000 range.

Framed photos hung on the walls. Couple of old teammates of mine. The current coach for the Saints. A famous jazz musician. I stared through a doorway flooded with dim light into an office and back wall with a view of another mirrored office building across the street. A red light blinked from an antenna on the roof. The sky was orange and black, dark clouds still hovering over Algiers. I hoped the streets would not flood tonight.

Brill walked in with a black man who looked to be somewhere in his twenties. The black man, really just a kid, carried a couple of helmets and footballs. He wore a navy polo shirt and khakis. They were laughing hard, and when the guy put down all the sports paraphernalia, Trey gave him a high five.

The other guy looked at me and his eyes narrowed a bit. Trey waited a second, checked messages on the secretary's desk, and then turned back. "One minute, Nick. Okay?"

We shook hands and his smile folded deeply into dimples. He divided his long frat-boy hair out of his eyes. "So, what do you need?"

He'd yet to introduce his buddy. The buddy crossed his arms over his chest and peered down at my dirty boots. I looked at him and he just watched me. No smile, no greeting.

"Oh, this is my friend Christian," Brill said. "We had to grab some of this stuff for a new sports bar a friend of ours is opening. They needed some more Saints crap. Man, we're going to be great this year. I can't wait."

I always hated it when men referred to the teams they followed as "we." I don't call drinking beer and yelling at the players doing the actual work some kind of true common bond. Especially the ones who think their affiliation is on a metaphysical plane and they are as responsible for the outcome as the guys on the field.

I followed Brill back to his office, where the walls were lined with more sports stars and photos of him with old NFL greats. One showed him running through some tires at some kind of NFL fantasy camp.

He reached into a small refrigerator by his glass desk and pulled out Evian water. He kicked out of his Nikes, rolled off his socks, and laid his bare feet on top of the desk. "Shoot."

"I need to look at Teddy and Malcolm's bank records, any account that was drained."

He sipped on the water as if it were a baby's bottle. A pacifier of some kind. He squinted his eyes and nodded with concern. "And what will that do?"

"Find ALIAS's money."

He nodded. "O-kay. Haven't the police already done this?" He gave a forced laugh.

"They tried, but Malcolm wouldn't let them," I said. "I need to know when you noticed the money was missing and copies of any withdrawals made."

He nodded again and downed half the bottle of water. He stood up and patted me on the back. "Listen, I appreciate you being such a good friend to Teddy, and if you hear of anything that can help us out with that missing money, I will let the detectives know. But it's not our policy to let information like that out."

"Call Teddy."

"We already spoke."

"And he said not to release these records to me?"

"And what would you do with them?"

"Make paper animals. Maybe a hat."

"They don't tell us anything. It just transferred to some kind of holding account that disappeared. The money came from Malcolm's joint account, and he doesn't want to work with you."

"What was the name on the account where the money was transferred to?"

He patted me on the back again and tried to steer me out of his office by grabbing my biceps. I didn't move.

In the other room, his buddy had strapped the helmet on his head and was trying to drop back like a QB. He had a puckered scar from a brand on his muscular arm, but his polo shirt was stiff and fresh. Expensive brown leather loafers.

"Teddy gets a little ahead of himself sometimes," he said. "I can only work with the police."

I pried his fingers from my biceps.

"Don't ever grab my arm again, kid."

"Whooh." Brill laughed and made a scary motion with his palms raised.

His buddy laughed and took off his helmet. He moved in close to me. I could smell a sourness about his clothes mixed with some kind of expensive cologne. He was light-skinned and his eyes were a brownish green.

"Listen, I know Teddy thinks he owes you something because you didn't really work out with the team and all."

"I look forward to getting those records," I said. "Why don't you just wait here for Teddy to call."

"All right, then," he said, holding the door wide. "Thanks for coming by."

His smile remained stuck on his face as if drawn by a stranger. He didn't even know it was there.

13

ABERCROMBIE & FITCH. Brooks Brothers. Crate & Barrel. Starbucks. Trey Brill liked the way his stores smelled. Uncluttered and clean. The dark coffee smell of Starbucks. The faded look to an Abercrombie hat with a cool old rugby logo. The way Brooks Brothers had the same ties and shirts every year. Everything the way you expected it. Trey finished up paying for a new suit and walked out with Christian, who'd hung with him since they left the office. He and his old friend side by side since the time they were twelve. Soccer practices to bars to business partners.

Trey and Christian watched Teddy from the second floor of the shopping mall, looking down at the fat man sitting by the wishing fountain. Teddy sure was sweating a lot today, the back of his silk shirt soaked. He seemed real jumpy, too, like when Trey mentioned that he needed to pick up a suit before they headed to Redfish for dinner. Teddy just kind of freaked out.

"He's fucked," Christian said, smiling.

"His own fault," Trey said.

"People like that can never handle money," Christian said. "They don't understand it."

"True."

He said good-bye to Christian, and as his friend was walking away, he saw Teddy peer up at the balcony. He was sure that Teddy saw Christian only from a distance and he was glad of that.

"I don't think that's a good idea," Teddy said when he met him at the foot of the escalator. The PA system played some Sting from his *Live in Tuscany* concert, one of Trey's favorites.

"He's my friend."

"Just don't think it's a good idea."

Trey tried to look concerned at Teddy's sweating and paranoia while they walked outside to the parking lot and stuck his suit in his trunk. Make him think he was flipping out about nothing. They decided to walk over to Bourbon Street and Redfish. Teddy said he couldn't breathe in the car.

"Are you doing okay, man?" Trey asked as they walked around the old marble Customs House. It was dark now and he could hear all the dance music and that awful Cajun stuff starting up down on North Peters and through the Quarter. Tourists in tennis shoes and shorts, carrying cameras and cups of Hurricanes, walked by the old brick storefronts and under wooden signs flapping in the warm wind.

"Yeah," Teddy said, huffing and puffing down Iberville and crossing over Decatur Street. "Just got some things on my mind."

"Your buddy Travers stopped by," he said.

"You help him out?"

"Yeah," Trey said. "Gave him what I legally could."

"Good."

Some homeless man wandered over, begging them for a few bucks. Said he needed some bus fare, behind him was the red curved neon of an all-night bar.

Trey laughed at him. "Get a job."

"Can't," said the toothless man.

"Sorry," Trey said. "Jeez."

Teddy didn't even notice. He just had his big head down kicking absently at a dirty Lucky Dog wrapper filled with mustard and stinking onions.

"You believe ALIAS?" Teddy asked.

"I don't know," he said. "I don't know him that well."

"I need that money."

"I know, Teddy."

"I don't think you do," he said. "Ain't worried about creditors, man. See, I borrowed some money from Cash."

Trey stopped walking by a used bookstore. He put his hand on Teddy's shoulder. "What's going on? Talk to me, dog."

Trey knew Teddy liked when he said "dog." Made him seem like a true Ninth Warder.

Teddy told the whole story about why he'd gone to Cash for money for ALIAS's video, said he thought they could make it up on the next record from this guy that Malcolm thought was so great named Stank. But Trey knew that Stank hadn't even cut the damned album yet. They were already getting killed by the latest releases from No Limit and Cash Money. Last year Ninth Ward Records was making those guys sweat.

Teddy said he had till morning before Cash said he was going to kill him. Trey led him into the restaurant, where they took a seat near the bar and ordered. They didn't talk until the waiter returned.

Trey took a sip of his dirty martini and looked concerned. Redfish had lots of chrome, yellow Christmas lights, a big fake oyster over the bar that had been turned into a mirror. Nice leather seats. It was all right to Trey, but he liked Emeril's a lot more.

The waiter brought them a couple of plates of Oysters Three Ways: grilled, fried, and raw on a bed of rock salt. Teddy slurped his right off his plate, gobbling everything up just like the street hustler that he'd always been. Or maybe because he thought this was his last supper or something. Pretty weird. Of course Teddy wasn't brought up with any class. He hadn't gone to Metairie Country Day or gone to Vandy on an academic scholarship that his parents bought. He hadn't spent his winters skiing in Vail or summers down in Baja sipping tequila and screwing girls from UCLA.

Teddy went to Freaknik in Atlanta and still paid women to be seen with him.

"Can we get money from anywhere else?" Teddy asked. "Did you check into the cars or the house?"

"Not in one night, man."

"Don't you know some people?" he asked. "People in Old Metairie. That kind of money like chump change to them."

"Teddy, you are my friend. But it doesn't work that way. I can't just call up somebody and ask for a half a million. I mean, they'd think I was crazy."

Trey stirred the martini with his finger. He knew he needed to call Molly, finally buy that sofa from Restoration Hardware, and maybe hook up with this gash who was in grad school at Tulane. A buddy of his had already fucked her. He'd buy her a drink and take her to the Hyatt or something. Heard she had an ass that just wouldn't quit.

Teddy buried his head in his hands. The redfish entrée came and Teddy pushed it away. "Nick's got to find it. He has to."

Trey played with his drink more. Two women, dirty blondes in halters and fake leather pants, walked into the bar. Their boyfriends behind them. Couple of tools in cheap Gap shirts and tourist running shoes. Last year's Nikes.

"I know this guy's your friend, but who is he, really?" Trey asked, trying to seem interested in Teddy's problems. "I mean, as a professional. He's a teacher, right? My buddy Josh is a lawyer and has three investigators working for him. They'd do a better job. This guy doesn't impress me."

"Yeah?" Teddy said. "Nick once got this woman out of jail after forty years. Also took down that L.A. motherfucker that owned that Blues Shack club."

"So he's muscle?" Trey asked. "That's not what we need. Let me get someone good on this. This guy, no offense, man, seems like a real loser. He was wearing a T-shirt with a cartoon on it."

"I have till the morning," Teddy said, head up and watching Brill now. "Ain't you listenin'?"

Trey shrugged. "Aren't you above this thug shit now? You worked too hard. You don't need people like that."

"What you got goin' on, Brill?" Teddy asked, looking Trey hard in the eye. He held his stare. "You wouldn't want to see me lose, would you?"

"After all we've been through?" Trey asked. "We're more brothers than you and Malcolm."

"You still meetin' with him tonight?"

"Should I cancel?"

"I guess not," Teddy said. "Don't have nothin' to do with my troubles."

Trey winked at him.

Teddy smiled. "You a hustla too, right?"

Trey smiled back and took a sip of the martini. "You know it, dog."

14

I CHECKED WITH CURTIS at his house—and got nowhere—dropped by the warehouse and fed Annie, leaving on Cartoon Network for her to watch *Superfriends,* and headed out to a strip club in New Orleans East where I knew I'd find ALIAS. It was about eight o'clock and the sky turned black and purple on the horizon as I drove I-10 toward Slidell and found the exit. I passed an old Shoney's and a now-defunct shopping mall that had become the place for local crack deals and gunfights. The cops didn't even like to patrol here anymore.

About ten years ago, New Orleans East was a suburb of corporate apartments and yuppie condos along with the usual strip malls and chain restaurants. But since the Hope VI federal housing initiative took off and local slumlords could get easy money through Section 8 housing grants, New Orleans East had taken over where the now-demolished Magnolia and Desire housing projects had left off.

But instead of brick and mortar sheltering the poor, it was Sheetrock and flimsy plywood—no apartment manager having to answer for shit while the slumlords grew rich and wrote off millions on their taxes.

The Booty Call Club was pretty much black-only with the loose gathering of basic out-of-town white businessmen with per diem cash to spend. Nothing special. A rambling building with no windows next door to a Denny's. By the parking lot stood an industrial plastic sign of a cartoon black woman covering her breasts with a Mardi Gras mask.

The inside was dark, lit in a few areas with track lighting and neon beer signs. The air smelled like cherry incense and Pine-Sol. Toward a main stage where some woman was twirling on a brass pole to George Clinton's "Atomic Dog," I found Malcolm sipping on a forty-ounce and smoking a Newport. His Saints jersey running down to his knees and his Timberland boots propped up in a chair before him. A couple of other teens I'd seen at the video shoot gathered around the girl's stage and stuck twenties into her garter.

She was brown-eyed and had long curly brown hair. She had a little pooch to her belly and her legs jiggled when she danced. But the more twenties she got, the more she shook it.

I pulled up a chair—the sound of the funk deafening—and leaned into Malcolm. He gave me a pound and offered me a Newport from his pack, his cigarette catching in the side of his mouth by his gold tooth.

"Where's ALIAS?" I asked. The music shifted to this old Prince tune about not having to watch *Dynasty* to have an attitude, and Malcolm ran with it, bobbing his head, cigarette dangling from his lips as he listened.

"You gonna get that man that took all that money?" Malcolm took a sip of the beer. He'd been smoking it up and his eyes were a little tight. He just kind of hummed each word out of his mouth. Told me he loved me. Loved me for helping his big brother out. He asked if I wanted a cigarette again and I said I did.

He handed me the pack.

"I know you always bummin' off people, right."

I appreciated the gesture; he was into respect. Last year when two shitbags had almost killed Loretta, the Paris brothers were the first at the hospital. Malcolm called me about every day after that wanting to know what he could do. He would've killed somebody if I'd asked him.

I took a cigarette and tucked the pack in my jacket.

"I need to borrow ALIAS."

"Take 'im," Malcolm said. "Boy played out."

"Was Dio like that?"

"Dio was nothin' but heart," Malcolm said. I still saw the boy's face in the hardened man. He still had the same soft eyes and nappy hair from when he used to come by practice with Teddy. Fifteen and running errands for his big brother.

Malcolm cupped a cigarette to his face, smoke fingering its way up over the lines and creases the last ten years had left.

"That what killed him?"

"I don't know what killed him, man," Malcolm said. He turned away and took a long drag off the Newport and a deep swig off the forty. "I always thought it was Cash that snatched his ass."

"Looking forward to meeting him."

"Be careful, brother," he said. "The man could turn Mike Tyson into his bitch. He likes to make you bow down. Bleed a little bit to his respect."

"You think Cash took ALIAS for the money?"

Malcolm shrugged. "Naw," he said. "Didn't you listen to ALIAS? Some white man worked him. That ain't Cash. He don't play."

"So I heard," I said. "What happened with Dio?"

His smile turned.

"Couple of men took him last year."

"Stuffed him in a van at that Uptown club?"

He nodded.

"And you don't think that's connected to ALIAS?"

"Why would it be?" he said. "Some hustlers took him down. He's dead. We'll never find him."

"Police said it was you."

Malcolm stuck the cigarette in his mouth and inched closer to my face. He mouthed the word "Shit" and turned his back to me. "Goddamn, I used to respect you," he said. "You just like 'em all. Fuck this. I don't care if I told Teddy to find you."

He got up and strutted away, his football jersey untucked, and took a long swig from his forty before wrapping his long arms around two of the dancers.

I found and followed a hallway through a back room where flickered patterns of red and blue lights played in small, individual coves.

ALIAS lay on a round bed with a young girl, really beautiful with her long black hair partially covered in a black bandanna and long slender legs. She stretched out on top of his back, hugging him tight almost like he was a life preserver, as he—oblivious to her—worked out some aggression on a video game with dragons and knights.

"You ready?" I asked.

"You get what you need?"

"No."

"I told you, Old School," he said, pulling on his baseball cap. "You wouldn't listen. These people done gone. No faces. No names. How you supposed to come through for Teddy? You best call him now and tell him to take a long ride out of New Orleans."

"Maybe."

"What else you gonna do?"

"I'm workin' on it."

"Better work fast."

"Come on."

He patted the young girl's right hand that gripped him tight, her body prone on his, and she slowly slid off of him. Wordless. Her eyes accusing me for taking him away. She tucked her hair back into her bandanna and stripped off a long shirt to reveal a complicated array of belts, garters, lace, and buckles.

She was fourteen and then she was an adult.

ALIAS checked himself in the mirror, grabbed a Saints ball cap that was perched on the edge of the chair, and nodded at me. "Let's roll."

15

ALIAS WAS HUNGRY and I was fresh out of ideas. But I'd made a ton of calls and hoped Curtis's countryfied lyin' ass would come through for once. I checked the cell phone, willing it to ring, but it didn't while we sat at the counter of the Camellia Grill waiting on ALIAS's hamburger. I'd ordered an omelette and a cup of coffee. It was about ten o'clock and I was tired. I washed my face in the bathroom with cold water and returned to the seat where ALIAS was already eating. I thought about Maggie's porch and these great old green chairs she had where we kicked back and talked all night.

The Camellia Grill was a little diner in a small white house at the end of the streetcar tracks near the turnaround in Carrollton. After being in the humidity all day, the air-conditioning felt nice, and for a long time, ALIAS and I didn't talk.

"You trust Malcolm?" I asked.

He nodded and took another bite.

"What about Teddy?"

"Sure."

"Malcolm ever ask you for money?"

He shook his head, looking confused. I passed him some ketchup and asked the waiter for some Crystal sauce. Just right on an omelette.

"Is Teddy gonna die?" ALIAS asked.

"No."

"How you know?"

" 'Cause Teddy can talk his way out of anything."

"What you mean?"

"I mean Teddy knows how to survive."

"So why you workin' so hard?"

"Just in case."

"Cash is evil."

"How do you know?"

"Me and him know each other. He offered me money to get on his label."

"You gonna leave Teddy?"

"Don't know."

"What do you want to be when you're grown up?" I asked.

"I am grown up."

"You're fifteen."

"I'm a man," he said.

"You like women?"

"They a'ight."

"Just all right."

"Yeah, I like them."

He looked away from me and dabbled a fry into the ketchup.

"I have a woman in Mississippi that's pretty pissed at me."

"You fuck someone else?"

"No."

"Get drunk?"

"No."

"Then what she bitchin' 'bout?"

"It's my birthday tomorrow and she had something planned."

He finished off the burger and carefully poured more ketchup in a neat little pile. He liked to keep everything separate. There was no mixing of ketchup and fries till he was ready.

"Who was that girl at the club?"

"Tamika."

"Who is she?"

"A friend."

"She's a kid."

"Maybe," he said. "She use her sister's driver's license so she can dance. She ain't bad. She can shake her ass and shit."

The streetcar passed underneath the oaks outside. A priest and a woman with a bruise under her eye walked in and found a seat by the bathroom. I finished the omelette and drank some more coffee.

"Where we gonna head next?"

"I don't know."

I excused myself and walked outside, trying Curtis again. The phone rang about six times before he answered. He [illegible]nded out of breath.

"Stella got me doin' this exercise tape, got that black dude that's some kind of big star in Hong Kong. You know he got that funny head that look like a turtle? Man, that shit kickin' my ass."

"What you got?" I watched my truck across the street and a couple of kids skateboarding around it. Crime lights scattered on my hood and I heard some bottleneck guitar playing at a biker bar in the crook of St. Charles.

"Pinky's Bar."

"Where?"

"It's in the Marigny but ain't no fag place or anything," Curtis said. I heard Stella yelling at him. "Ask for Fred. You'll get what you need."

16

PINKY'S SPECIALIZED in kick-ass punk music, explosive drinks, and a Tuesday-night bondage show, or so I heard from Curtis. I'd left my leather mask back home and I never owned a whip in my life but decided I'd be safe. I told ALIAS he could wait in the truck, but he said he wanted to see this place. He said freaks were interesting and wanted to know if it was like that shit in *Pulp Fiction*. I'd parked off Elysian Fields and Chartres by a methadone clinic and a vegetarian restaurant that offered discounts to same-sex couples. A few years back, I wouldn't have even driven through this neighborhood; the gunshots and violence were constant. But a few years ago, the homosexual community had taken over the Marigny, cleaning it up and making it their own. But now the historic district right by the Quarter was going through another change. Gentrification. Now it was hipper than Uptown and way too cool for the Quarter.

And Pinky's, I think, was supposed to be too cool for anyone.

A nice neon sign of a forties pinup in a pink nightgown hung over the vinyl padded door with a diamond glass for a window. Nice curvy butt and shoulders and blond hair on top of her head in ribbons. She winked at you, holding a hand of cards. Pink neon surrounding her body. From inside, Johnny Cash was singing "That Lucky Old Sun," the Ray Charles number.

A grizzled white dude with multiple piercings and a shaved head smoked a clove cigarette behind the bar and flipped through a copy of *Newsweek*. A photo of George W. Bush on the cover looking intense. He nodded along with the article as I waited for a little service.

"What'll it be?" he asked. He was British.

"Two Cokes."

"I want a beer," ALIAS said.

"One Coke and a Barq's."

"Man, that's root beer."

"No shit."

ALIAS walked off to the jukebox.

"I'm also looking for a guy named Fred Moore," I said.

"She's not in."

"She?"

"She'll be back in a minute," he said. "She had to pick up the band."

We waited as the bar really opened up. The lights dimmed. More pink neon. Black-and-white photos of forties B actors and movie posters for these noir films that I didn't even know lined the walls. A few Bettie Page flicks. Some sixties Roger Corman stuff. ALIAS loaded up the jukebox with some rap music I'd never heard.

The waitresses walked in and started getting ready for the night. Brunette and blond. They were all beautiful and young and hard as hell. Their pasty white faces never saw the sun. Deep red lips outlined in black and hair up in Andrews Sisters configurations. Tight black Ts with glitter sayings: BITCH and HOT STUFF and double dice on snake eyes. They all wore combat boots and black socks.

ALIAS gave me a wild stare over the back of one of the girls and mouthed the word "Freak."

A few minutes later, an older woman with hair so blond I wasn't too sure it wasn't white walked in the door with a group of tired kids hauling guitars and pieces of a drum kit. She pointed out the stage cast in a red light, walked over to the bar, and asked the pierced Brit for the mail.

He handed some stuff to her but didn't mention me. She had on large black sunglasses in the darkened bar. Long black shirt, tight black pants.

I introduced myself and said I'd like to talk to her about some business in private. Johnny Cash came back on in the shuffle and sang about God havin' a heaven for country trash.

"I do my business here. You don't like, then fuck off. This is my place."

She sat at the bar stool next to me. She was in her late forties or early fifties. She reminded me of Deborah Harry if Deborah Harry lived an even tougher life. She lit a long cigarette.

"Who was Pinky?"

"My mother."

"No shit."

"No shit," she said. "I've heard that more GIs jacked off to her than Betty Grable."

"You must be proud."

"Fuckin' A."

"I had one of those posters of Farrah Fawcett. Got me through puberty."

"You must be proud too."

"I have guilt."

She took a long draw of cigarette and nodded about ten times, letting the smoke just float out of the corner of her mouth. Her mouth looked like a shrunken, dead rose. She kept looking over my shoulder at ALIAS. She watched him as she played with her cigarette.

Fred motioned for the bartender. "Watch that kid."

The bartender nodded.

"The kid's with me."

"What are you, into some kind of Big Brother program?" she said. "Get rid of that guilt you got."

"I heard you could lead me to someone who conned a friend of mine."

"What's in it for me?"

"Great question," I said. "I can arrange money."

"Who sent you?"

"Curtis Lee."

"Thought he was on the Farm."

"Got out."

"I would've stayed if I was married to that wretched woman."

"He loves her."

"Curtis has problems."

"Maybe."

She walked off, spoke to the band for a few minutes, and then returned to the bar. Punks began to fill up the place, all black-T-shirted and pierced, tattoos muraling their arms. Heads shaved. Hair moussed up in impossible directions.

"What do you want to know?"

I repeated the story about Teddy, the kid, and the con. The man with cauliflower ears. She listened.

"How much money did he lose?"

"That's for you to find out and then tell me who I need to find."

She shrugged. "How much?"

"Has to come through first."

"I haven't run a game in five years."

I ordered another Coke. She paid for it and I appreciated that.

"Anyone run the big games around here?"

"Used to be this cocksucker named Fourtnot but he died in the eighties. I don't know. Mostly freelance. Lots of Lotto games. Big cons on old women down at the lakefront. But what you're talking about is impressive. Good imagination."

"Not bad."

She reached out with her long fingers and slowly raked her red nails across my arm.

"Tell your boy to get lost and come with me," she said.

"Where would you start?"

She flipped her hair back and lit another cigarette. She looked at herself in the mirror, not finding what she was looking for, and mussed her hair with her fingers. "I will. You won't."

Her fingers were stained with nicotine and her breath smelled of garlic and mint. She looked at me and sighed. "I want five thousand."

"Has to come through tonight," I said.

"I'll work on it."

"I need it within a couple of hours."

She nodded.

"What happened to Pinky?"

"She jumped off the balcony of the Fountainebleau in Miami."

She stubbed her cigarette into an ashtray filled with peanut shells and walked away.

17

I DROPPED ALIAS at his mansion a little past midnight. He told me that the place—a Mediterranean Revival number on Pontchartrain with bonsai-looking trees—was going to be plowed under someday and updated with something he'd seen on *Deep Space 9*. We walked inside an empty house and I noticed a little spot for him in the living room with a GI Joe sleeping bag and a small CD player. Dozens of rap CDs lay on the floor by his pillow and a couple of discount packs of chips and warm liters of Pepsi. Little indentations from missing furniture spotted the white carpet. Moonlight crept into his paneled French doors from the pool.

"You sure you're going to be okay?" I asked.

"Yeah," he said. "Why not?"

I gave him the number to the cell and watched him as he tucked himself into the blanket and turned his back to me.

I drove back home, hoping that thing from Fred would shake out. Without that, I didn't have much. Teddy wouldn't respond to my messages about that dick Trey Brill. I was beginning to lose patience and I was tired as hell.

But as soon as I got close to my warehouse on Julia, I felt something was out of place.

Four cars were parked in broken patterns in front of businesses that had closed up for the night. A black Cadillac Escalade, two red Ferraris, and a green Rolls, all their bright silver rims shining down the stretch of asphalt.

I didn't turn into the warehouse. I parked down the street and walked.

The convertible top was down on the Rolls. A box of .38 slugs sat empty in the passenger seat. The light to my warehouse burned bright through a huge bank of industrial windows. The small blue door that leads to the second floor was closed.

I slipped a key into the lock and slowly pushed it open with both hands. I reached for the Glock in my jacket. The seventeen rounds waited jacked inside.

Upstairs, I heard Annie's high-pitched barking. She yelped in an urgent rhythm.

I crept up the stairs and heard a crash in my loft and a couple of men laughing.

I moved forward, my heart skipping pretty damned quickly in my chest. I tried to control my breathing and slip silently to the landing. Annie kept barking, her yips working into a howl.

The huge sliding door had been pushed open and inside about a half-dozen men rifled through my shit. A man with a puckered burn mark across his cheek drank my Jack Daniel's from the bottle and then spit a mouthful onto the floor. Two of the men were shirtless and muscular, wearing stiff, wide-legged jeans and clean work boots. Gold and platinum in chains hung around their necks and molded into their teeth.

I couldn't spot Annie.

I slipped my finger tighter on the trigger and backed down the stairs to call the police. My heart began to palpitate, my breathing quick. The man with the burn mark asked for a lighter.

I took another step backward.

I felt the sharp prick of a flat, wide blade in my side.

The knife moved up to my neck.

"Slow down, motherfucker. We waitin' on you."

He pushed me forward on the landing while I slipped the gun into my jacket pocket. In the darkness, he hadn't seen it.

As we entered the large open space of the warehouse, a couple of tool shelves by the window where I kept my field interviews had been toppled. Several VHS tapes—loaded with interviews of people who'd died years ago—lay in piles on the floor.

A short, muscular man in a net shirt walked toward me, his palms open on each side as if waiting to begin prayer. His teeth were platinum and jeweled and he had a red tattoo of a heart that seemed to be live and beating on his muscled chest.

His right hand darted to the small of his back and he came up with a snub-nosed .38 that he jammed and twisted in my ear. I was so intent on not moving, I didn't even notice his feet kicking out my legs.

I fell to the floor. He inched closer with the gun to the bridge of my nose.

"You like scrambled eggs?"

He called 'em "aigs."

His group ringed me. Their eyes were red and squinted tight and they gritted their teeth while I squirmed.

"What you doin' with them Paris brothers?" the man asked.

The man with the scar pulled out a book, *Catcher in the Rye,* from my kitchen table and held a Zippo against its pages. He dropped my book next to the pool of whiskey and I watched its pages curl with smoke.

I didn't move. I didn't breathe. Annie's yelps came from inside my bathroom.

The leader knocked me across the face, holding the gun in my ear.

"Teddy's my friend," I said.

He laughed at that, his platinum teeth feral and wild. He yanked me halfway off the floor with one hand and an arm the size of my leg. His arm didn't even tremble as he held me there.

I smelled the fire burning into the book's musty pages.

"I take it you're Cash?"

"How you know my name?"

"Luck."

He let me go. As I got to my knees, I heard the clicking of guns around me. He kicked me hard in the ribs. I tried to breathe but couldn't. My bones felt like they were made of splintered wood. He thumped my head with the back of his hand. "Who got that money?"

I gasped that I didn't know. Cash picked up the smoldering book, nodded at my shelf of first editions, and asked if I thought it was too cold in the room. "Need some heat."

One of the thugs gripped the back of my neck and I could smell his rancid body odor, like that of spoiled milk, seeping through his bare chest. He threw me forward, my head connecting hard with the wood floor. I rolled on my stomach, wheezing and groaning a bit, and reached into my jacket for the Glock.

Two of his boys tackled me and wrestled the gun from my hand. Annie kept yelping. One of the boys let her out and she came running to me, licking my face. I held her close and stayed on the floor.

"Teddy Paris sold out the kid," Cash said. "You keep out ALIAS' business. He roll with me now. You hear? Don't come round Calliope no more. That's my world."

I wiped the blood off my mouth and stood, holding Annie's collar. "Someone conned ALIAS."

"Ain't my trouble."

"If anything happens to Teddy, a detective from NOPD will be coming for you before you can take your morning piss."

He smiled some more. I got to my feet. Annie stood by me and began to growl.

"You set Teddy up?" I asked.

He laughed and pawed at his chest. His mouth shined in the light.

"We goin' for a ride," Cash said.

I could taste the blood in my mouth and my hands shook uselessly at my sides.

"And if I refuse?"

"Then we'll kill your ass."

18

CASH AND HIS ENTOURAGE drove me over the river to Algiers, where they ate greasy sacks of Burger King, traded stories about women they'd done, and passed around joints as fat as rolls of quarters. All this while I waited for someone to put a bullet in my head. I was too tired to be scared. My hands had stopped shaking a few minutes before and I just listened to the river moving past us and the sound of tugs and faint music from the Quarter. The air smelled of sulfur and old dirt.

We were in the dead zone. Nothing but warehouses and vacant shotguns. Rusted cars and spare parts from the World's Fair in 1984.

Their Rolls, Ferraris, and Escalades ringed me like some kind of old wagon train. Cash was doing business in his car. Someone had built a fire from some driftwood. I kept thinking about my dog. Wondering why such a group of thugs would've let me lock her up before coming along.

Cash climbed out of his ride and strutted over.

"You know you used to could ride over the river in a bucket," I said, growing tired of the silence.

Cash turned to me. I thought I heard him growl.

"It's true," I said. "It was like Disneyland; you could pay a few bucks and get a nice view of the city and everything. Those were what I like to call simpler times."

"Shut the fuck up."

"You want some of your boys to hold me down while you beat me again?"

"You sayin' I ain't hard?"

It was so dark that a few of the thugs had turned on their headlights to spot the high grass where we stood.

"I think you're a pussy who needs help winning a fight," I said.

Wrong choice of words. Cash pulled off his net shirt and moved in for me. His fist cocked back, eyes wild. He pushed me with his right hand.

I led with my left and connected with his ear with the right. He leapt on top of me and started hammering at my face, but I kneed him in the nuts and he fell off me. I wrapped his bald animal head into the crook of my elbow and I squeezed until he started trying to gasp for air that would not come.

All his boys circled us, drawing their guns back on me.

I let him go.

He stood, started to laugh, and walked to me with a smile. He bent his neck to the side and I heard his spine pop.

I thought I'd gained his respect up until the point he punched me in the stomach.

I fell. I breathed in as hard as I could, feeling the air narrowly pass into me. I noticed all the lights across the river. Everything grew muffled around me.

"Punk?" Cash yelled. "Punk!"

I used a concrete block to find my feet and I wavered in front of him.

I punched for his temple, but he ducked. I tried another shot and he ducked again.

I gave up on boxing and tackled his legs out from him. All of his boys whooped and hollered as he tried to get off his back like a fallen turtle and I wrapped him up in a headlock. I tasted blood and dirt in my mouth.

"We even," he said. He spit in my face.

"Stay away from Teddy."

"Stay away from my boy ALIAS," he grunted.

I let him go and for several moments we both tried to catch our breath. He paced around and talked a little shit about me being a cheater and then moved in close, his eyes wild like he wanted to go again.

"Teddy needs more time."

"Fuck him," Cash said. "Teddy tell me that he need more time too. How come his brother paid off that bitch Nae Nae then? Dropped off a goddamned Mercedes truck yesterday. Now does that sound broke-ass? He just wavin' that shit in my face. That I cannot stand."

"Who's Nae Nae?"

"Stay away from ALIAS," he said, reaching for a shirt a flunky held open for him. As soon as he looped his arm into the fresh silk, he reached out for the man's joint and took a hit. "Tell Teddy I'm ready to deal."

His breath expelled into a big fat ganja cloud and then dissolved into the wind.

"He won't give you the kid."

"Well, I ain't gonna let him fall like Dio. Man, that boy had some heart and he dead 'cause of it. Tell Teddy to stay in the city."

"Teddy didn't kill Dio."

"You sure?"

I looked at him.

He sucked on the joint. "Why you fight me? You crazy in the head?"

"Maybe."

"Ain't nobody takes on Cash like that."

I nodded.

He did too. He looked down at his watch. "That dawn come mighty early. Tell Teddy we lookin' forward to taking him for a ride."

"What'd you want with me?"

"How 'bout you just stay home tonight?" he asked. "What happenin' between me and Teddy is our own thing. This shit been comin' for a long time. He don't need to come up with that money. You see?"

I left my hands at my side and Cash shook his head like I'd just given an incredibly stupid answer to a very simple question. He ran his fat tongue over the platinum and diamonds in his mouth. His small pit-bull eyes lazy but still intense.

As he drove away, he threw my Glock 17 into the ditch along the road. I wiped the dirt on the side of my leg and tucked the empty gun into my jacket.

Their wagon train of SUVs and Italian imports looped back onto Powder Street and the old rusted bridge that stretched over to the city. I walked behind them, rubbing the blood from my face, straightening out my clothes and calling a United Cab from the cell still in my pocket.

19

TREY LOVED THAT SCENE from *The Grifters*. The one when Cusack walks into that TGI Friday's place and holds a twenty in his fingers but has the folded dollar flipped underneath his palm. When the bartender gets ready to make his change, he coolly flicks out the buck and no one notices a freakin' thing. Trey didn't like to keep things from Teddy. Didn't like to hide things from the big guy. He'd always gotten along with him, enjoyed picking out his clothes, decorating his home, and shaping Ninth Ward into a national company. But Teddy didn't have to know everything.

Trey looked over at Malcolm, drunk and stoned, sleeping on the couch in Trey's office in the CBD. He clicked off his e-mail and reached into his desk drawer for two CDs he'd burned earlier today. Nothing but a white paper label.

On his walls hung pictures of his travels with his fraternity brothers from college. All of them in that little bar down in Costa Rica listening to that reggae band and singing like hell. Another of him and Christian in Switzerland when they climbed that mountain and drank some really good German beer, both flashing their wrists with freshly built Rolexes. The good one. The Submariner.

Trey tucked the CDs into Malcolm's coat pocket and shook him awake. The overhead lights had been shut off by his secretary and only small little table lamps glowed. Malcolm stirred a bit and Trey made himself a Ketel One martini at the minibar. No vermouth. He hated vermouth. A clean twist of lemon.

On the bar, he kept a small CD player and flicked through the CDs. No fucking rap. But he did have some awesome Dave Matthews. A little Widespread Panic and some Limp Bizkit. Great driving music.

He cranked up the Bizkit. It was Friday night. All the offices were closed and he could play a little. Malcolm grabbed a beer beside him and began to wash his face in the tiny marble sink.

"What are you doing?"

"Cleanin' up," Malcolm said.

"There's a bathroom down the hall."

He began to walk away, shaking his head, his Hornets jersey slipped over a white T with some hundred-dollar jeans. His face covered in shadows.

"Why don't you turn that shit down?" Malcolm said.

"Check your pockets while you're out."

Malcolm looked at Trey for a second and then walked back to his stiff jean jacket, searching through each compartment. When he found the CDs, he froze.

"How many more?"

"Twenty-two tracks, enough for a double album."

"Don't make no sense."

Trey took the martini and walked back to his desk and plunked down the drink on the table. He just started to dance, rocking his head up and down. Feeling that music. All that energy. He might be a businessman but he could still rock.

Malcolm turned down the music. He walked over as Trey started giggling a little and reached his right hand in the air for a high five.

"Where you gettin' this?"

"His mother."

"Dio said his mamma died."

"Then it was his aunt."

"Damn, man," he said.

"A little extra kick that we needed," Trey said. "Right?"

"Teddy will want to know."

"And you'll tell him about his aunt," Trey said. "I keep up with all his family. They're all part of the estate. Teddy will understand."

"Is it good?"

"The best."

"Don't want to be known for producin' a dead man all my life."

"Dio is forever," Trey said, reaching for Malcolm's hand.

Malcolm didn't take it. "You startin' to make sense."

Trey stopped smiling and had to catch his breath. "What are you talking about?"

"You know, Brill," he said. "Quit tryin' to fuck me."

"Keep cool."

Malcolm's face turned inward. "This shit got to stop."

Trey walked over to the window. From the outside, they just looked like mirrors. Dozens of silver glass frames. But on the inside, everything was so fucking clear. The Quarter. A gambling boat drifting down the river. Some women lining up down by Harrah's.

"Let's roll," Trey said.

"I'm done."

"Nope," Trey said. "We're hangin' out Uptown. Some wicked women I know going be down at F&M's later. You're a celebrity after that spread of you and Teddy in the *Picayune*."

Malcolm stared at Trey. Trey could hear Malcolm's breathing.

Trey didn't even look back. He'd come back around. They always did.

He downed the martini, cranked the tunes, and danced. It was Friday night every night of his life.

Malcolm flipped the CDs onto Trey's desk and walked away.

20

I EXAMINED A SMUDGE of blue welts along my rib cage as I stepped out of the shower and got more pissed off. *I hurt.* I could smell the sour-milk body odor of that one thug and see flashes of the fire. I looked down at the remnants of my old book and rubbed Annie's head, checking her over. She seemed fine. A little wired and confused, but fine.

I needed to call Teddy and tell him about Cash. He'd want to know about the deal for ALIAS, although he wouldn't take it. Everything was about the kid. His money and his talents.

As I was about to pick up the phone, I kicked my toe at the copy of *Catcher in the Rye* that I'd found in my mother's things when I was fifteen. It was scorched, the dust jacket destroyed, but some of the pages remained intact.

The book had been my only insight into a woman who'd killed herself the day she'd turned thirty-two.

She left me with my father, an alcoholic high-school football coach, who let our farm in Alabama become overgrown in high grass and filled with rotting fences and barns.

I brushed off the blackened edges of the book, flipped through the pages that weren't fused. I checked the cover page, as I often did.

To Alice,

H.C.'s alter ego—accept this humble offering (condition, etc.) but I wasn't sure if you had a hardbound copy.

For myself, the chief in "laughing man" is easy to identify with. It's in Nine Stories *(find included).*

Hope you enjoy (if you haven't already read it) and accept these from,
Your secret admirer

I stood for a few minutes trying to catch my breath and slipped into a pair of 501s, a King Biscuit Festival T from 1991, and my boots. I thought about the Chief and wondered who he'd been to my mother and sometimes got mad at him for not trying to save her.

I called Pinky's Bar. Fred wasn't there and I hung up.

The phone rang in my hand.

"What you got?" Teddy asked.

"Who's Nae Nae?"

"Nick, man, I told you to stay out of Malcolm's business."

"Who is Nae Nae?"

"Bitch he got pregnant last year," he said. "What she tellin' you about Malcolm? Ain't nothin' but lies, man. Did you know she even set up a goddamned Web site about her havin' Malcolm's baby and him not giving her any money. Ain't that some shit? A Web site, man. Somethin' like malcolmsbaby-dot-com. Shit."

"Cash said he wants to trade ALIAS for your life."

"No way."

"Where does Nae Nae live?"

"Nick," he said. "Come on."

THIRTY MINUTES later, I pulled into a short driveway off Elysian Fields with Teddy and Polk Salad Annie by my side. Teddy was in his silk bathrobe and working cell phone calls trying to borrow the money Cash wanted, while Annie chewed on a bone I'd brought.

"Does that animal fart?" Teddy asked. "Or was that you, Nick?"

"She's a lady."

"So it was you?"

"It was the dog."

Teddy snapped shut the cell phone and tucked it into his pocket. He wore a black fedora on his head and had an unlit cigar in his mouth. A dry wind kicked up some elephant ears and palm trees. Across the street, I heard a child screaming.

"You feelin' better?" I asked.

"I ain't leavin' town," he said.

"Cash just wants the kid."

"Cash will do what he says," he said. "That's his way."

"I know his way," I said, feeling the bruise beginning to form beneath my eye. I opened the door from my truck and stepped out onto the gravel and into the darkness. "Don't tell me about Cash's way."

Nae Nae's house was painted pink with green trim and had children's toys scattered across her weedy lot. I saw the strobelike flashes of a television coming from the inside. It was almost 2 A.M.

Teddy knocked on the door and relit his cigar.

Nothing.

He knocked some more.

A woman in her early twenties opened up with a kitchen knife in her hand. She wore an old Saints T-shirt of Ricky Williams and her long braids whipped across her face as she jabbed the knife near Teddy's heart.

"What the fuck are you doin' at this time of night?" she asked in a high-pitched whisper. "Don't you know my baby still asleep in here? Your goddamned nephew and all you got to say is nothin', standin' there with your white hoodlum friends tryin' to get me up to get yourself some of that ass that you always wantin'. Well, you ain't gettin' shit from this girl, and you tell that greasy-ass brother of yours that I ain't satisfied for shit."

She dropped the name of a local attorney who was known throughout the black neighborhoods as "Pitbull" Sammy. I'd seen the billboards and they were good.

"Hey, Nae Nae," Teddy said, taking off his hat and moving the knife down at her side. "Good to see you."

"What he want?" She pointed at me with the knife.

"He's my driver," Teddy said. "Listen, did Malcolm give you something this week?"

She pulled at the frayed bottom of her Saints T-shirt and tucked the knife into the elastic band of her panties. "Maybe."

"Nae Nae?"

"You try and take that away," she said, shaking her little fist at Teddy. "And I'll kill you dead."

"Get in line," Teddy said. He slipped the hat back on his head and motioned for me to wait back at the truck with Annie. I did. Teddy knew what I wanted. I let him take the lead.

They talked for a good fifteen minutes in the yellow light of the porch. Bugs flitting about their heads. She eventually moved up under the bridge of Teddy's arm and looked up at him, laughing. Teddy picked her up off her feet right before he left and swung her back down to the ground.

He'd turned a knife-wielding woman into a friend. I couldn't believe how good Teddy could be.

"Son of a bitch," I said, my voice sounding hollow from inside the truck. Annie moved, her head between the two front passenger seats with the bone stuck between her molars, curious about my musings.

Teddy slid back in and kept puffing on the cigar. I reached over him and rolled down the window.

Teddy rubbed the back of his neck, the seats cracking under his weight. "All right."

"All right, what?"

"Let's go see him."

"You sure?"

"My brother givin' away fifty-thousand-dollar cars on the week Cash is about to take my ass out," Teddy said, gritting his teeth and slamming his fists into the dash. His breath came in jumpy spurts.

I started the truck and we drove north toward Lake Pontchartrain where Malcolm kept his house across the street from his brother.

We didn't talk the whole way. Teddy just kind of leaned into the wind as we rode, puffing on his cigar and searching for answers in his mind.

21

AT 3:45, TEDDY BOOSTED me onto his shoulders to grab the second-floor balcony of Malcolm's house. I reached the lowest edge of the iron, got a good grip, and pulled myself onto the ledge. We'd spotted a French door ajar by his bedroom and outdoor Jacuzzi after ringing his doorbell about thirty times. Down from the patio, Teddy told me to come down and let him in. I looked down at Teddy, still in the bathrobe and slippers, and said, "No shit."

I walked through the darkness of the house, white carpet, gold albums on the walls, and down onto the slate of his foyer and the front door. I saw a Brinks security system by the row of switches but it didn't seem to be armed. But really I couldn't tell if the red light meant it was on or off. I opened the door anyway.

Teddy strolled in, punching a code, and turned on all the lights.

Malcolm had a big open den with three big-screen televisions lined up side by side and a back bookshelf filled with CDs and dozens of pieces of Sony stereo components and Bose speakers. A few books on the *Kama Sutra*. *Playboy*s going back to the mideighties in leather cases.

"Quite a collection," I said.

"He's always been into freaks."

"A man of classics."

"Why you always makin' jokes, Nick?" he asked. "This shit ain't funny. Goddamn."

"It's gonna be all right," I said. "Be cool."

"Ain't your ass."

We moved upstairs to Malcolm's bedroom. He had one of the last water beds I'd seen since the seventies and a ceiling that was completely mirrored. Prints of Janet Jackson and Aaliyah and some woman named Gangsta Boo hung on the walls. Gangsta Boo had even signed and dated hers. *Thanks for that night in Memphis.* In the photo she was grabbing her crotch.

"What happened that night in Memphis?" I asked Teddy. "With the upstanding young woman?"

"Don't ask."

Teddy and I looked through his chest of drawers and found a lot of sweats and Ts and jewelry but no check stubs or deposit statements. He had a small desk by a window but the drawers were all empty. The room smelled of cologne and sweat.

We walked downstairs and Teddy opened up his brother's refrigerator, pulling out a couple of Eskimo Pies. He handed one to me.

I grabbed the wooden stick. I hadn't eaten in a while.

We walked through the house like a couple of kids in a museum, eating ice cream and talking. He pointed out some family photos hung on the wall and a ten-foot-tall oil painting of Teddy leaning against his Bentley. "That was his Christmas present."

The house was still and hummed with the quiet AC.

"I don't think we're going to make it," I said. "I'll stay with you, Teddy. All right?"

"No way."

"Make me leave."

He nodded and pulled me into his big meaty arms and rubbed the top of my head.

"Shit, man, cut it out," I said.

"I love you, Nick," he said. He hugged me like he always did after a game, whether we won or lost. He always acted like he just wanted to savor this one moment and keep it forever fresh in his head.

"Son of a bitch."

"Really, man," he said. "You the only one I trust."

I found a little room by the kitchen with his washer and dryer, a bulletin board, and a tiny little desk. I rifled through the drawers and saw nothing, but reached high on a ledge and found a large box filled with bank statements and credit card bills.

Teddy helped himself to another Eskimo Pie. I had the same.

"What you think of ALIAS?" he asked as I pulled out a few slips of paper, looked through them, and passed them on to him for a second opinion.

"I don't know."

"He's a good kid," Teddy said. "Grew up in Calliope and lost his mamma about two years back. Heard she'd been dead for a couple of weeks before anyone called the cops. ALIAS wouldn't call 'cause he thought the child welfare people would take him away."

I didn't say anything. We kept working, looking through the box.

"Guess we all know about that," he said. "Right?"

"What's that?"

"Losin' family."

I nodded.

"But you got JoJo and Loretta now and I still got Malcolm, that sorry sack of shit. Man, look what he did to me."

We walked back in the TV room and sat down on the leather couch. The room was dark except for a couple of tall stainless-steel lamps Teddy had turned on by the windows. We were in a large cavern, twelve-foot ceilings, space big enough for a scrimmage. The place felt hollow, like the inside of a whale.

"ALIAS talk to you about ball?" Teddy asked.

"No."

"Kid wants to be a DB," Teddy said. "Sometimes I have him pickin' off passes when me and Malcolm be jackassin' around the studios. Man got vert, you know. If the kid could read, man, I think he could play."

"He can't read?"

"Can't even spell his name."

"I hadn't noticed."

"Not somethin' he talks about," Teddy said. "Don't mean he ain't bright, though. You know that. Just never been to no real school."

Teddy crossed his big fat legs and propped them up on a glass coffee table with the latest issues of *XXL*. He dropped the fedora's brim down in his eyes, switched the old cigar—now just a nub—into the other side of his mouth.

"Good Lord," he said, scanning a picture of a rapper in a gold bikini. Unfazed he was a few hours away from Cash.

"So we wait?"

"Nothin' else to do."

I looked at the television. Something had been taped on its blank screen but I was too far away to read it. I walked close and pulled off a piece of paper Scotch-taped to the fifty-inch Sony.

Someone had typed a note and torn the paper in half.

I read the note and then reread it:

To my big-brother Teddy and all my people at Ninth Ward,

Thank you for a great ride these last three years. Y'all made it happen. Put the Ward, NOLA, all of it, up on top.

But some of us make mistakes. Money make men be some evil people. Do evil things against family.

I ask for the Lord's and my family forgiveness.

I can't live another day takin'. I set up ALIAS and killed the best friend I ever had in Dio.

Lord forgive me. Bury me in the Ninth.

Y'all party, roll, and remember what I used to be.

I handed the note to Teddy.

I had to help him get to his feet. His whole body shook and he dropped to one knee. "Where's the kid?" he asked.

"Home."

"You sure?"

22

YOU ASLEEP WHEN CASH KNOCK *on your window holdin' a tall forty and that little girl from the strip club by the hand. He say he want to take you on a ride and you crawl into your P. Miller jeans and Lugz shoes fast as hell. You want to be lookin' tight for that girl, show you Uptown all the way.*

Y'all soon kicked back in his Escalade, ridin' past them projects that you share. You gettin' high with Cash, that man promising you the world just to make him millions if you leave Teddy and the Ward. You marvel at that, the way your mind works, the way it brings in that gold, as you float by the strawberries givin' out fifteen-dollar blow jobs and thirteen-year-olds on BMX bikes shufflin' off that crack for grandmamma pushers. Grandmammas who watch their soap operas while their little boys carry Ravens and Glocks.

"That white man won't bother you no more," he says.

The girl, still don't know her name, snuggle into your arm and play with that platinum necklace like a little drunk cat.

The blue-and-red neon in the all-night liquor stores and those hard crime lights over oak trees almost make your mind drunk while Cash tellin' you why you should get out from Teddy and Malcolm.

He say they don't want him tellin' you the truth about yo' man Dio.

You don't ask questions. He don't serve up no answers. To you, Dio was God. He started the whole sound. He played the block parties out in the yard. Showed you that you could break out of Calliope.

Sometimes you wear Dio's clothes. Malcolm even give you that Superman symbol that the man used to keep on his neck. Sometimes you wonder if his spirit don't move your rhymes.

Cash is smart the way he play you. He come from Calliope too and turned himself into a billionaire. That nigga just made a deal with some label in NYC that jacked him up about $10 million. Now that make him 'bout light-years away from Teddy and his brother. Cash don't hustle. He don't sell from the back of his car. He run with the big dogs.

He say he still tied to CP3. Still get his hair cut in the 'hood and rolls block parties. He say Teddy and Malcolm are just country-ass Nint' Warders. And you can't trust 'em. Cash been you, he says. He know what you need.

Even before it's out his mouth, you down at this club off Airways Boulevard where nineteen-year-old women are grindin' their sweaty asses in your lap and rubbin' your head with their soft fingers and rakin' their long red claws over your neck. Cash and his playas watchin' you as you strut from that VIP room while he sips on a bottle of Cristal and nods to move on.

You do, leavin' the girl at work. You move on to three other clubs before he drop you back lakefront, to that mansion you was designin' from a space movie you seen on cable. High humpback gates like you seen on MTV, all surrounded by cement mixers, stacks of plywood, and plastic sheeting popping in your empty windows.

"Why Teddy kick you out and now he say he want you back?"

"Mad, I guess."

"Friends don't play like that."

Cash's boys crack open some Cristal and y'all drink it straight from the bottle. You take a couple hits from a joint, making it wash deep into your lungs, and listen to all them boys talkin' shit 'bout their new Italian cars, freaks they met out on the road, and high-dollar restaurants with pink shrimp as big as yo' big toe.

Cash tell you again about Teddy and Malcolm and all about what happened to Diabolical. He say that Teddy and Malcolm finally gonna pay for what happened to the man who made Dirty South. He say the Paris brothers only killed that young nigga so his sales would double. And truth be known, Dio weren't nothin' till they jacked his ass at Atlanta Nites.

You remember that thug's face and his rhymes when you was a kid and now all them T-shirts and lost albums and tributes. Death make you live forever.

All that talk about Dio and your own chances and risks make you want to take the boat out.

When you start that motor, Cash flashes a smile loaded with platinum and diamonds on the dock and then you disappear. His dogs playin' with green-and-yellow bottle rockets out by your pool and hills of green grass on the levee.

You take that boat way out in the lake, where the lights don't mess with the crisp stars. You smoke a blunt to take it all down, flat back in that skinny little boat, just driftin' in loopy choppy circles trying to figure out what happens next. You think about that, the way you drift, and that's cool with you. Because you are a puzzle. Them pieces come to be known as you grow. Ain't that right?

Because evil can't touch you. You away from that evil and men that can pull a young brother apart. It makes you smile as the blunt stinks up your clothes—the Little Dipper burnin' so bright it reminds you of the Christmas lights that used to frame your grandmamma's window—to know you are safe. Goblins and them mean ole ghosts have disappeared from your life like the edges of the smoke into that cold wind at the lip of the boat.

23

WE SEARCHED ALL NIGHT LONG. We took Teddy's black Escalade with silver rims with a few of his people following. We used a ton of cell phones and followed a trail through so many strip clubs that I started to smell like smoke and could guarantee that they'd play some Aerosmith song before I left. We checked out late-night diners like the Hummingbird and clubs where he'd hung out. We checked out this Uptown apartment he'd shared with a woman who'd borne two of his children and even deep down into the Ninth Ward to the leaning shotgun houses where the Paris brothers had grown up.

Teddy told me stories about their grandmother and that an uncle of theirs had been some kind of soundman for the Ohio Players. He told me about his first business running dime bags for some local hustler in the early seventies and how Malcolm once had a box haircut so tall it bounced when he walked.

He talked about his brother's talent and how he recognized hit songs the first time he heard them on the radio. Teddy talked about how Malcolm had found Dio and how it had changed him from a man selling CDs out the back of his Buick Regal to being one of the richest African-Americans in Louisiana. He smiled.

"We worked together, all right," he said.

He steered the Escalade with both hands.

"We done all right."

We drove.

No one knew a thing about his brother. ALIAS still wouldn't answer his phone.

From cinderblock bars in Algiers to some backdoor clubs in the Quarter, we were worn-out by 6 A.M. I was outside the Ninth Ward Studio leaning against the gold brick wall and smoking when I heard Teddy walk back out.

The sky had just started to turn purple at dawn. The air in the Ninth Ward smelled salty and mildewed from the channel. I could smell the diesel fumes from the trucks and hear the hiss of the brakes as they moved on. I watched Teddy as he rolled up his sleeves and made a couple more calls, pacing.

ALIAS came down to the studios about 7:30 wearing the same clothes from when I'd left him at his house. He gave Teddy and me a tired pound and said, "I heard."

Everybody had heard. Everyone Teddy knew—a big crowd—was looking for Malcolm.

We all drove. The thought of Cash seemed weaker now. Teddy almost welcomed it.

"The deal's off," Teddy told me with such confidence I almost believed him.

"What do you mean?" I asked.

"My family's in trouble," he said. "That will make sense to him."

"And you being dead wouldn't cause trouble for your family?"

"It ain't the same," Teddy said, wheeling the Bentley with me and ALIAS back down Canal and onto St. Charles and then to the Camellia Grill at the end of the streetcar line. He bought breakfast for twenty-three people who'd been out looking for Malcolm and gave a big speech right outside the diner as the rain first started to come about 8 A.M.

He offered a reward for anyone who could find his brother alive. He never mentioned the note or suicide or anything other than that something had happened. I got the feeling that most people blamed Cash.

I had just gotten my third cup of coffee to go and was walking outside when I saw Teddy leaned against his Bentley crying. He just kept nodding and nodding but his words made him sound like a child who was confused.

I watched ALIAS disappear down the streetcar tracks and then turn his walk into a run as if he could escape from the sadness that was about to wash over people he knew.

I walked slow across the tracks and stood by Teddy.

He looked down on me.

"They found him," he said. "He's come home."

"What?"

"He's finally come home."

Teddy had cracked. I just helped him into the car and aimed it toward the parish line. That's where Teddy said they were keeping the body.

The rain started hammering the hood of the car just as we made the turn by the Metairie Cemetery.

BAMBOO ROAD ran flush along a dirty concrete canal that stretched from Pontchartrain to the Mississippi. The road was the edge of the Orleans Parish line and I slowed Teddy's Bentley along the muddy shoulder, where NOPD, Orleans, and Jefferson Parish patrol cars all parked at weird angles. The sun rose into a thick mass of high, gray-black clouds and the spinning lights made the drops of rain on his windshield come out in colors of red and blue.

When we got out of the car, my mind numb, heart breaking into hard slivers, I heard the sound of bamboo canes knocking against one another as if someone was waiting at an unseen door. Their narrow leaves flickered in the wind of the approaching storm.

Someone grabbed Teddy's big arm, a cop, and led him down to the bank of the canal. The bamboo continued to knock as the sky opened up and a thick, warm shower of rain began to cover our faces.

I was glad. Teddy didn't like people to see him cry.

A black man in a tight Italian suit and a hard woman in a black jacket met us on the path. Behind them, there was a tangle of cops standing at a clearing of trees. Jay Medeaux was there and I hung back with him. The canal was long and narrow and dry except for a few puddles of brown water. Someone had left a bicycle without tires on its steep concrete slope.

"Where is he?" Teddy asked Jay.

He didn't say anything. Jay just let Teddy pass, walk down that muddy path, through all that knocking bamboo, to the police on the hill. Rain full-out all over them now. I saw a few scatter, holding notebooks and jackets above their heads. A cracking sound of thunder far off in the lake.

Teddy's thousand-dollar shoes were caked in mud and leaves and moss.

I hung back. The smell of the green leaves and dirt strong in my nose.

My vision tilted as my friend moved among them, the way the camera does in old movies when they want to make you feel like you're on a ship.

I felt some acid rise in my throat.

Malcolm would not face us.

He was strung up in a dead oak tree by the neck. Twirling slightly as if he could still control his movements. His platinum chain twisted deep and red into his neck behind the rope.

Teddy walked to look at him but strong hands held him back.

"You can't," the woman cop said.

"Why?"

"Please wait, sir," she said.

He shook her off, walked through four other cops who tried to hold him back, oblivious to any strength but his own.

He stared up at Malcolm. I bent down and toyed with some wet grass, shaking my head.

Bamboo knocked as if in applause. The sky above closed in like a dome.

Dark gray rain coated Malcolm's face.

24

FOR THE NEXT THREE DAYS after we found Malcolm's body on Bamboo Road, it rained. I'm not talking about a slow drizzle or boring patter that we get almost every spring afternoon in New Orleans, but real out-and-out thunderstorms that flooded the lower Garden District and closed parts of the city. I had to drive with water up to the running boards on the Gray Ghost just to make it to this community center in the Ninth Ward where there was a remembrance ceremony for Malcolm. Basically it was just a fancy word for a big wake open to fans and friends. They'd already had a more private ceremony the night before at this Uptown funeral home. I was there but chose to stay outside and offer a few kind words to Teddy. We spoke. But I don't think he noticed me.

The gravel lot outside the community center was packed with cars. I had to park four streets over on Desire beside some abandoned food mart and walk the whole way past rotting shotgun shacks. The red, green, and blue faded and bleached like something out of the Caribbean. Water had soaked through my boots and into the black blazer I'd picked from the back of the closet for the occasion.

But the rain hadn't discouraged the onlookers and fans. Some held up fluorescent yellow-and-orange posterboards with words of love for Malcolm. The words, written in black ink, ran and smeared over the paper and down on the arms that held them high. News crews from local TV stations waited in vans with open doors for the right time for a live shot. I saw one cameraman with a BET T-shirt on standing beside a tall black woman with extremely long legs and soft relaxed hair. I followed the echoing sounds of a preacher's voice into a basketball court where rows and rows of folding chairs had been set up.

"No Jesus, no peace," said the gray-suited man at the podium. "Know Jesus. Know peace. Our friend brother Malcolm knew peace. Knew it before the Lord came knockin' on his door. Knew he had family. Knew what family meant. Y'all hear what I'm sayin'?"

I looked around the basketball court and at the elevated stage where there was a purple casket with an inscribed *P* on the side. Teddy sat wide-legged on a small chair by an older woman who I'd met last night. I think a distant aunt who'd helped raise them. Several long-legged beauties, some holding children, sat closest to the coffin. Many wearing dark sunglasses and nodding to the preacher's words. Nae Nae was absent.

The thunder rattled the high panes above the bleachers and kept cracking out in the distance. We weren't far from the channel and I suddenly had the thought of all that dirty rainwater washing out into the port and then into the Mississippi.

Teddy walked up in a draping black suit, jacket falling to his knees, and spit-polished boots. He kept on his shades and the size of his earring made an impact at even forty yards.

"We all family," Teddy said, holding his hands tight on the podium. Old preacher-style. Even his cadence reminded me of two-hour sermons I'd heard sitting between JoJo and Loretta. "That name. Our name. The Paris name. That's what it all about. Malcolm and me used to talk about that. When we was growin' up and used to take the streetcar past all them fine homes, he used to say some hardworkin' man made that family about two hundred years ago. Ain't that a trip. We just layin' it all down for our grandkids . . ."

Some of the well-dressed women with children shifted in their seats behind the coffin.

"And their kids. That Paris name. We always gonna have that, Brother," Teddy said, dropping his hands to his side and walking to the coffin. I could only see the profile of Malcolm's gray face and the edge of a satin pillow. I didn't want to see. I'd had problems with these kind of things since I was a child.

Teddy kissed the tips of his fingers and touched them to the coffin. He reared his shoulders back and strutted to the edge of the stage, where he stopped. I saw his head drop, his arms shake, and he fell to one huge knee, rocking the entire platform.

I stood.

But two rappers I'd met, T.H.U.G. and Stank, grabbed each of his elbows and helped him down the stairs. He'd reached the back door, near the locker room, when I heard the cry. A deep gut-churning moan and scream that made me drop my own head and pray.

After the ceremony, people stood and talked. The television news crews moved in. Hundreds of flowers continued to be dropped at the base of Malcolm's body. Cards and little notes written on napkins. Rain-streaked signs and CDs of his music. Some dude even dropped a baggie full of weed into the casket. One woman dropped her red panties.

I pushed past them to find Teddy but he'd already emerged from the back locker room and had a strong gait as he walked through the huge crowd on the court. You could hear his shoes click above all the talking. Strong and confident.

He smiled at me. And I believed he was headed toward me when *they* entered.

Beneath the exit doors, right beside the "Drugs Kill" sign, stood the entire crew that had wrecked my warehouse. They all wore identical black leather jackets and shades.

Cash grinned at Teddy in the thirty yards that separated them.

He tossed down a white wreath and it skidded for about ten yards before stopping way short of my friend's feet.

"That's the way it go," Cash yelled, his platinum teeth shining with the fluorescent light.

I looked at Teddy.

"He's a little upset," Teddy said.

"Why?"

"I had his Rolls torched last night."

"Why?"

"He set Malcolm off."

Cash nodded. "Sleep tight, Teddy. Watch out for them bedbugs."

He and his thugs disappeared.

25

IT WAS DARK AGAIN and I knew I'd slept through the day. I awoke to a cracking sound rattling my warehouse. It sounded like the floor, but in the darkness I heard a deep roll of thunder and knew the storm from the Gulf was blowing over the city. The air smelled of ozone and salt. The bank of windows facing Julia Street shook and I turned back into my pillow, hearing Annie get to her feet and start into a low growl. I'd been dreaming about Maggie. I was at her house in Taylor and we'd been staring up at the branches of a huge pecan tree and the blue sky beyond.

"Annie," I whispered. "Annie. Lay down."

I pulled the pillows over my head, waiting for the sleep that would come to me so easily from the *tap-tap-tap* of rain against the windows and roof above me. Another flash of lightning broke close and the air became charged with electricity and white light. The brightness startled me and I opened my eyes to see Annie had disappeared.

She was growling near the front door.

I padded my way through the warehouse, scratching the hair that was sticking up on my head and calling her name.

Another flash of lightning.

A man stood in the corner. He had a gray face and wore a tattered overcoat.

He looked to be a thousand years old.

I didn't even break stride. I ran for the kitchen in the darkness, feeling my way through the drawer where I kept my Glock.

I wanted to make it to the switches and light up the floor. I couldn't see shit. I thought maybe I was just tired, dreaming of ghosts the same way I did when I was hunting old blues singers. Robert Johnson at the foot of my bed.

But there was a different smell to my room. It smelled of fish oil and mothballs and tattered winter clothes left too long in storage. A musty basement odor.

I held the gun strong in my hand.

Annie kept growling.

Then she yelped.

Hard.

I fired off a round in the direction where I'd seen the apparition. High above the range of my dog.

She trotted back to me and I felt her stand at my side. Her back was wet and sticky.

My eyes adjusting in the darkness and then lit up again with lightning.

The sliding door rolled back. I heard it. I saw a flash of brown coat and then it disappeared into my stairwell.

I ran to the door and flicked on the lights. I stooped down to Annie and looked at her bloody flank. She's been scratched hard but not deep, like another animal had clawed her.

I left her and ran down the steps with my gun. The door to the street was wide open and I saw a sweeping mist of rain hitting the asphalt outside in the dull glow of the city's crime lights.

I carefully peered out, making sure I didn't get my head blown off.

A block away and across the road, I saw the darkened shape of a man in a long tattered coat, his face hidden into the lapels. He seemed to be made of nothing but shadows. His weight did not shift. He did not move.

I squinted into the rain as I walked to him, half in a dream, half expecting his shape to dissolve into my hands when I touched him.

He turned and walked into the hole of another warehouse covered in plywood. The wood over the lower windows ripped away by the homeless. I guess I needed to know if this was one of Cash's boys back for more or some crack addict from the Hummingbird ready to make a score.

I held the gun in my hands.

On the lower floor, the vacant building shined silver from the crime light. My feet were still bare. I felt discarded pieces of wood and wet cardboard on my toes. The air smelled the way it had in my warehouse and I tried to slow down my breathing, already growing nauseous.

The silver light leaked through like vapor.

I could not see the man.

No shadow. No ghosts.

I found stairs leading to the level above me. But I did not follow.

The light had ended. My heart beat in my chest so fast.

I could not think. The smell overpowering.

I walked back through the wind and rain to my stoop.

At the base of my stairs, there was a gold pocket watch hanging from a tarnished chain.

When I flicked open the cover, the old blues song "Love in Vain" played. I could not breathe. I felt someone had entered my head.

I snapped shut the cover, walked back upstairs, and bolted my door three times before calling the police.

26

THE GIRL'S HAIR smelled of cigarettes early that morning. Her breath like Jack Daniel's and old cherries. Trey moved out from under her and grabbed the suit pants that he'd kicked out of last night and carefully counted out the money in his wallet. His AmEx and ATM cards were where he'd left them. He slipped into his pants, the white sunlight crawling through the girl's Pottery Barn curtains. The checked ones from page fifty-eight. Painful light that hurt his head a lot. He couldn't remember when he'd lost count.

Thirteen dirty martinis. Some bar owned by retired surfers down in the Warehouse District. Not far from his loft. There was blurry stuff in his head. A round of drinks for some girls from Loyola. Some dancing in the middle of a crowded bar. Some rap. ALIAS's song. White girls singing along. Two more martinis. Three. The nineteen-year-old snuggled into his neck. Her grabbing his crotch by the cigarette machine. A cab ride to somebody's house by Audubon Park. A pass-out, more drinks, some beer this time. The girl's roommate's boyfriend putting an X tablet into his hand. All that good feeling. That alertness. Her eyes rolled into the back of her head, not even fucking moving last night.

He pulled on the linen shirt, the good one from Brooks Brothers that his girlfriend Molly liked. Molly was always mothering him. She bought his food, did his laundry, made sure he was working out when she came in from Atlanta.

He found the latch of the door, never taking another look at the girl in the bed.

He took a cab back to the bar, found his BMW, and made his Saturday-morning calls. He called Molly, told her he had a cold. Made sure she hadn't called last night. She had. He'd been too sick to pick up the phone. Poor baby, she said. She'd make him feel better next week. She talked about cooking for him or something. He wasn't listening. He just wanted to make sure she was lined up. Her father was so damned close to investing in his company. All that old Atlanta money, lunch at the Cherokee, Buckhead parties where he could get even more. More contacts.

He parked, opened the door to the loft, and found Christian lying on his leather couch. The one he'd had delivered from Restoration Hardware. Christian's feet were rubbing around one of those Tuscany pillows.

"Bitch, get your nasty feet off my shit."

Christian rolled over. "Eat it."

Trey walked back to the kitchen. Everything stainless steel, the way Molly liked. She ordered them. He opened the refrigerator, grabbed a beer, watching himself in the warped reflection. Fuck, he needed a haircut. All shaggy and low, could barely see his eyes.

"What's up, Chaseboy?" Christian hated to be called that. All of that going back to Country Day. One black boy in the class. Some kind of Martian.

"That dude Travers called."

Trey stopped drinking the beer, his stomach twisting.

"I said you were at work. But it looks like you were out on pussy patrol."

"Hell, I think she was passed out for most of it."

Christian pointed at him and said, "You got game, motherfucker. You got game."

Trey nodded. Still feeling a little fuzzy with the X and the martinis. Really play up the whole sick thing. Call Molly. Have her mother him more.

"Was she as good as Kristi Lynn?"

"God damn, that redneck whore will never wash out. You know? I mean, who really gives a shit anymore."

Christian threw the remote at the brick wall and stomped into the bathroom, where he took a hard, long piss. He wandered back, laughing, no longer mad, and wanted to go down and score a dime bag from some niggers who lived down by the Riverbend.

"What's Travers want now?"

"Maybe he thinks I took ALIAS's money." Trey laughed.

"Why would you con out your own client?"

"Exactly."

"He any good?"

Trey's head hurt more. He walked to the edge of the sink and held himself there. Williams-Sonoma towels. A rack of ten types of olive oil. Some with oregano and black pepper inside.

"Yes," Trey said finally.

"You worried?"

"I got it under control."

Trey looked over at Christian, suddenly remembering the fall carnival at Country Day, five years before that redneck bitch who changed their life. The families had paid some trash down south to bring in a Ferris wheel, some kind of ship that rocked back and forth till you about puked, and these little swings where you'd get strapped in for your ride and be twirled until you were almost horizontal. He remembered Christian being kind of gay about it and trying to catch his leg when they swung close. He held on to his leg and laughed and laughed like it was so funny. Why would he do something like that?

"I'm just wondering if this badass rap star is worth all this trouble."

"Don't get much meaner," Christian said. "Man don't like it when you talk that way 'bout him."

27

FOUR HOURS AFTER THE POLICE LEFT, Teddy called to let me know he'd come up with a way to pay Cash. Just like that. He was at the airport about to fly to Los Angeles to strike a deal with Universal for distributing the final Dio album. He didn't want to do it but he said the offer was his only option. While we were on the phone, I tried to talk to him about Malcolm and why he should try to work with Jay Medeaux at NOPD. But he didn't want to, instead asked me to leave town with ALIAS. He needed me to keep the kid out of New Orleans until peace was made with Cash.

"I'm not worried about ALIAS," I said. "I'm worried about you, man."

"I have a dozen of the baddest motherfuckers in the Ward lookin' out for me," he said. "What's a white boy from Alabama gonna add to the mix?"

I told him about the man from last night.

"Some ratty-clothes fucker?" Teddy asked. "Man, that some ole homeless dude lookin' for a place to squat and a sandwich."

I loaded up my army duffel bag, called JoJo in Clarksdale, picked up ALIAS, and headed the Gray Ghost west on I-10. We drove north on 55, passing supersize truck stops, Cracker Barrels, and rest areas. We stopped for gas outside Kentwood but kept rolling for a few more hours. ALIAS slept. I listened to a new album by Jim Dickinson and some old Ry Cooder sound tracks.

At about 3 P.M., ALIAS and I pulled off at an exit in Vaiden, Mississippi, for supplies and some chicken-fried steak at the All-American Diner. Eighteen-wheelers blew diesel fumes from their exhaust. Fords and Chevys nestled by a bank of glass windows, their owners inside shoveling in chicken-fried steak and fries.

"What the hell is that shit?"

"It's steak."

"Then why they call it chicken?"

"They don't call it chicken, man," I said to my young road Jedi. "They fry it like a chicken."

"That sounds nasty."

"Wait till you try it," I said. "Best in the state."

I imagined ALIAS's do-rag and thick platinum chains would draw some stares from the truckers who were hunkered over their lunch platters. But I needed some good, warm food and often stopped here on my way to Clarksdale.

I let Annie make a deposit on the grass and left her in the shaded car with the windows down. ALIAS mumbled and planted his feet on the ground outside the truck. He yawned tall and hard and motioned at the windows of the restaurant.

"You takin' me to a Klan meeting, Old School?"

"Bring your sheet?"

"Come on, man," he said. He looked at all the spindly pine trees in the forest across the road and pickup trucks in the lot. The air was silent except for the roaring of semis every ten seconds on the interstate.

Two black truckers in tall cowboy hats—toothpicks wandering from the sides of their mouths—pushed the front doors open and gave long looks at ALIAS in his baggy FUBU jersey and low-ridin' jeans.

I ordered coffee from a teenage waitress who looked as if she'd just woken up and the world held a million possibilities. Her smile plastered and hard, eyes so wide open that they gave me a headache. ALIAS got a Coke.

"That was some fucked-up shit, man, in New Orleans," ALIAS said, playing games with his fingers. They fought one another as he refused to look me in the eye. "Don't want to be part of that."

"I'm sorry about Malcolm."

ALIAS shrugged. "Nigga made his play."

"That's hard."

"What ain't?"

He looked away from me for a moment and I nodded.

"You want me to drive?" he asked.

"No one else drives the Ghost."

"That ole piece of shit?" he asked. "I got some silk underwear that cost more money."

"Probably runs better too."

The waitress came back and I asked for the Texas-size chicken-fried steak and ALIAS ordered a cheeseburger and fries.

"You want to tell me more about your buddy Cash?" I asked.

"Cash ain't my buddy."

"Teddy heard he was at your place the other night," I said. "He sent some folks by to find you and they said you were outside smokin' it up with Cash."

He didn't say anything.

We stared out into the parking lot at the trucks until the food arrived.

The country-fried steak sat brown and covered in white peppery gravy in front of me. ALIAS ate a few fries and looked around for a ketchup bottle. There wasn't one, and he tried to show he was so damned interested in finding the bottle that he wouldn't look me in the eye.

"You made up your mind?"

"Man, Cash want me to join his label," he said. "You know that? Said I'm a punk for runnin' to the Ninth Ward when you got a straight-up Calliope brother with L.A. connections."

I watched his face. He blew out his breath and rubbed the top of his head. He'd quit eating his food.

"So you're gonna stay with Teddy?"

"I'm gonna do whatever ALIAS want to do."

"That have anything to do with Tavarius Stovall?"

"Man."

"You know that your name comes from a plantation where we're headed."

"Slave name."

"Sort of," I said. "But someone in your family came from Clarksdale. I'd bet money."

"My people come from Mississippi?"

"Where did you think they came from?"

"All I know is Calliope."

"Maybe we can stop by," I said. "Always good for the soul to know your roots."

He looked up at me, in the eyes, and smiled. " 'Cept when those roots are rotten."

"Why would you say that?"

"Just repeatin' the words my grandmamma tole me," he said. "She said my mamma was a drug addict and a whore. Said she was sick in the head and I was just like her."

The waitress came back and leveled a ketchup bottle on the table. She smiled at us and looked pretty even though she had crooked yellowed teeth and brown frizzy hair.

"I saw your video on BET," I said. "You got talent."

"You watch BET?"

"Frequently," I said.

"Which one you see?"

"I don't know. You were driving a Mercedes in the Quarter with three girls in bikinis. You looked pissed off talking on that cell phone."

ALIAS laughed. "So where you takin' me?" he asked, happy with the ketchup and tapping the bottle.

"I told you, we're going to stay a few days with some friends of mine."

"That old dude."

"Yeah, that old dude," I said, cutting into the steak.

"What he to you?" he said. "Some kin?"

"He and his wife took me in when no one else wanted me," I said.

I watched ALIAS in his wrinkled shirt. His face covered in oil and sweat. Then I looked at two truckers by a window drinking a cup of coffee and enjoying a moment of silence. I could not see much beyond the road.

28

JOJO AND LORETTA LIVED in a turn-of-the-century farmhouse a few miles outside Clarksdale in a town that once had a name. I'd learned to recognize the county roads by piles of rocks or trees, since signs were rare. Soon I crossed their old footbridge and headed down a gravel road. The house was two stories and white with a wide screened-in porch where Loretta had draped blue Christmas lights right below the tin roof. It was just before sundown and JoJo and I slipped into some metal chairs flecked with green paint and rust and drank whiskey. The whiskey was hot and warm but surprisingly mellow.

Annie lay at JoJo's feet.

"See?" he said. "That dog's smart. She remember me."

"Maybe she just wants some food."

"Dogs remember who save their ass," he said. "She'll always remember me. Right, girl?"

He scratched the back of her ears and she barked.

Loretta had shown ALIAS a bed in the back room of the old house and in the last few minutes had began to make us dinner in the kitchen. I could smell the greens simmering with a fat, salty ham hock and cornbread baking in the oven. She served sweet tea and scowled at JoJo's whiskey.

I returned to the porch with JoJo. The sun slowly headed down over his pastureland to the east in a slice of yellow. Dark patches of shadow hung beneath his hickories and pecan trees as I sipped on the tea and told him about ALIAS and Malcolm.

JoJo propped his feet up on the ledge and continued to run an oilcloth on his old .22. Chickens cackled behind the house.

"When did you get chickens?" I asked.

"When I decided I wanted eggs," he said.

JoJo was in his late sixties now. Broad-shouldered and black. His arms starting to thicken from his return to farmwork and his rough fingers tough and quick over the stock and the barrel.

"What you gonna do with the kid?" he asked.

"Stay with him around here for a few days," I said. "If you don't mind."

"Why he got them gold teeth?"

"They were out of diamonds."

"He's street, Nick. Watch your ass. I don't mess with those project folks in New Orleans."

"Kid's a millionaire."

"You got to be shittin' me."

"I shit you not. He owns a big mansion on the lakefront. Has a Mercedes and doesn't even have a learner's permit."

JoJo put the gun down on an old table. "You brought a drug dealer to my house?"

"Worse," I said, and laughed. "A rapper."

"No shit," JoJo said, laughing too. "Kids will listen to anything these days. Man, when I was a kid, we all wanted to be Muddy Waters. The way he sang about women and whiskey. Made me want to play that ole blues."

"Not much has changed," I said.

"Except plenty," he said. "That music is against God. Makes thugs into heroes, women into things, and money above all."

I wanted to ask him about the stories he'd told me about Little Walter and his dice games and fistfights, but I didn't.

The smell of Loretta's cooking made my mouth water despite my stomach being full of that chicken-fried steak. I sank harder into the porch chair and rested my boots on the plank floor and took a deep breath. The old sun had touched the edge of JoJo's farm, just nudging it a bit.

"Felix found a new job."

"What?"

"Pours drinks into plastic peckers," I said. "Says to tell you hello."

JoJo stood. He walked to the screen door and opened it. The spring squeaked as he held it open and spit outside. "Lots of bad shit happened in New Orleans."

"You ever think about coming home?"

JoJo held his eyes on mine. He had some deep bags under there and I suddenly thought that I was making them worse. "This is my home," he said.

I laughed. "The Quarter is fresh out of good music."

He pointed to the rolling acres past the porch.

"This is where I'll die."

The dozens of cattle he owned chowed down and swatted flies with their tails. A smooth, easy swat that looked effortless. Brown-and-white ones just enjoying their day eating in the morning sun.

"We can find a new building."

"That place on Conti Street has always been the bar and always will be."

"Except for now they serve martinis and play techno music."

"What the hell is that?"

"You don't want to know."

"If you want a bar so much," he said, "you open it up."

I laughed. "You're kidding."

"Why not?" he said, and held up the gun, sighting the barrel into the field. "You can't open a beer?"

"You know there's more to it than that."

He shrugged. Loretta's deep voice called us in to eat.

"I'm too busy."

"Working for Teddy?" JoJo asked, laying the gun down. "You crazy? Teddy would sell you for a quarter. Quit taking these jobs for folks. What you carryin' inside of you that makes you feel like you got to pay the whole world back?"

"I want to see this one out. Then maybe I'll think about it."

"You think long and hard, son. 'Cause this old man ain't comin' back to the Big Easy for nothin'. I don't care if I hear Miss Raquel Welch walkin' naked down Bourbon Street waitin' to give me a kiss."

"Come on," I said, knowing about the secret photo JoJo kept of Raquel in his desk drawer. She was his ultimate, the way I kept the calendar of Miss March '91, although secretly guessing that Miss March would find me quite dull.

"All right," he said. "I'd come back for that. But if you talkin' to me about Sun and Felix and that crazy-ass friend of yours—what's his name? Oz. Then no dice."

Loretta called to us again.

"Kid stays clean. If he fucks up—if I smell him smokin' some weed out back—he's gone. This is my home and that kid don't have the sense God gave a turkey."

"Put him to work."

"I do have a fence needs to be tended to."

"He's a teenager. Thinks he knows it all."

"Like you did?"

I smiled. "Exactly."

JoJo walked inside the old house, his feet beating hard on the hundred-year-old floors. Over his shoulder, he muttered: "Let's hope he's different."

29

YOU DON'T LIKE *to get fucked wit'. But the ole man and Nick did it to you every damned day. They get you up when it's still dark and make you shovel shit out of some nasty-ass dirt yard—light comin' from some little lantern—where some goats have crapped or somethin'. Nick make you jog with him before breakfast, right when the sun runnin' down some dirt road and you can't even keep up a mile. But on that sixth day, man, you keep up. You run strong by his side. He tell you that you fast and you like that when you eatin' bacon and sweet-potato pancakes on that ole porch and that old woman warm you with a hand on your back.*

You like the taste of the pancakes. The way the hot syrup is warm and flows right through them.

When you there for ten days, you ask him about that dream you been havin' since you was a kid, to play pro. Nick say that you got to get back in school and the ole man ask how long you been out.

You tell him a few years.

That ole man shake his head and walk back into the red barn where he's tearin' out planks of wood that's rotten with termites and making a heap to burn. He like tearin' out all that old shit and puttin' something right back to replace it. Good wood, he say, make it strong.

Sometimes y'all ride into Clarksdale inside JoJo's old truck. That ride old as hell, smell like rust and funk, and JoJo make you listen to some station out of Memphis about Soul Classics and he think there's something wrong with you 'cause you don't know some singer named Al Green.

That's when church start. And man, that church shit don't let up. Wednesday too. Even Nick go to this country-ass thing by the highway where some fat-belly preacher start talkin' for about four hours while your stomach gets all rumblin' and you lookin' at the bulletin. Bored as hell. Ain't nothin' goin' on in town. Even the girls—and they do know you—ain't that ripe.

They wear these lace gloves and hats and can't look you in the eye when y'all talkin' at the picnic after the service.

"I seen you on TV," one of them says. But she smell like onions or some shit and has a little black mustache over her lip. Maybe she be all right she shave that thing off.

Nick take you down to some movies at some drive-ins a few nights those first two weeks. Some nights y'all roll into the Sonic, where y'all get burgers, chicken fingers, and Cherry Cokes.

Y'all keep cleanin' up JoJo's world. You run with Nick.

Sometimes he talk to you. Sometimes he just stare outside at all the people movin' by him.

That makes you wonder 'bout him.

Something just ain't settin' right in his head.

"You all right, man?"

He look at you like you the one who's crazy.

"Just tryin' to figure out some thoughts."

30

MAGGIE LIVED A FEW MILES outside Taylor—about an hour from JoJo's—in a small white farmhouse surrounded by rosebushes and rows of tomatoes and corn just planted. The hickory tree leaves made brushing sounds as we walked toward her front porch, the sky overhead the color of water in the Florida Keys. I held her hand and she gripped me hard as she told me about a new photo exhibit she was working on for a gallery on Oxford Square.

"It's more than just headstones," she said, pulling her sticky white T-shirt away from her chest. "I mean, we've seen that about a hundred times. I've done pictures of graves of woodworkers. They had some kind of fund that kicked in when they died and some of the monuments are incredible. There's this man who died down in Paris and his headstone looks like a log stump."

"Want to show me?"

She stepped back and closed one eye, trying to read my mind.

Maggie was tall and thin with muscular arms from working horses and she had these bright green eyes that made you just want to look at her all day. Her smooth skin was tanned from working outdoors and her hair was the color of black ink.

We took a drive down a backcountry highway, past the freshly planted cotton and small clapboard buildings and around an old gas station that sold hot boiled peanuts and warmer beer. We drove through the Yocona River basin forever flat and brown, waiting for the cotton to twist up out of the earth, and up into the Mississippi hills around Paris. We drove on a highway cut through a long forest of oaks and pines and poplar and hickory and pecan. Green leaves still in the early-summer heat. Dogs trotted loose in gullies and tractors drove slow, headed to turn over some more soil. The air smelled of rich dirt and green leaves.

We turned off the main highway and passed some loose storefronts, all sun-bleached and bare of paint, that had once been a town. Around a small curve and down an unpaved road, we found it.

We parked under an old oak bare of leaves, slammed the Bronco's doors with a thud, and walked out onto the dirt hill of a cemetery. Children and old people and some lost in accidents and others from yellow fever or world war or Civil War. Marble crosses and lambs made of mortar and sculptures of open Bibles. The rocky earth was filled with them.

"What happened to the town?" I asked.

"This is the town."

"Oh."

"This was where Theora Hamblett lived," she said. "You know? The folk artist." Maggie brushed her hair from her eyes and squatted down near a grave covered in mud. She wiped away the dirt so she could read the headstone better. "You ever think about dyin'?" she asked.

"Not when I can help it."

"I think it's good," Maggie said. "Makes you remember life."

I liked the way she said "life," really strung out that *I,* and told her.

She raised up off her haunches and stood up in front of me, nose to nose. So close I could smell the mint on her breath. "Can you stay?"

"Just tonight," I said. "I've got to get back to New Orleans."

"Because of that kid?" she asked. "ALIAS."

I nodded and kissed her on the forehead.

"Didn't that man who stole his money kill himself?"

"No," I said.

She squinted into the sun behind my back. "When will you be back?"

"Soon."

"What did you do for your birthday?" she asked.

"Slept and watched *Hud*. It was on TV."

"I love that movie," she said.

"I knew you would," I said. "Why do you think I hang out with you?"

"I hired a sitter tonight," she said.

"We can take Dylan."

"He'd like that," she said. "Then what?"

LONG AFTER dinner and two Disney movies later, Dylan fell asleep and I watched Maggie hoist him into her arms and take him back to his bedroom. *Saturday Night Live* was on her old TV that flickered when the volume got too high and we drank some Abitas and kissed for a long time on her old plaid sofa.

In her bedroom, windows cracked so we could hear the early summer of crickets and hot wind in the tall skinny pines, I watched her strip out of her gray T-shirt and kick out of her boots and jeans. The numbers on her AM radio said it was almost 1 A.M.

Moonlight scattered across her body. I watched her as I tripped out of my boots and clothes. She hooked her thumbs into her cotton panties and rolled them down her long legs.

We met in the middle of her old iron bed and I wrapped my right arm around her waist, feeling her small breasts against my chest and her long legs hooked around mine. She kissed my ears and my cheeks and mouth. I felt the heat and softness between her legs.

In the small room, I only heard her breathing. A bright bit of sweat on our bodies. In the end, she gripped the back of my neck and bit into my shoulder, only the slightest scream escaping her lips.

"Do you love me?" she asked. As she broke away, I heard her breathing hard.

I wanted to say yes but the answer seemed too easy, so I just kept kissing her, hoping she'd forget the question.

31

TREY FOUND TEDDY sitting on the steps of his brother's tomb smoking up a fat one and telling old stories about when they were kids. Trey wiped off the edge of the marble and sat down, just kind of listening, and trying to find out if the big man had finally lost it. Teddy took a hit off the joint and passed it over to Trey. He took a hit too and stared around him at the little cemetery wedged between a bright red shotgun shack and a tiny white church. He'd heard from someone that Fats Domino lived around here. Trey couldn't name a single song that dude wrote but his father talked about the man like he was freakin' God. Trey always wondered why a man who made so much money would still live in a shithole like the Ninth Ward. All those little shacks shoved together about ten feet apart. Crappy junk cars parked out front and a bunch of restless blacks just trying to make it day to day. Paycheck to paycheck.

"What's up?" Teddy asked.

"You haven't called me back."

"Been busy."

"I'm sorry, man."

Teddy smoked down the joint and tucked a carton of Newports on the tomb. He wiped away the pigeon shit from the steps and stood. "I ever tell you about when Malcolm findin' sound for his records?"

"No."

"He was always lookin' for that perfect cut," Teddy said. "That right guitar or beat. He find this weird shit off these old records. He'd mix some album about science projects and shit and some Tito Puente. Malcolm could keep people movin' with the beats and breaks."

Trey nodded. He watched an old woman shuffling down the sidewalk in her curlers and nightgown. Her hand was on her hip, black skin slunking off of her like a Shar-Pei.

"Hey, Miss Davis," Teddy yelled.

"Hey, Teddy. You seen Kenny?"

"No, ma'am."

Teddy lowered his voice and kept talking, hands in his black pants pocket, Hawaiian shirt untucked and flowing over his belt. Sandals. Straw hat.

"I used to take him to this record store called Elysian Fields," Teddy said. "They had some right shit upstairs, you know? Rap, blues. Even some country. But downstairs is where all good records went to die. You know? Real humbling lookin' down in that basement among all those leaky pipes and shit and seeing thousands, no, man, I'm talkin' millions, of records down for the count."

Trey pulled the joint from Teddy's fingers and smoked it down to the edge. "You want to go get drunk?"

"Na, man," he said. "Can you see it? Stacks and stacks of records as high as you is tall down in Elysian Fields, that ole record smell comin' in your clothes and down into you lungs and you can hear people walkin' upstairs in the store. Man, I didn't want to have no part of it. Here I was makin' all that money, wearin' the Armani and drivin' a Mercedes and tryin' to get my family out of this."

He waved his hand in the little cemetery. "You know? But all my brother wants to do is rescue sounds. He just want to save the soul of musicians who ain't really never made it. A dead man's voice. Maybe some weird-ass beat or guitar."

“Come on,” Trey said, hand on Teddy’s back. “Let’s go. You smokin’ too much hyrdro.”

“No,” he said. “Make me see it all. I want to be back down in that little record shop and feel that energy that young nigga felt. Man, he’d carry them ole records in crates and boxes all over this city. All he wanted from me was to go down in that basement with him. Rescue records. Find beats.”

“Teddy, why don’t I get you a girl?”

Teddy’s red eyes turned on him and he spit on the ground. “Fuck that shit, man. I don’t go for that.”

“Fine,” Trey said. “I’m leavin’.”

“Those L.A. folks don’t want nothin’ from Nint’ Ward but—”

“Dio.”

“You right on that.”

Trey pulled out two discs from his suit pocket and handed them to Teddy. “Are we cool, dog?”

Teddy smiled.

“Make that deal,” Trey said. “We need to keep your brother’s dream alive.”

32

THE NEXT DAY, I could smell the dust boiling under the tires of JoJo's tired white F-150 while we followed a long row of split-rail fence we'd built in the last five days. ALIAS sat in the back of the truck with Polk Salad Annie and sipped on a Coke as we rounded a turn and headed into some flat, strip-logged acres JoJo wanted to turn into some pastureland for his cows. I pushed the bill of my Tulane hat from my eyes and looked into the rearview at ALIAS. JoJo stopped abruptly, making me reach out and hold on to the cracked dash of his truck.

He bounded out of the truck and opened the stainless-steel toolbox, pulling out a Glock 9mm and an old .38 he used to keep on him when he closed up the bar. My Glock was tucked under the driver's seat in the Ghost. I wanted no part of this.

The dust gathered in the afternoon haze and I squinted into the light. I needed to get on the road to New Orleans but still had a favor to ask.

JoJo laid out some old blue medicine bottles on the side of a dirt mound and handed the kid his gun. "You show me how to shoot, then," JoJo said. "You want to talk all tough, then back it up."

The argument had started at Abe's BBQ right off Highway 61 after we'd worked for three hours on a section of split-rail fences. The kid said he'd wanted the Glock back that JoJo had confiscated while I was over in Oxford. I hadn't known ALIAS had brought a gun. I didn't even know ALIAS had a gun. But I wasn't surprised.

I tried to cool them down but then backed off when JoJo got a little hot. We didn't even have time to eat the damned barbecue we bought. Instead, we rode in silence to get this thing finished. That was tough because Abe's made very good barbecue.

"You first," ALIAS said, taking off his basketball jersey and tucking it into the pocket of his jeans.

JoJo pulled the .38 from his waistband, leveled it with one hand in a side stance, and cracked open three bottles in a row. He smiled and handed me the gun. The barrel felt hot and a slight haze of gunpowder hung biting in the air.

"Forget it," ALIAS said, leaning back into the truck. "Let's go, man. I need to get back to my crib. This place is a joke."

I started to say something but JoJo held up a hand.

The kid pushed himself away from the car, ejected the magazine from the Glock, thumbing through the rounds. He leveled the gun at the targets.

In a one-two pop succession, he cracked open the shards of JoJo's run, breaking some tiny blue pieces of glass into slivers. The shells from his 9mm bullets popped out in brassy confetti down at his feet. He missed only one of the six.

I smiled.

ALIAS dropped the gun at his side.

JoJo looked at me. "Good shot. But that don't give him an even head."

He pulled the gun from ALIAS's hand and tossed it back in the truck. He grabbed the .38 and arranged six more bottles in the same order as before.

"Make you a deal, kid," he said.

ALIAS looked at him.

"You get more than me and you can keep the gun," JoJo said.

"So?" he said. "I'll keep it anyway."

JoJo held up his hand. "But if I take them all out, then you have to follow through with something."

ALIAS looked up at JoJo.

"You got to take some readin' lessons with Loretta."

"Who said I can't read?"

"Them things you mouthin' off the cereal boxes don't make no sense," he said. "That rappin' ain't gonna last long."

"I got money."

"We got a deal?"

ALIAS flashed a golden smile. "Whatever you say, old man."

JoJo didn't seem to like those final words as he took aim about five feet back from where ALIAS stood and blasted every single bottle into shards as if he'd tapped them with the electric finger of Zeus. JoJo smiled.

"Shit, can we eat lunch now?" I asked. "A growing boy needs that barbecue."

"You that hungry, kid?" JoJo asked ALIAS.

"I was talking about me," I said.

"When you headed back to New Orleans?" JoJo asked, his face covered in sweat.

"After I say good-bye to Loretta."

JoJo nodded. "What about him?"

I looked over at ALIAS, who stood with his fists on his hips, grinning big and gold as he leapt back into the truck bed. Annie followed.

"You're gonna like Clarksdale," I said.

"Ah, man," ALIAS said.

"JoJo, I'll be back in a week," I said.

JoJo eyed the boy. The sun was yellow and full. High beams on the back of our necks and forearms. Cicadas screamed their high-pitched sounds all around us in the distance of trees just starting to fully leaf.

"That okay with you, kid?" JoJo asked.

He shrugged.

"Could use some help painting the barn."

"Shit, man." ALIAS spoke up. "I ain't no slave."

JoJo walked over to the pile of broken glass and examined a sliver

ALIAS had blown apart with his gun. The light refracted hard in my eyes. Multicolor prisms twisting and playing on the earth.

We piled into the truck.

In the grind of the truck's engine and crunching of gravel and dirt under his old tires, JoJo asked: "Why do I think you've just brought me some kind of riddle I can't figure out?"

33

WHEN I DROVE BACK to New Orleans, I checked my messages. I'd received six since I'd been away, four from credit card companies, one from an old student working on her thesis, and one from Jay Medeaux. I didn't even stop to unpack, only poured out a little Dog Chow for Annie and jumped right back into my truck and headed up Canal and down Basin to the Ninth Ward. Teddy and I needed to talk.

When I arrived at the studio, I felt I'd entered some type of medieval castle. A high chain-link fence surrounded the warehouse made of gold cinderblocks and a black tin roof. Saints colors. Young men in bandannas and stocking caps stood tough, their arms across their bodies, guns tucked into their fat belts. Wide-legged jeans down low. Some smoked cigarettes. None talked. They wore sunglasses, Secret Service–style, and held on to radios. Muscled and hard, they watched me as I parked the truck, my Creedence still playing loud, and walked up to the front of the building. They didn't seem to appreciate John Fogerty the way I did.

A kid I didn't recognize squashed a cigarette under his foot. He wore a thick platinum rope around his neck with the Ninth Ward "9W" symbol. The air was so hot outside it felt like radiation off the asphalt.

"You that white dude?" he asked. His skin glowed with a feverish sheen.

"That's the rumor."

White, red, and yellow roses had been laid on the leather seats of Malcolm's Hummer.

"Teddy waitin' on you," he said.

Two of his rappers, or guards, escorted me into a backroom studio. The studio was dark and about thirty degrees cooler than outside. They'd set red and blue bulbs in floor lamps to create a mood. Thick glass hoodoo candles flickered in the air-conditioning. The air smelled like incense and weed.

"Where you been, man?" Teddy asked. His black silk shirt was rolled to the elbows. Pizza boxes and Chinese food cartons lay in huge piles on tables near the console. On the other side of the glass, I saw some kid with headphones on studying a small spiral notebook. He looked pissed-off with himself and kicked a stool across the room.

"Malcolm knew this was gonna be Stank's ride," Teddy said, watching him and shaking his head. "This thing called 'Project Girl.' He'd laid down this track straight on, sampling some ole Louis Armstrong shit. You know, workin' that Louisiana sound like Mystikal? Man, he had it. But damn if I don't know what the fuck I'm doin' and I've seen him work this shit all my life."

I took a seat by him in the cramped control room watching Stank in a black muscle shirt and a hooded parka. I could smell Teddy's Brut aftershave but it disappeared when he fired up a plump cigar. The room suddenly became clouded and thick. I wedged the door open gently with my foot.

Teddy's face had grown gray and he sweated in the sixty-degree coolness of the room. Great bags hung under his eyes and his fingers shook around a big plastic bottle of Mello Yello. Stank tapped on the glass and startled me.

He circled his index finger in the air.

Teddy squashed the new cigar into an empty coffee can filled with roach clips and the beat started once again. He slid his fat fingers across the mixing board, that same bounce that every other rapper in the country had tried to copy ever since it had been born in the South. The sound track to every black neighborhood in the U.S. Women and ice. Cars and clubs. Stank took a deep stance, hat sideways on his head, and rolled into it.

I watched Teddy's head bobbing up and down, almost hearing the cash falling from the sky in green rain as he moved with his arms. I smiled.

Teddy smiled too until he swung his big arm too close to his food and knocked the Mello Yello all over the console, seeping into all those tiny knobs.

The equalizer's green and red lights dimmed and then shut down. The music ceased in the monitors above us and I watched Stank's hands turn to fists. "What the fuck's up?"

Teddy grabbed his Italian leather jacket and started dabbing off the console. I pulled the jacket from his hands and found some napkins near a pizza box. I wiped the metal and plastic clean but knew it was no use. He'd shorted out the system.

He stood and kicked open the door, leaving the room. I sat there for a while and watched the others clear out. Some more of Teddy's men walked around, prowling, making sure I didn't start any shit. I saw some accusing stares and I smiled back. These boys were in their late teens. Twenty if they were lucky. Their scowls and the hard-edged violence in their eyes reminded me of angular men who'd worked the Delta land and had been beaten down for generations. They were teens; they were old men.

I grabbed a cold Coke from a cooler and found Teddy in his office. Glass desk. Black leather furniture. Boxes and boxes of CDs obscuring the windows. He yelled for everyone to leave him the fuck alone. About a dozen men streamed from his office, a couple of obscenely beautiful women. Black with ringlets of soft hair, T-shirts cut off below their breasts.

I found a comfortable place on the sofa and lay down like you would in a shrink's office. I noticed one of Teddy's old game balls from the Saints and read the writing. It was a play-off game against Atlanta where Teddy had picked up a fumble and ran it back fifteen yards for a TD to win the game.

I tossed the ball up in the air and remembered the party at Teddy's house when we got back to New Orleans. He'd shook his fat butt on the counter of his kitchen with two women and an honest-to-God midget someone met in the Quarter.

I tossed the ball up in the air again. "ALIAS is safe," I said. "He's with JoJo. But in case anyone asks, you don't know shit."

"A'ight," he said, burying his big head into his beefy arms. I heard him sniffle and cough, his body shaking loud and hard deep inside, and the rippling pain hurt my heart so badly I worked to change the subject.

"You can buy a new mixing board. That's what, five thousand? Man, that's how much you paid for those rims on that Bentley."

"If I don't get another album from the kid, man . . ."

On the wall, he had a picture of him and Mike Tyson and Don King. Another showed a picture of Teddy and Sherman Helmsley. He signed the photo "Movin' on Up."

"He'll be back," I said. "I promise."

"He always come back here," he said. He nodded to a long row of keys that hung from gold hooks behind his desk. "You see all that? I let all my talent see where I can take 'em. You see I got two Bentleys. Three Escalades. And that little one there, the one with the platinum fish? Man. That's my baby right there. Sweet little Scarab boat. Got to slap ALIAS hand every time he come in here tryin' to take them keys. I said he cut some platinum albums and he can have it. That's how I know he'll be back. He want it so bad it hurt him."

"This album was the trade with those people in L.A.?"

"No," he said, pulling his head free from his arms and settling into his large desk chair. "That's the last of the Dio tracks. This is for somethin' else I owe."

"What about Cash?"

"Don't worry about Cash," he said. "He know the money comin'."

"You paid him back?"

"Waitin' on the call," he said. "We got to meet. Calm things down. Smooth it over."

Teddy's face sagged and his expression turned inward, looking down at the calluses on his hands and the manicure on his fingers.

"Talked to Jay Medeaux," I said. "Cops don't think Malcolm killed himself. Didn't think he could hang himself in that tree."

Teddy shook his head. "He hung himself."

"Maybe," I said. "Can I see his papers now?"

Teddy shook his head and buffed his nails on his pant leg. "It's over," he said. "We straighten this thing out with Cash and we done. What Malcolm done was not right. He took a kid's money and killed the best rapper we ever had."

"He was your brother."

"Let's not talk," Teddy said. The room quiet as hell, Teddy's face only lit with a small banker's light. "Okay?"

The phone rang and Teddy took it, slumping back into his leather office chair. He grunted a couple times and then said, "I got it."

I raised my eyebrows.

"You roll with us?" he asked.

"Where to?"

"Antoine's," he said. "Cash ready to make the deal."

34

ANTOINE'S ISN'T MY FAVORITE restaurant. Most of the places I enjoy are far out of the Quarter in little neighborhood pockets where the food's cooked on broken-down stoves by women who look on their customers as extended family. But I used to eat at Antoine's and Commander's Palace—one of my favorites—for special occasions with JoJo and Loretta. They found it very important that I know how to handle myself in nice places. Sit up straight. Use the right fork. They also taught me how to order and how to dress and how to recognize the better foods. "Don't be so country," JoJo said to me about a thousand times. Antoine's used to have a menu printed completely in French with waiters who held their jobs as lifelong professions.

But recently I'd noticed a change in the old place. You saw more and more out-of-town businessmen walking from its century-plus doors chomping on toothpicks, wearing golf shirts without a tie or jacket. The waiters had grown ruder, the food a shadow of what it had once been. The menu printed in English.

We rode in a stream of Bentleys and Escalades rolling into the Quarter.

I'd grabbed the sport coat that I'd worn to Malcolm's wake over my white T-shirt. Jeans and boots were at least better than a golf shirt. The music battling from each car didn't even stop when we rolled onto St. Louis near the old Wildlife and Fisheries Building and Teddy's flunkies were left to go park.

We were seated at a huge rectangular table in the center of the restaurant. White tile floors. Café chairs with tables covered in white linen. The walls lined with pictures of dead starlets and U.S. presidents.

A man in an out-of-style Italian suit sat with a peroxide-blond woman with mammoth breasts. He fed her ice cream from his spoon and nearly dropped the white mess in his lap when Teddy's boys walked in.

We didn't even have time to settle our asses in our seats when Cash parted a scurrying group of waiters with about ten of his men and found a seat opposite Teddy. He wore a white linen suit without a shirt. Platinum weighing hard on his neck and fingers. Teddy nodded but did not get up.

Bad energy filled the room.

He saw me but didn't look at me. My hands clenched at my sides and my mouth grew dry.

Teddy motioned over the waiter, ordered chilled shrimp for his people and five bottles of Dom Pérignon.

The weight of his eyes stayed on Cash, who had dipped a shrimp as large as a cat's paw into some cocktail sauce. When the waiter brought the Dom to Cash's side of the table, he told the man to pour it straight up into his water glass.

The waiter blanched, so Cash took the whole thing from the man, popped the top with his bare hands, and drank off the running foam like a child at a fire hydrant in summer.

I motioned to the waiter for a Dixie. I hated champagne.

"Big family," Cash said, his mouth full of wet shrimp meat and champagne. "Got you a white boy and everything."

"What?" Teddy asked. He had yet to touch any food. He waited for the waiter to splash a bit into his glass. He took a small sip, nodded, and waited for the man to pour.

Teddy placed the glass to his lip and tasted the champagne. The waiter nodded and ground the bottle deep into an iced bucket by his elbow. Two waiters filled everyone else's glass from other bottles.

"We through?" Cash asked.

Teddy nodded.

"You know you should be in the ground."

All the men at the table were quiet. They didn't take a bite of their food. The chatter from the small islands of tables around us sounded like insects against a screen door.

"Sorry about your brother," Cash said. "You know? We ain't neva seen alike. But shit with your family tears your heart out from inside."

Teddy nodded.

The waiter brought my beer.

"That white boy and me played a couple weeks back," Cash said. "He tell you about that? Yes, sir, me and him got down in Algiers for you, nigga. Why he do that for you? Crazy, man. He's a crazy motherfucker takin' on Cash like that. He lucky he alive too."

Cash moved his fingers around his bare chest. He still wore sunglasses. I didn't say anything. Teddy looked at me and shrugged.

"You got that money?" Cash asked.

"It'll be loaded in your trunk."

Teddy tasted some chilled shrimp. Then everyone started eating. I tried a few. They tasted thawed and tasteless to me. Even the cocktail sauce was a grade over ketchup. Teddy ordered those french fries loaded with hot air that he liked so much and even started talking among us for a while.

I ate. But I watched too. Cash swigged down his own damned bottle of Dom. His platinum teeth gleaming, a black tattoo of a pistol on his left hand, a blue cross burning bright on his right. Sweat drained from his face and slick bald head and onto his chest.

In the middle of it all, just as the lights had dimmed in the restaurant when a bunch of tourists had ordered crêpes suzette or some shit, Cash spoke loud. "I want the boy. I want ALIAS. He's my blood. We the same."

"Ain't no boundaries at Nint' Ward," Teddy said. He sipped down the rest of the champagne, crooked his finger at the waiter, and whispered something in his ear. The man looked confused and walked away. "I respect what you sayin', man. I respect that you tryin' to make the peace. But you made the play."

"You can keep your respect," Cash said. I could tell his eyes were reddening and he was a little drunk. "Or we can play."

"Play what?" Teddy said, leaning back into his chair. His arms spread across his chest. Full Marlon Brando mode. "You ain't had no business interruptin' Malcolm's thing."

"You burned my Rolls," he said.

Cash tucked four shrimp into the pockets of his right fingers. He gnawed off each one as if eating parts of his own flesh and laughed with shit stuck in his teeth.

The woman with big boobs next to us sucked in her cheeks and turned her head away. Cash smelled her action and got up out of his chair.

He leaned down to her and said something to her that made her clutch her chest and then run to the bathroom. He sat back down at the table and wiped his mouth as if his dirty words had spilled on him.

"The kid?"

Teddy hadn't moved from the Brando pose. He stroked under his chin with the tops of his fingers. "ALIAS is my company."

Teddy stood.

All of his boys stood and for a moment I felt like a kid who didn't attend church enough to know the rules. I stood too, a few seconds later.

"I appreciate the dinner," Teddy said. "I look forward to concluding our business in the future. You'll get your money but you ain't never gettin' ALIAS."

Just as he turned his back, there was a mammoth crash. Cash had flipped the table, splattering the champagne and shrimp cocktail and sending my beer into a foaming skitter across the floor.

"You're dead, motherfucker," he screamed. "Goddammit, you're dead."

35

FOR TWO DAYS, I didn't see or hear from Teddy. I worked on my long-delayed book on Guitar Slim, planned another trip to Mississippi, replaced the radiator in the Ghost, and took Annie down to this place on the levee called Dog Park. I'd taught her to sit and stay, her reward some pepperonis off a pizza from Port of Call. I finally called Teddy on his cell Tuesday night and asked him on his voice mail when I could come by and look through Malcolm's papers. He didn't call back and I was beginning to think I was done. I figured he'd worked out his deal with Cash, maybe had accepted the idea of his brother being a thief and a killer, and wanted to mourn in peace.

I reached into my pocket and found the pack of Newports that Malcolm had handed me a million years ago.

I crumpled them into my hand and dumped the mess into the sink.

Before I knew it, the rains would be here and then that first little fall chill and I'd be back trapped in a Tulane classroom teaching nineteen-year-olds about singers who'd been dead for fifty years. On Thursday, I was ready to go. Duffel bag packed with clean jeans, T-shirts, shit-kickin' boots, and enough underwear in case that bad accident ever happened. I just needed some good CDs—fill up my case of fifty—when the phone rang.

I should have ignored it. I wanted very badly to see Maggie. Check out ALIAS's progress with JoJo and Loretta. Heard he'd actually followed through with JoJo's deal. Loretta had bought him some kids' books and he'd been working on the words. On the phone, she called him a genius.

I packed up Big Jack Johnson, Tyler Keith and the Preacher's Kids, Robert Bilbo Walker. The phone rang more.

I grabbed it.

"Man, Nick," Teddy said. "Where are you?"

"Home."

"No, you ain't," he said. "You in Hawaii."

"How's that?"

"Twenty minutes from the Paris abode," he said. "We havin' a luau."

"I can't."

"Just stop by."

"I'm on my way out."

"It's about JoJo."

He hung up.

FROM THE porch in back of his Mediterranean Revival mansion—all creamy pink stucco and red barrel tile—I could smell the hog meat roasting in a spit and plantains frying in a blackened skillet. Teddy had hired a local reggae band to set up near his dollar-shaped swimming pool and a crew of women to give free massages. I pulled a Red Stripe from a galvanized tin bucket filled with ice and sat down on the diving board. Women in string bikinis and men in thousand-dollar suits roamed the patio. On the driveway sat a car lot full of Escalades and Bentleys, with those chrome rims shining like silver dollars in the afternoon sun.

The patio was a jungle of palm trees, banana plants, and fat magnolias filled with white Christmas lights. Pounding rap filled the backyard from some speakers inside his living room and a rottweiler and a pit bull—someone told me had belonged to ALIAS—roamed the backyard, eating barbecue pork from unsuspecting partyers' plates.

Trey Brill held court at a dock on the lake, teaching some former Calliope and Magnolia kids the perfect swing. He let them take turns hitting golf balls over the levee while he sipped on a Heineken from a little chair.

He caught me watching and gave me the two-finger salute and turned back to his pupils.

Teddy walked by and handed me a paper plate laden with black beans and rice topped with shaved onion. He settled onto the base side of the board and began to eat too.

About ten people suddenly rushed the pool and splattered us. But Teddy didn't break stride with the fork. He stared into an empty field beside the house where a contractor's bulldozers sat idle.

The men in the pool had plucked a couple of women up on their shoulders and were chicken-fighting. A young kid had a circle of men around while he freestyle-rapped about the women he'd slept with and the cars he owned.

I tried to find what Teddy saw in the open field.

I think he was just numb.

"Sold Malcolm's car today," he said to himself.

"Jay Medeaux said you still believe he killed himself."

He nodded. "I don't hate him, Nick. I don't. Even after what coulda happen to me with Cash when that money disappeared. Still don't change nothin'."

"I'm leaving town," I said.

Teddy shook his head and drank down the rest of the Red Stripe in one gulp. He smoothly shifted from the diving board, stood, and disappeared back into the house. I followed.

The inside of his mansion was all slate and tile, all big chunks the size of flagstones in the Quarter. He had a couple of paintings of jazz scenes on the walls, a USS *Enterprise*–sized entertainment center with four big screens. Only one couch and a couple of chairs. Half of a furniture store display.

Teddy handed me a Dixie. "That's your brand, right?"

I nodded.

"I need you, Nick."

"Teddy," I said. "You're all right now. Talk to the police."

"Naw, man. Not for that. I need you to hang. You know? Like we did back at camp. Remember how we used to watch them soap operas and shit, laughin' at them women with those big titties who couldn't act? Remember that dude who had that eyebrow and shit? You would turn the sound off and make up his voice. Man, that was hilarious."

"I need to get back to ALIAS. JoJo can't handle him on his own."

He reached inside his bulky pants pocket and then pressed a brass key into my palm. He gripped my hand inside his meaty fingers and held me there, looking into my eyes. "There you go."

I looked at him. He winked.

"It's the bar," he said. "It's yours."

"I don't understand."

"I bought JoJo's back," he said. "It's yours. You were there when I needed you. You came through."

"I can't take that," I said. "I didn't do anything. I didn't help you."

"How you supposed to know it comin' from my own backyard?" Teddy smiled. "You my brother?"

I nodded.

He shook his head as two women in bikinis came up to him and started tickling him on his side. One of them, a black girl with ringlets of soft brown hair and softer eyes, had a squirt gun tucked into the elastic of her thong bikini. "Come on, Teddy," she said, teasing. "You promised."

The other one, a blonde in a red-checked bikini, reached for my hand, her stomach flat and hard. Brown eyes and smooth rich tan. I shook my head, wanting to stay.

"We cool?" Teddy asked. He nodded at me, waiting on my answer as if I had another to give. I nodded. The blonde smelled like cocoa butter and strawberries.

I heard his booming laugh, the splash of water from the pool outside, and smelled the hog meat roasting in the air. I remembered something I had not thought about for years. About ten years ago, we had this smart-ass fullback from Nebraska who thought he was the ultimate practical joker. Sometimes his jokes were funny, like putting child-size jockstraps in all the coaches' lockers, but sometimes he crossed the line. His jokes a little too mean.

One season, after a few losses on the road, he started giving Teddy a hard time about never having a woman. He said if we won the next game, that he'd get Teddy a date with the best-looking woman in Louisiana.

We won, unexpectedly, in San Francisco. When we stepped off the plane, there was a beautiful black girl in a cheetah print coat and spandex pants holding a sign that read TEDDY.

Teddy, his long coat draped over his arm, stopped cold because he was the only Teddy on the team. He pointed to himself, a smile forming on his lips while the smart-ass fullback patted Teddy's huge back and said "Good luck, Tiger."

I drove down to JoJo's and got drunk because that's what I did back then, only to find Teddy waiting at my apartment when I got back. He sat on the curb in the parking lot, his head in his hands, sobbing.

He'd apparently taken the woman to Commander's Palace and to the top of the Trade Center for drinks. He walked with her under gas lamps in the Quarter, holding her arm in the crook of his, telling her about growing up in the Ninth Ward with a brother he loved. He told her that she felt special, that he knew things like this just happened, and that maybe he was in love.

She just smiled at him, rarely talking.

She held his hand back to his car, where she unzipped his pants and performed acts on him that he'd only read about as a small fat child growing up in a poor neighborhood.

He kissed the top of her head and told her that he loved her.

In seconds, she sat upright in the car and fixed her coat, asking for the money that she was promised. Teddy asked what she meant and didn't understand until she reached into his pocket, pulled out two hundred-dollar bills, and climbed out of the car.

Teddy cried and fell asleep on my sofa that night. In the morning, he was gone.

He never mentioned it again. Ever.

I drove back to the city and called Maggie on the way, letting her know I'd be late.

"What happened now?" she asked.

"I was paid for something I didn't deserve."

"What are you looking for now?"

"Respect for a friend."

36

I NEVER HEARD BACK from the woman at Pinky's bar in the Marigny. I never called her and she never called me. No messages, no letters. After Malcolm died, I didn't see there was much point. Since that morning we'd found him hung in the tree, I'd been bothered. What had happened to the money and the people who'd been working with him? I never was much for neat endings and lost cash. Besides, I was a little pissed-off that Fred at Pinky's never called me back. If only I'd let her tie me up.

I drove to Frenchman, parked on the street, and walked over to Pinky's, the pinup girl winking in neon. It was about 2 on a Sunday and the same British bartender was sweeping up the floor, the radio tuned to some Iggy Pop as he danced with his broom.

When I walked inside, he turned down the radio and held the broom close to his chest. "We're closed."

"Back to see Fred."

"Fred's asleep."

"Where?"

"Upstairs," he said, giving me that "you dumb-ass" look. "Where else?"

He pointed to a flight of stairs hidden behind the bar by neatly spaced spindles. Above the rows of multicolored bottles sat a small shrine made from skulls, cow bones, and a large pentagram. Someone burned incense in the mouth of the skull.

I bounded up the creaking steps covered in mildewed red carpet and knocked on a door that was already ajar. Near the door was a neat grouping of old plaid furniture and a coffee table made with legs from a mannequin. The more I opened the door, the more mannequins I saw. Black and white. Male and female. Some with pants. Some with whips. Some with bright green wigs, others with dated sixties hair. Even one dressed as a nurse.

I knocked on the door, hearing a woman giggle in the back.

A teenage girl, who looked about fifteen, a little plump with black nails and cherry-red hair, bounded out of the room wearing nothing but a long Jazzfest T and said, "You're not Bob."

"No."

"Fred?"

Fred emerged from the door wearing a pink terrycloth robe and holding a Sno-Kone, eating off the top. Her white witch-blond hair packed on top of her head. She had a naked Barbie doll clutched in one of her hands.

"Yeah?"

"Nick."

"Yeah."

I smiled. She walked back into the bedroom. The girl followed, looking at me. I heard her say, "What's with the dipshit?"

I crossed my arms on my chest and waited.

Fred came back. Her breath smelled like the Jack distillery in Lynchburg, a brownish coating on the Sno-Kone. In the back, I heard the girl flip the channels from MTV over to a cartoon featuring fighting Japanese robots.

She looked up at me, red-eyed and sneering, and belched.

She stuck a piece of paper in my hand and stumbled back.

"Five hundred for this," she said. "It's all I could get you."

"Let me see if it pans out."

"It will."

I nodded.

"I talked to Curtis and he knows where to find you," she said. "Leave the money with Bob. If you don't, I'll have Stella pay you a visit."

She laughed and left the room. She started giggling and I heard her jumping on the bed with the little girl.

Written in almost illegible cursive were the words *Alix Sentry. Orleans Parish Jail. Waiting for you.*

I heard the Japanese robots kicking ass in the next room and watched the still mannequins watch me as I left the little apartment, not sure where this was headed.

THE ORLEANS Parish Jail stands right next to the police station down on Broad Street. Someone, probably another inmate, had decided to paint the cinderblock topped in concertina wire with faces out of those eighties Robert Nagel prints, the ones with the women with very white faces and black hair. I walked along the wall and found the front desk, where I checked in with a deputy. I told them I was a friend of Alix Sentry and we had a meeting set up.

He made a call to Sentry's holding cell.

"You're going to have to wait," he said. "Takes us about thirty to bring the prisoners in."

"What was he charged with?"

The deputy looked down at the computer screen. "Two counts of fraud and four counts of possession of child pornography. Oh, and drug paraphernalia."

I smiled. "We're not that good friends," I said. "Really just acquaintances."

I waited in a little family-room area close to the desk with two women and five children. One of the women was white and wore a black halter top cut away with straps in the back to show off a tattoo of a dolphin. Her long brown hair had been moussed and puffed up on her head circa 1987 and she'd painted her lips probably a half inch over where they ended. Her kids, I guessed, ran around the sofa while I watched an old console television playing *Wheel of Fortune.*

Her kids were scrubbed clean and wearing crisp T-shirts and new jeans.

The other woman kept trying to guess the answers with words and phrases that didn't quite make sense. She became very frustrated when this guy on TV never said "Pretty in Link."

A deputy called my name and led me through a metal detector. I had to take off my belt buckle and leave my keys in a little plastic bowl on the second try.

"Does anyone ever try the ole nail file in the birthday cake?" I asked.

The guy handed the keys back to me and scratched his hairy neck before leading me into an empty room filled with about ten plastic slots, little cubes where you could talk through the plexiglass. I was hoping to see the woman from *Midnight Express* pressing her boobs against the glass, but I was going to be alone with Alix Sentry.

The back door opened and a black woman deputy led out a man in handcuffs. His smile so waxen and stiff when he saw me that I had to look away from his face.

37

ALIX SENTRY STOOD about five feet eight, bald with just wisps of brown hair ringing his head, with small brown eyes and a pointed nose. He sat on the other side of the partition and folded his hands under his chin. He stared right through the glass, twisting his nose like he was trying to smell something. He wore an orange jumpsuit reading ORLEANS PARISH JAIL and watched me in silence.

An intercom system separated us. I waited about thirty seconds for him to talk while he stared.

"You're a nice-looking man," he said.

"Aw, shucks," I said.

He smiled. I leaned back in the seat.

"Maybe we can write," I said. "Pen pals."

He smiled. "I'd like that."

"Fred Moore call you?"

"She's such a sick little bitch."

"Everyone likes Barbie," I said. "A woman on the go."

"She likes real ones."

I nodded. "You going to help or not?"

"Depends on what you'll pay me."

"Same as Fred, five hundred."

He laughed. "I wouldn't give up Fred for five hundred."

"I'm not asking you to give up Fred."

He started playing with the zipper on the jumpsuit. "Isn't this thing so ugly? I feel like I should be in the Ice Capades."

"What do you have?"

"You know what I do?"

"Yes."

"Then why would you think I'm so fucking stupid?" he asked, raising his eyebrows.

"I don't think you're stupid."

"You know what they arrested me for?"

"Yeah."

"Someone set me up," he said.

"I don't care."

He blew out his breath and slumped back into his seat with his arms crossed over his chest. He was so average that I could see him living in Metairie with a wife and a Volvo.

"I want five thousand."

"I don't have it."

"Fred said you did."

"Fred isn't my accountant," I said. "I can pay you if I find the money."

"That's a big if."

I looked over at the female deputy watching us and up at the water-stained tile ceiling buzzing with dull fluorescent light. "You have something else to do?"

He looked at the back of his hands and stretched.

"He sold me out," he said. "He's the one that planted those magazines of young boys and all of it. I don't play like that; I never have. He trashed my house and made a phone call to the police that I'd been harassing his kids. Said he was a concerned father and I'd been walking around in a Speedo giving out toys."

"What did you do to him?"

He laughed. "Got somewhere first."

"Where?"

"To this old woman," he said. "She gave me her jewelry and furs. Made her feel better. I was her friend. He wasn't."

I nodded. The room smelled of Lysol and urine. Words had been carved into the stall where I sat. A hundred phone numbers and names, a couple of business cards of attorneys.

"I'll pay two if I get the money back."

"Five," he said. "I know it's worth that."

I blew out my breath and rubbed my face with my hands. Stretched the legs.

"I've been led to you through a few people and now I feel like I'm bargaining for something that doesn't exist. I don't think you know shit. I think you're bored and just want to practice up while you're waiting for your court date."

"ALIAS told you about him, right?"

I leaned in. His eyes grew larger and he moved within inches of the glass. He bit off a cuticle and spit it on the floor.

"He said his ear was bad, right? A really ugly left ear."

"I can pay you only if the money comes back," I said. "And I mean all of it."

"It's a lot, isn't it?"

"How do you know?"

"I think he's gone."

"Who?"

He laughed.

"Give me something," I said. "You want him in jail and you want some cash. What else are you going to do?"

"I read," he said. "I like Dickens. Poor kids making good for themselves. Finding out they're really rich. Class struggle."

"Is that it?"

He leaned back into the glass and spoke into the two-way intercom. "Don't fuck with me. I can ruin people's lives."

I waited. He took a breath.

"You know that hotel in the Quarter with the fence made out of corn. It's iron but looks like stalks."

"Sure, on Royal. The Cornstalk."

The place sat about two blocks over from JoJo and Loretta's place.

"There is a street right there. It's Dumaine or St. Phillip. I don't remember, but he used to live there. It's an old apartment. Used to be one of the motels where the rooms open up outside."

"Right."

"That's all I have."

"A name?"

"Marion Bloom."

"Worked with a woman, too."

"That would be Dahlia. You find Marion, you'll find Dahlia. She does the work for him when she's not stripping. When it's a man, she can turn any boy in about five minutes."

"Pretty?"

"If you like that," he said. "You'll know her when you see her. Real tall with light skin. Almond-shaped eyes. Makes her look kind of Asian. She's a real doll."

"That's it?"

"From what I hear, five thousand is good."

"You know who they were working with?"

He shook his head.

"Just the job," he said. "Dahlia talks in her sleep and I talk to those people."

I got up to leave.

"You have a gun?"

I nodded.

"Excellent."

38

A COUPLE OF HOURS LATER, I walked with Annie down by the Cornstalk Hotel and let her take a piss on the cornerstone of a building that sold gourmet dog bones for five dollars each. Annie was more of a Milk-Bone woman; I was sure of it. I took her by the leash and trotted her down St. Phillip and across Bourbon and back down Dumaine. Right as we were getting close to Royal again, I saw a two-story building with doors facing outside. Old clothes had been left on the crooked railing and junk cars stood in a small parking lot. A pile of air conditioners sat stacked three high on the bottom floor, where an old man in a plaid shirt beat them with a wrench.

I walked down Dumaine holding Annie's leash, passing the open door of a voodoo museum where incense blew out. Inside, I could see dozens of lit candles and an old oil portrait of Marie Laveau.

I crossed the street and into the lot of the old motel. The old man didn't look up from his work, he only kept cussing.

Annie sniffed his leg and he jumped.

"I'm looking for Marion Bloom."

"No one lives here," he said. "We're renovating."

"Did a guy named Bloom live here?"

He shook his head and patted Annie's head. "Good dog."

"This your place?"

"Yeah."

"Was this a rental?"

"Yeah, but I'd let it turn to shit. I rented it out to a bunch of fucking losers. Had some guy leave his needles right out on the street; another guy took a crap in the sink."

"Maybe he got confused," I said. "Did you rent to a guy with a bad ear? You know, like wrestlers get. Lots of extra cartilage."

He nodded. "I think he said his name was Alix."

I laughed. "You know where he went?"

"No," he said. "You a friend of his?"

"Something like that."

"Well, he left a bunch of shit here. You're welcome to it. If you don't get it, I'm throwing it out. Just a bunch of bills and crap."

I followed him to the back of the old motel, where he had a metal storage shed filled with lawn-mower parts, ratty mattresses, and boxes of soap. He left the door open and light cut in through the dust. I waited as he dragged out an old box marked ALIX.

I looped Annie's leash into my belt—she kept pulling, smelling something that was dead—as I rifled through the box. Two pairs of Wrangler jeans, an Official Bourbon Street Drunk T-shirt, a box of Polaroid photographs, a loose-leaf binder filled with notes and Bible verses and bills addressed to Marion Bloom.

I searched through the photographs, finding a couple of Bloom at Pat O'Brien's piano bar. Drunk with a couple of women at his side. His head was turned to the right and I saw the infamous ear. He was short with black hair, big eyebrows, and a larger nose. He looked like a rodent.

One of the women was a light-skinned black woman with long black hair. She wore something on her top that looked more like a bandanna than a shirt, showing her taut midriff. The bikini string from her underwear showed above her tight black pants. She had Asian-looking eyes and thick lips. Thin-boned and standing like a ballerina, with her shoulders back and her hips pushed forward. Her lips were squeezed together as if she were kissing the camera.

I grabbed the photos, the journal, and bills, thanking the man.

"You don't want this T-shirt?" he asked, rubbing his neck. "Funny as hell."

"You keep it."

I tied Annie at an old iron horse post at the C.C.'s coffeehouse on Royal. The owner knew me because JoJo and Loretta used to hang out here a lot.

I bought a café au lait and read through Bloom's journal. He'd been taking notes on how to be a minister, inserting important Bible verses to use and even a fake résumé of places where he'd "pastored." Inside the notebook was a real estate booklet with a photo of an old Captain D's restaurant near Fat City circled in red.

I looked through the pocket, finding some other similar properties and a couple of flyers from a travel agency about cheap flights from New Orleans to Tampa.

In the reverse pocket I found a tabloid-size little newspaper called *Big Easy Dreamin'* that advertised strip clubs and massage parlors and all-night XXX video stores. The paper had been folded onto the sixth page. The ad read for a club on Airways Boulevard called Body Shots, where you could drink tequila out of a woman's navel for five dollars.

In the black-and-white ad, I saw a picture of the woman I figured to be Dahlia. She had her arm around another woman, both wearing bikinis and sombreros, inviting everyone to come on down.

Annie barked at some people passing by and then took a few laps from her water bowl.

I finished the café au lait and walked outside. I called Teddy and got him on his cell. It sounded like he was in his car.

"You know some strip club called Body Shots?"

He grunted. "Man, I don't go to places like that no more."

"Do you know it?"

"I can make some calls," he said. "Sure my boys know."

"I need you to take me there."

"Thought you was leavin' to see your woman in Mississippi," he said. "Why you want to go out and party?"

"I think I found the folks who took ALIAS for his money."

"What you mean?"

"A con man named Bloom and a stripper that goes by the name of Dahlia."

"They workin' with my brother?"

"I don't know."

"But they got the kid's money?"

"Pretty sure."

"Where you want me to pick you up?"

"The warehouse."

39

"I TOLD YOU, I ain't never been to this place Body Shots and never use to hang with Malcolm and ALIAS at the Booty Call," Teddy said as we pulled away from Julia Street in his new white Escalade with gold rims and Gucci interior. "What kind of shit is that? That was some half-assed movie with Will Smith's wife and I don't do strip clubs. Not anymore."

"ALIAS said you owned a table there."

"That's not true."

"Teddy?"

"A strip club is like goin' to some buffet where they show you the food but you can't eat," Teddy said, wheeling up Canal and down onto I-10, headed to Airline Highway, the beginning of old Highway 61. The old road now filled with abandoned roadside motels and diners and places once used by travelers before the interstate. Now it was empty pools and crack dealers and motel rooms rented by the hour. "You know? Like, look at all these beautiful steaks. And all that baked potato with sour cream and chives and shit. But if you try and get one mouthful, you get arrested. Ain't that fucked-up?"

A 1950s drive-in movie theater sat between a decaying motel advertising AC and color televisions and a defunct steak house. The lot had been surrounded with wire but the tall screen and speaker boxes still stood. Everything still neat and tidy, only a few weeds growing through the cracked asphalt as if the owner waited for the day that the old highway would be back. Until then, it seemed the movie would remain private, only something a few could imagine.

"I just bought this," Teddy said, thumping his steering wheel. "You like it?"

"Did you really need it?" I said. "Why don't you put that money to some good use?"

"What, you a communist, Travers?" he asked.

"No, man," I said. "I just don't like to see a waste."

"You remember that community center where we had Malcolm's wake?"

"Sure."

"Ninth Ward Records built that shit, man."

"Good."

"But you think all the jewelry and cars and homes and women are . . . what did you say? A waste."

"Aren't they?"

"See, you still don't get it," he said. "The culture of our world, right. That's what my people want to see. They want to see you livin' large and steppin' out with the Gucci and Vuitton and all them suits from Armani and your woman wearin' Versace and gold and platinum and diamonds."

"Maybe you could be different," I said. "Maybe you could set a better example for the kids who buy those CDs in Uptown, spending the only thirteen dollars they have on a Ninth Ward record."

Teddy turned down the Master P and looked over at me, the highway whizzing past. "You ever been black?"

"One night," I said. "But I was very drunk. Someone told me about it later."

"No playin'," he said. "You got to know what it feels like to walk into a restaurant or bar or Saks or some shit and have people not wait on you.

Have security guards followin' you while you tryin' to pick out some goddamned gloves for your brother's Christmas or bein' asked to leave a movie theater 'cause you talkin' too loud."

"What does that have to do with anything?" I said. "I never thought you wore blackness on your sleeve."

"I wear something else, man," he said. "I wear the car, the jewelry, the two-thousand-dollar suit 'cause that makes people respect me. When I walk into Canal Place, man, people waitin' for me at the door. They don't see black no more; they see green. You understand?"

Teddy parked close to the door of the strip club and we could hear the bass-driven funk rattling the corrugated tin of the building. He locked up the Escalade from his key chain and buttoned up his black suit.

He carried a carved wooden cane under his arm as we walked inside.

He didn't even try to pay a cover.

The little black girl in leather pants and snakeskin bikini top just giggled when he walked in, and ran to get the manager.

"Clout," I said. "You got it."

"I got the cash."

Teddy didn't look around at the women or the layout, he just took a quick turn and walked up a small flight of steps where there was a circular table and booth. A card on the table read RESERVED.

"This is Stank's place," he said. "He called ahead."

We took a seat. A waitress came over, tight T-shirt with no bra, hoop earrings, and bleached hair, and asked what we wanted. I ordered coffee and Teddy wanted some brandy. He asked for the best they had and I was wondering if Teddy thought the Body Shots had some kind of private reserve.

"What ever happened to that good-lookin' girl you was seein' when we played?" Teddy asked.

"The blonde?"

"Yeah."

"She left me when I quit," I said. "I wasn't as good-looking without a salary."

"Wasn't into that whole cool blues professor shit?"

"She thought McKinley Morganfield was a former president."

"Who the fuck was McKinley Morganfield?"

"Never mind."

As the waitress laid down the drinks, the manager of the bar—a short, swarthy little guy in a black polo shirt and pants—took a seat with us. He shook Teddy's hand and presented him with a few cigars. Teddy handed one to me but didn't introduce us. I nodded at the guy and drank my coffee.

The song changed to "Don't Mean Nothin' " by Richard Marx. I wondered if I'd just entered some kind of eighties time warp or if Richard Marx singing about having self-worth had somehow made him a patron saint to strippers.

"You like Richard Marx?" I asked the little manager.

"Sure, yeah," he said, snorting, giving Teddy a "you believe this guy" look. "Whatever."

"Beni?" he asked. "Stank drop some money here."

"You know it."

"He works for me."

"I know."

"Nick, show him the picture."

I reached into my back pocket and pulled out the photo of Dahlia. The good one from Pat O's.

"Know her?" Teddy asked.

Beni nodded. He looked up at me and back at Teddy.

"She don't work that way," he said. "The girl onstage. The little one with the chain-mesh bikini. You have an hour with her in the back room for free. On the freakin' house. For him, how 'bout a hundred."

"We don't need our dicks jacked, Beni," Teddy said. "We need a name."

"She rob you?" Beni asked.

I shook my head.

"Cut you?"

I shook my head again.

"Don't tell me you're in love."

"That's it, Beni," I said. "I'm in love. What's her name?"

"He ain't in love," Teddy said. "What's her name?"

Beni looked down at his hands and adjusted some horrible gold rings on his hairy knuckles. "How much?"

Teddy reached into his wallet and laid down four hundred dollars.

"I shouldn't pay you shit with all the business that Stank give you."

Beni scraped up the cash and said, "She quit last week. Left with some other rapper."

"Who?"

"I don't know."

"What did he look like?" I asked.

"He was a freakin' black guy. What can I say?"

Teddy shook his head and then shook it some more.

"What's her name?" I asked.

"Dahlia," he said. "That's all I know."

"What's her Social Security card say?"

He looked over at Teddy and raised his eyebrows. "Is this guy joking?"

"Didn't she fill out anything to get paid?"

"Let me check."

He returned about ten minutes later with a little index card marked with the name Dahlia, a social with the name Dataria Brown, and an address in Midtown off Esplanade.

"You won't tell her that we seen each other," Beni said.

"Why do you care?"

"I just don't like her is all," he said. "The way she'd look at me made me not want to turn my back. Like she'd stick a freakin' knife in it if I looked the other way."

"Dataria," I repeated. "You know a guy named Bloom? Boyfriend or something. Has a bad ear?"

"That's all I know."

"You sure?"

"She danced, got naked, took her cut, and left," he said. "What can I say?"

"Was she a good dancer?"

"What?"

"Was she a good dancer?" I repeated over the music.

"Yeah," he said. "She was. The best I'd ever seen. She could move."

We drove back in silence. Teddy just kept watching the road, steering with those two fingers like he always did.

"Sure would like to find that money," he said.

"I know."

"You want me to go with you?"

"No, I'll handle it."

"Nick?" he asked.

"Yeah."

"Open that bar up," he said. "Be true to your dreams."

40

I LEARNED HOW TO TAIL people when I was traveling through the Delta with my tracker mentor Willie T. Dean, and Willie T. wasn't too big on taking no for an answer. I remember we'd once been searching for this man outside Jackson who knew something about the last days of Tommy Johnson and we were tired as hell. We'd been in the Delta for two weeks collecting stories and recording them on video and audio, and here was this guy who thought that white people were an abomination.

He'd rather sell his soul than have us sit up on his porch and ruin his reputation with his neighbors.

So instead of driving back to Oxford, where Willie T. had been teaching blues history for the last thirty years, he told me to park down this dirt road and wait till the old man's pockmarked red Ford pulled out from the trailer.

We did. After a near fistfight, the purchase of a case of beer, and Willie T. warming him up with stories from our road trips and a little song he played on his 1920s Dobro, we got him talking.

But New Orleans wasn't the Delta and this Dahlia woman was no bluesman.

I wanted to work alone, so I'd dropped Teddy at home. I soon found out the address in Midtown was bogus and had to have a friend of mine in Memphis run the social. Ten minutes later, he gave me an address back in Uptown, not far from the streetcar line. He used the same computer service as bill collectors, no one more tenacious.

I didn't know how long it would take for Dahlia—if she even lived there—to pop her head out of the little carriage house where she lived in the Garden District. You could always tell someone lived in a carriage house when the street number contained a "½."

I sipped on a Barq's, ate some Zapp's Crawtaters, and leaned back into the seat of the Ghost, my stereo tuned low on some '68 Comeback, a band out of Memphis. The air was sticky and thickly humid. Huge brown elephant ears grew in rotted rows along the steps to the second floor. A collection of rusted wind chimes and flowers rubbed against one another in the summer heat.

I was parked under a huge oak on a little side street near the cross of St. Charles and Napoleon. The streetcar clanged and rolled in the distance. I could smell the Mississippi and the sugary-sweet smell of decaying magnolia flowers. I finished the bag of chips.

I could not see inside the carriage house—the building leaned a little to the right, probably a casualty of the city's termite plague—but could see blue light leaking through her curtains. I heard the wind chimes ringing and the sound of drunks on the patio of Copeland's restaurant at the corner.

Forty-two minutes later, Dahlia ran down the creaking wooden steps, past a car covered in a mildewed tarp, and down the narrow gravel drive to a brown Miata. I started to grab her right there, but she was too fast and I was curious about where she was headed.

She started the car, drove a block down Napoleon, and then circled back to St. Charles. I did the same, keeping about three cars back. We passed rows of restaurants and dry cleaners and Victorian houses, up and around Lee Circle. Neon and brightly fluorescent in the night.

She turned on Poydras, headed to the river, stopping down by Peters by Harrah's Casino. I found a pretty quick parking place, slapped The Club on my steering wheel, and followed. I stayed about eight yards back. I was pretty sure she was headed into the casino, but two seconds later, she ducked into the W Hotel.

I watched from a large bank of windows along Peters as she gave a kiss on the cheek to the bouncer at this place called Whiskey Blue, a bar I'd heard was the top place to be seen in New Orleans. One of those beautiful-people hangouts where everyone dressed like they're trying to imitate Dieter from the Sprockets skit on *Saturday Night Live*.

The bouncer—of course dressed in all black—waved me in, unconcerned about my age.

The bar vibrated with techno music and had been softly lit with track lighting and candles. All leather and velour. Soft cushioned sofas and high bar stools. Lots of health-club-muscled men with goatees. A few of the golf-shirt crowd with cell phones on hips. The bar was spare and obsessively clean.

Martinis and Manhattans. Few smokers. These people were too beautiful to smoke. Too rich. Too perfect. Maybe she was moving up from Airline Highway, found her a little sugar daddy.

Dahlia had found a place in the far back corner of the bar. A little cove of low sofas and curved love seats. She'd taken up a comfortable spot on the lap of some white man in a black suit.

I ordered a Dixie from the bartender.

"A what?" asked the bartender. She wore a tight black tank top and a very short miniskirt. Long tanned legs and knee-high black boots.

"A Dixie."

"Is that with rum?"

"Hops."

She wrinkled her nose. "What?"

"It's a beer," I said.

She pointed to a shelf of imports and other microbrews. I accepted a Sam Adams and waited at the bar, the techno making my ears bleed, some jackass next to me talking to someone about where they "were going to hit next" and a "kick-ass deal" he'd made with a client. I watched Dahlia, keeping my head turned away. The man in the black suit swatted her butt playfully and wrapped his fingers around a frosted martini glass.

About five white people around them laughed at something he'd said. But I could not see his face.

I took a sip of the Sam Adams.

Dahlia snuggled her face into the man's neck.

He took a broad, self-indulgent smile. Martini in the right hand. Dahlia's muscular ass in the other. He turned.

Trey Brill.

41

BEEN A DAY. *Been a year. You ain't sure. All you know is that you left in some broke-ass town with two T-shirts to your name and an old man ridin' you hard about work. You become just a slave to him. He's about a hundred years old and old school as hell, the way he play records on this phonograph and sip beer out on his porch with his old lady. You like the old lady. She buy you some new clothes and cook you some food that's 'bout the tastiest shit you ever put in your mouth. Chicken pie. Greens.*

She respect you. She call you ALIAS.

Not the old man. That old man call you kid or Tavarius or just Stovall with a laugh. You ain't nothin' but a punk to him, puttin' up fences till you have blisters, paintin' some raggedy-ass barn till it get dark. Yesterday he take you fishin' and think you a fool for not knowin' how to work a hook.

He don't know shit.

Tonight he brought you downtown and you think this gonna be all right. You down off another road called Martin Luther King. He tellin' you all about when he was your age, like you give a shit, and all about whiskey and women—all the money that was floatin' down these cracked asphalt streets.

But you can't see it. Clarksdale had to be a broke-ass city from the start, man. The stores have sheets of wood in the windows, just like the places round Calliope, and boys work the corners with their rock just the same. The old man just shake his head at those fools and take you into this old brick building that look out onto the corner. A yellow light comin' from the door like a candle glow in a skeleton's mouth.

The corner is workin' tonight. You can smell the funk sweat off the crackheads' bodies and that lazy eye from the women in tight skirts. You don't mess with that. You got your life.

Old man take you inside. The floor is concrete but worn smooth from dancin' feet. There's a pool table in the corner with some green felt burned by cigarettes and a small bar where they only serve beer and whiskey. Christmas lights—blue, green, and red—hang from the walls.

You order a forty and get one but the old man swipes it from you.

Two old men sit down with you. Just as old and black and gray as the man and you gettin' tired. You walk over to the jukebox and check out the tunes while the old men start talkin' about cotton and farming and some man named Sonny Boy.

Juke has some old-school joints. Run-D.M.C. like Malcolm used to play for you. Music made before you was born. Something called "It's Like That and That's the Way It Is."

You kick it up. Even other punks noddin' with the music, 'cept the old men.

In the dark bar, concrete cave over your head, you get the mean eye.

Just for playin' music.

"Tavarius," the old man call you. "This man is Bronco and his brother, Eddie Wilde. We went to school together here. We was you once."

You look at his face and don't see it, listenin' to Run-D.M.C. and then flippin' that song to "Rock Box." You think about Malcolm and the way he died and you clench your jaw real hard. Sweat workin' hard in this concrete room.

"You still got it?" JoJo ask.

The man he call Bronco, black with green eyes and a face like an Indian, show the back of his forearm and four scars runnin' like tracks.

"What happen to you?" you ask.

"We had some women trouble."

You smile, take a swig from JoJo's beer. He don't say nothin', like he can't see it.

"In fact," Bronco say, "her name was T-R-O-U-B-L-E. And wadn't worth the time."

Eddie Wilde, thin and tall and in a black suit, shake his head. "Pussy make you do some dumb shit."

"You right," JoJo say. "Ever think about that? Everythin' a man do is for pussy. His job, his clothes. Even drivin' a silly-ass car. But he ain't never believe it."

"I remember when you wore your first suit to church," Bronco say. "You just met Loretta, I do believe, and just about lose your mind."

"Shit," JoJo say, snatching the forty away from you and takin' a sip.

Y'all sit like this a long time. You can hear the trucks and cars prowlin' down MLK and hear the country thugs talkin' shit outside. The air is so hot your T-shirt sticks to your skin and soon you start lookin' at yourself in the mirror when JoJo send you to get beers. You look back at the old men and flex the muscles in your arm.

JoJo start playin' blues on the jukebox and the old men come alive. Eddie Wilde dance with himself out on the smooth floor, waggin' his old black-man finger. Bronco sing along with a song call "Feel Like Goin' Home."

You could swear that your old man's eyes get heavy with that, his lips moving over the words. "Late in the evenin'," he say. His mind forty years behind.

They all slammin' beers and talkin' shit when you see those young thugs walk into the joint. They little older than you, wearin' black Ts with no sleeves and thick gold around their neck. They watch you from the end of the bar with their red eyes.

Under the table, you feel for the knife in your pocket.

While laughin' at one of JoJo's jokes, Bronco take the blade from you hand and starts cleanin' his nails with it.

The country thugs come to you.

You kick the chair out. Ready to fight.

One of the boys smiles. "You right," he say. "ALIAS, my man."

Everybody slappin' you on the back, pullin' you away from the small corner where the old men drink.

They keep talkin' but no one is listening.

42

"HAVE YOU TALKED TO JOJO?" Maggie asked, very early and very bright the next morning. I rolled off the mattress I kept on the warehouse floor and cradled the phone closer to my ear.

"No."

"He seemed pretty pissed," she said. "You know, like he didn't have time to talk."

"He always sounds that way."

"You doin' okay?"

"Fine."

"You know what I did yesterday?"

"No, but I'd like to know," I said, growing awake thinking about Maggie. I knew she'd been up since dawn. Her skin would be flushed from taking care of her horses, the smell of hay on her sweaty T-shirt and in her dark hair.

"I rode for about two hours up in the north county," she said. "You know the land that Abby's parents had?"

"Yeah."

"Just me," she said. "I tried to keep in trees but I got all sweaty and my jeans and boots got hot as hell."

"I like you sweaty."

"Well, Tony finds this little creek that I hadn't thought about since when I was a kid. I just kind of kicked out of my boots and clothes and jumped right in. Nick, it was so cool in there. Some nice big rocks to dry yourself in the sun."

"You lay in the sun without your boots?"

"Nothin' else."

"Nothin'?"

I rolled over on my back and stared at the tin-stamp ceiling. Red chili-pepper lights burned in my kitchen. Morning light shot through the cracks in my bookshelves like lasers.

"Nick?"

"I wish I was in Mississippi."

"Me too."

"You're in Mississippi."

"But not in Mississippi with you."

"The entire state is better with me?"

"Not really," she said. "I just need some help shoveling out the shit in my barns."

"That's me," I said. "Shit shoveler first class."

"Glad you finally found your calling."

"Oh, you know," I said. "It's a gift."

I showered and shaved. Annie needed a short walk to fertilize a little tree and I grabbed a croissant and cup of chicory coffee down at Louisiana Products. I made some phone calls. Finally I got one back.

HIGH GLASS walls surrounded Alyce Diamandis in the little fish-bowl office where she worked on the third floor of the *Times-Picayune*. File cabinets filled almost every other inch of the research library, long and thick as coffins, loaded with newspaper clippings going back to the twenties.

Alyce was a tall, thin woman who wore her black hair twisted up into a bun and held in place with chopsticks. She had on cat-shaped glasses with small rhinestones and a red Chinese dress embroidered with gold dragons.

"Somewhere there's an Asian drag queen running around naked," I said, walking into the little cube.

"I was feeling a little yin and yang."

I'd known Alyce for years through my longtime ex, who once worked at the paper as a crime reporter.

Alyce kept on typing and pushed the glasses up her nose. Wall-to-wall books lined her office and reference guides waited crammed between metal bookends of an *A* and a *Z*. A Rubik's Cube and a copy of *Bridget Jones's Diary* sat on her desk. "One minute," she said. "Al-most."

I picked up the Rubik's Cube and began twisting it around. "I used to have one of these."

"I read this morning that when you turn thirty-five," she said, still typing, "you are officially no longer in a cool demographic."

"Already passed that."

"But soon Rubik's Cubes, Pac-Man, and Duran Duran will be like our grandparents' nostalgia over Benny Goodman or Clark Gable," she said. "You know? When Generation X all passes over thirty-five, it's all over."

"All those Corey Feldman movies on American Movie Classics."

She finished clicking, laughing, and turned to me and crossed her long arms across her chest. A small candle burned by the computer monitor, some kind of chocolate aromatherapy. There was a little Zen sand garden and two open Mountain Dew cans.

"I need you to run a name."

"Can you leave it and come back later? I'm swamped."

"I don't need you to dig around in those old clips," I said. "It would be recent."

She turned around, gave a small grunt, and typed away. "Name?"

"Trey Brill."

"You know you could've probably gotten this off the Internet?"

"What's that?"

I stood watching the screen over her shoulder. Five hits. "Football player?" she asked. "Wait. Sports agent?"

"Yeah."

She clicked more.

I also asked for her to run the name I'd gotten from Teddy's secretary, Robert McClendon Brill III.

Twenty seconds later, the printer hummed to life and she handed me a couple of hot sheets of paper.

"Sick," she said.

METAIRIE—A college student charged with the rape of a Chalmette teen made his first appearance in court Monday.

Christian Chase, 18, a freshman at LSU, pled not guilty to four counts of sexual battery. The charges stem from a March 5 arrest when a 16-year-old girl from Chalmette accused Chase and another young man of finding her passed out at a Bourbon Street bar and taking her to Chase's family home in Metairie.

The girl—not identified because she is a minor—told deputies the boys fondled and performed sex acts on her with foreign objects before dropping her in a Dumpster behind a nearby shopping mall. The girl's face and body had been covered in lewd words and pictures written in permanent marker. The girl's family has filed a civil suit against Cherries, the bar where police say the girl passed out.

Last week, prosecutors dropped charges against Robert McClendon Brill, 18, a freshman at Vanderbilt University, who deputies say was with Chase that night.

"It's him," I said, shaking my head.

"You might want to make sure," she said.

"When did this run?"

"Ninety."

"It's him," I said. "He's about thirty."

"Let me run an AutoTrak on him to make sure," she said. "Can you give me some connections?"

I told her about Brill & Associates in the CBD and his connection to Ninth Ward.

While I waited, I flipped back to the first story that ran on the arrest a few months earlier in 1990. About how Brill's father was a local attorney and member of one of New Orleans's big Krewes and Chase's father owned one of the city's biggest construction companies. Members of the Metairie Country Club. The boys had attended Metairie Country Day School and had academic scholarship rides. Both had been all-stars on the private school's soccer team.

"You're right; it's him," Alyce yelled to me from her fishtank office. "Same address in Metairie. God, that's evil."

I wondered how Christian Chase felt about being left to hang for what happened to this girl. I wondered how much he knew about Trey Brill now.

"You know the guy who covered this?"

Alyce looked over my shoulder at the byline and smiled. "Of course."

"Still around?"

43

TWO HOURS LATER, I sat in the Hummingbird Diner having a late breakfast with a seventy-year-old reporter named Orval Jackson. Apparently the paper had tried to force him into retirement a few years ago by taking his longtime beat. But as a man who'd started covering news when he was sixteen in Kansas and continued with decades at the UPI, he didn't let a bunch of management assholes tell him what to do. He told me a little about covering the Kennedy White House with Helen Thomas and some about the early days of NASA in the sixties before we got to his stories on Trey Brill and Christian Chase.

"So you remember them?"

"I wish I could forget those two arrogant little pricks."

"How did Brill get off?"

"His rich daddy."

Orval had a full head of white hair and clear blue eyes. He wore a short-sleeved blue dress shirt hard pressed and a red tie printed with tiny Tabasco logos. A white Panama hat lay by his elbow where he kept his coffee.

He glanced around the old diner.

"You eat here much?" he asked.

"It's a block from my warehouse."

"Hope you have all your shots."

The Hummingbird was a combination flophouse and diner where you could still get a room for twenty bucks a night. Orange vinyl booths, brown paneled walls, a big board painted with breakfast specials available twenty-four hours a day, 365 days a year. Outside, a red neon sign blinked the word HOTEL. Two homeless men fought outside over a stuffed rabbit and a half-eaten cheeseburger.

We ordered eggs, bacon, and toast. The waitress, a woman I knew named Jennie, plunked down a pot of coffee as a streetcar passed by the windows and shook the glass.

I smoked a cigarette, trying to blow the smoke away from Orval, while we waited for our food.

"Brill just called Daddy from jail," Orval said. "His father had this lawyer from Baton Rouge named Newcomb swoop in, make a few calls. The boy only spent maybe two minutes in front of a judge before the case was dropped."

"And Christian Chase?"

"You ever heard of Booker Chase?"

"No."

"He started his construction company when he was nineteen with one dump truck," Orval said. "Now most of the new building going on in New Orleans has his name attached. He grew up in the Irish Channel. Scrapped for everything he owned. He expects his kids to hold their water."

"Didn't make that call," I said, stubbing out the cigarette as the plates were laid on the table. I cut into some eggs.

"No, sir," he said. "Kid got six long years in Angola."

"Where's he now?"

"I heard he's working for his father," he said. "Booker has the boy driving a dump truck, just like he had to. He's got an office over in Old Metairie, not far from the country club."

"Think he'll talk to me?"

Orval shrugged, buttering his toast and taking a bite. "What's going on with these kids now?"

"Brill works for a friend of mine," I said. "His brother was just killed."

"What's his name?"

"Teddy Paris."

"Football player, right?"

I nodded.

"I read about that," Orval said. "Sounds like his brother was a thug."

"Yeah, I read that too. The reporter called him a gangster rapper. This kid was a music producer. I'd known him since he was fourteen."

"Good kid?"

"I liked him a lot," I said. "He was always respectful and smart. One of those kids wise beyond their age."

Orval looked at me, still sizing me up, but so good at it that it didn't show much.

"You work for Teddy Paris?"

"Kind of."

"What's that mean?"

"I sometimes research stuff for friends," I said. "It's what I do at Tulane and sometimes people hire me for favors."

"What's that pay?"

"Teddy bought me a bar in the Quarter."

Orval nodded. "Maybe I can do something like that when I retire," he said, taking a bite of toast. "Don't want to sit on my ass and learn how to drool."

We ate for a while and I thought about finding Christian.

Orval pulled a business card out of his shirt pocket and wrote a few notes on the back. "This is a Belgian beer I've been trying to find for ten years. It's brewed by monks and called Orval, spelled the same way. Can you ask your distributor about it?"

"When I get the bar up and running, I will."

"When will that be?"

I shrugged.

I looked outside and noticed the sun was gone. Rain began to splat the hoods of Yellow and United cabs parked along St. Charles. The hammering of the hoods grew more intense and I sank into my seat. I knew I'd be soaked all day.

My day was just starting.

"Kid won't talk to you."

"I have to try."

Orval looked around at a prostitute sauntering into the grill with a stained dress and two Japanese tourists in black leather. Both men ordered a couple of Budweisers.

"Jail changes people," he said. "But you still live a long way from Old Metairie."

44

OLD METAIRIE WAS NEW MONEY that had grown old. Big houses and big cars huddled under sprawling oak branches and lined idyllic streets; children rode bicycles and played football in between the rare traffic. There was a pink stucco country club and a ton of small boutiques, coffee shops, and little bistros. A little oasis away from downtown. The neighborhood streets disappeared off Metairie Road under a dome of oak branches as if to hide the secret garden. Marble statues. Stone walkways.

Ferns grew on oaks in the richness of the humidity as a light shower hit the top of the canopied trees and dropped down with a splat on my windshield. The sky had turned a dark gray and pink in the north. I slowed to a stop down on a street called Nassau.

The Chase house was whitewashed brick with big green shutters held down firm with wrought iron. A white lawn jockey showed his lantern to the walkway. I rang the bell. Christian hadn't been at his father's office and I'd found his family's home address in the White Pages.

A black woman appeared, laughing and holding a highball in her hand. Her gray hair pulled straight and tight into a comb. Green eyes wrinkled at the edges. She wore a black pantsuit with a white silk shirt splayed open with several buttons loose.

"Yes."

"Mrs. Chase," I said, guessing.

"Mmm-hmm."

"Is Christian around?"

She looked back into the house and I heard several people talking and some jazz playing low. It sounded like Earl Hines. Mrs. Chase looked into my eyes and then turned away back into the house, her heels clicking on the marble floors.

I heard her call her son's name.

I took a few steps back and saw a couple of Mercedeses and Cadillacs parked in a little cove by the four-car garage. No one came to the door for a while. Mrs. Chase did not ask me if I wanted to join the party or have a drink with a few of her friends.

I walked down a stone path back to my truck to make a call when a young man in his late twenties opened the door and followed.

Blue-jeaned and shoeless. A tight black T-shirt hugging his muscular upper body. I almost didn't recognize him as the man I'd seen with Trey at his firm in the CBD. As he walked toward me, I remembered him playing ball while we waited and the foul smell coming from his body.

Shit.

Christian Chase flexed his arms across his chest and I saw the scarred brand on his arm. The flesh on his biceps had grown pink and swollen where he'd been touched by a hot iron. He smelled like a ton of Calvin Klein.

"Good to see you again."

"What's your problem, man?"

"Kenny G, Michael Bolton, Dave Matthews, and Fred Durst. I call them the Four Horsemen of the Apocalypse."

He tilted his head at me, his green eyes seemed to glow as a slow smile sliced across his face. He chewed gum and stuck his hands into his pockets. He hunched his shoulders while he watched and chewed, almost cheetahlike in the roundness of his muscles.

"Things working out for you since you left the Farm?" I asked.

His gaze loosened and he squinted one eye at me. "What do you know about that?"

"I go to Angola to record musicians," I said. "One of the finest guitar players of this century, Leadbelly, was once there."

He popped his gum. "Quit fucking with Trey."

"He never looked out for you."

He walked in close, his hands still in his jeans and eyes focused somewhere on the ground below me. He inched in to my face. "You can't work me. It can't be done. You can try, but you're gonna lose."

"I heard Trey took most of his vacations in Aspen while you were inside. I guess those nice cold beers tasted mighty fine. But I'm sure you met friends."

"I don't suck dick."

"Did Trey come visit you, man?"

He looked away. Stepped back and watched me.

"You think you can come up to my home and disrupt my mother's party telling me shit about my best friend? You've got to be fucked in the head."

"He conned that money from ALIAS. I need someone to lead me through how it was done."

"Trey has been my friend since we were six."

"Whose idea was it to take that girl from Chalmette? Why do you think a black man got stuck with it?"

"Didn't have anything to do with that," Christian said. "You liberal fucks always want to play race like we're cripples. Fuck off."

"Brill sure didn't push his daddy away," I said. "You could've used just one person to stand up. But no one did."

Christian Chase turned and walked away down the narrow stone path. The rain fell harder on me while he opened the porch door and walked inside to the music. He just kept shaking his head and laughing.

The door closed with a solid thud.

45

FOUR MEMORIES OF MALCOLM played in my head. I didn't like to remember him. I didn't want to keep making myself sad and sick over something I had nothing to do with. But these were so personal and old that I was glad this was what my brain had selected. It was the kid, not the man, that stayed. Malcolm remained fifteen in my head: catching balls at the old Saints camp on Airways, hustling players for money the moment we'd step off the plane, smiling on his sixteenth birthday when his brother bought him a Mercedes, and watching him steal the dance floor the night we'd made the play-offs for the first time in years.

He was not hard or scarred. He was unbearded and smiling. He wasn't left swinging in a tree like a tattered photo from a nineteenth-century lynching.

I drove into my garage and bounded up the steps to the second floor of the warehouse. I heard the laughing. Voices rebounded off my high ceilings and into the metal stairwell like an echoing funnel. I was soaked with water and grew cold on the landing.

I was too tired for another round with Cash or any other random freak who'd broken into my house. I crept back to my truck and grabbed my Glock.

When I returned to the landing, I slid back my metal door, ready to face whatever shit I'd been handed.

"Goddamn, boy," a voice said. "Look like someone shit in your Cap'n Crunch."

JoJo, ALIAS, and some friend of JoJo's I'd met years ago sat at my kitchen table playing cards and feeding Annie leftovers from a Burger King bag. I slowly tucked the gun back into my belt.

"Made some coffee," JoJo said. "Left it warmin' on your stove. Why don't you get some Community Coffee? This cheap shit taste like mud."

I found a towel in my kitchen and dried my hair, offering my fist to ALIAS.

He gave me a pound but kept his gaze down at the table. I noticed he didn't have any cards. He leaned his head into his hands.

I shook JoJo's friend's hand.

"You remember Bronco?" JoJo asked.

"I'm sorry," I said. "We met a long time ago."

"Back when Pinetop come back," Bronco said. "It has been a while."

Bronco was about JoJo's age and black, but with green eyes and high cheekbones. A strong Native American face.

"Bronco rode down with me to help me get some things for Lo," JoJo said. "You know we sold our place on Royal? Need to clean out by end of the month."

"No," I said. "I didn't know."

I took off my jean jacket and hung it on a peg by the door.

"You helpin' out?" I asked ALIAS.

ALIAS shook his head, dug his sneaker heels into my floor, and pushed back his chair. He stomped off to the bathroom and slammed the door.

"Okay, no help from the kid."

"Kid's upset," JoJo said.

"This I see."

Bronco sipped on some coffee and rearranged the cards in his hand. "He forgot his head in my home."

"And?"

"He took two hundred-dollar bills from my wallet."

I blew out my breath. "Fantastic."

"I gave him two days to come to Jesus Christ," JoJo said. "But he wouldn't. He's back with you. I can't do nothin' with a kid that steal from me. You know my rule."

I did. Any employee even suspected of stealing was gone. I knew a waitress who once pocketed maybe five bucks from a table. She was let go on the busiest of nights. It was a reputation that had only grown since JoJo opened the bar in '65.

"Okay," I said. "I got him now."

"Me and Bronco goin' down to Anchor to get dinner," he said. "You wanna come?"

"Can I bring the kid?"

"Why not?" JoJo said. "He's yours."

I looked at the floor for a few moments before walking over to the old gas stove and pouring the coffee JoJo had made. It had been sitting on the burner a long time and seemed slow to pour from my old speckled pot.

"I got the bar," I said.

JoJo nodded.

Bronco laid down a hand. Three queens and two tens.

JoJo said, "Shit." He tossed his cards facedown into a pile of matchsticks on the table. Annie followed me from the kitchen.

"I'm gonna ride down to the bar and check things out."

"Thought you said it was some high-dollar place now."

"It is," I said. "It was."

JoJo looked at me strangely.

"Teddy gave it to me," I said. "But it's yours. It's your bar."

JoJo laughed. "Bronco, did I not say this was gonna happen?"

"Yes, sir, you did," Bronco said, shuffling his cards into each hand and keeping his eyes trained on me and JoJo at the same time.

"You want to go check it out?" I said. "See what we can do."

"You."

"What?"

"What *you* can do."

I nodded, lowered my head, and sipped the coffee.

"We'll come by after we eat."

"Fair deal."

"Last fair deal gone down."

"On this Gulfport island road," I said, completing the Robert Johnson lyrics.

ALIAS walked back from the bathroom and took a seat at my sofa. "Y'all give me a phone. I'll have my people come for me."

"No," I said.

"What you mean, 'no'?"

"I mean, you're comin' with me."

"Where?"

"Help with some things."

"Fuck that, man," ALIAS said, leaning forward, his Superman symbol dangling off his chest.

"Thanks," I said. "Come on. Let's go."

The kid followed, shoulders slumped and hat down far into his eyes.

I said to the men: "We'll see you at the bar."

JoJo winked.

I grabbed a clean shirt, a toolbox, and a flashlight.

At the bottom of the landing and on into the garage, ALIAS turned to me and said, "Man, fuck all this. That man call me a thief."

"Is that not true?"

"Shit, no."

"That old man only deals in respect."

"You got to give it to get it."

I climbed in and started my truck. We backed out onto Julia Street.

"You know Trey Brill?" I asked.

"Yeah," he said. He shook his head and made a wry smile.

"Don't like him," I said.

"He's like this white dude that's always tryin' to be down and shit. Calls me dog and tries out words he's heard on BET. He's just some white boy on the lake tryin' to call on me. Come on, man."

"You know a friend of his named Christian Chase?"

ALIAS laughed. "Na, man. Don't know no dudes named Christian."

"Was Trey tight with Malcolm?"

"Yeah," he said. "Malcolm and him rolled."

"Where?"

"You know, clubs and shit."

"He ever talk to you about money?"

"Na," he said. "What's up?"

"Just askin'."

"You think he played me?"

"I think he played a lot of folks," I said.

"Why he do that?" he said. "Boy gets a cut of Teddy's money all the way."

"People like that you can't figure out," I said. "Their souls are polluted."

"What about you?" ALIAS said. "Teddy bought you a bar. Ain't nobody in it for nothin' else but themselves."

"That's a cold attitude."

"Cold keeps your ass alive," he said, sliding down deep into the seat, watching the gray buildings and neon weather the rain.

46

DOGS LIKED BEER. I had just cracked opened a Dixie when Annie craned her neck in the slot between the driver and passenger seats and tried to get a good gulp. I gently pushed her into the backseat of my truck with the flat of my hand and pulled out a po'boy from Johnnie's for ALIAS. He grabbed it and unwrapped the fried oyster sandwich, eating while we waited for the rain to quit pelting the Quarter. I soon learned that ole Polk Salad liked po'boys better than beer. I had to push her back about a dozen times.

The sky turned a deep bluish green and black and the little wooden signs under the crooked wrought-iron balconies swung in the wind. A stripper, bathed in red light, smoked a cigarette by an open door, her black silk robe open to show a pasty white belly.

"You mind if I start calling you Tavarius?"

"Na, that's cool. But if you holla at me, you know, with my people, call me ALIAS."

"You think that stripper would like a beer?"

"Man, I wouldn't let that woman lick the rims on my Mercedes."

"I see what you mean." I flicked the switch for my windshield blades on my truck to clear the view. "Good God."

We laughed for a while. Tavarius worked on his sandwich and I stared across the little street. I felt my breath change. "You want to tell me about what happened in Clarksdale?"

"Ain't nothin' to tell."

"That's not the way I heard it."

"All y'all think I'm a thief."

"You didn't take JoJo's money?"

"I got a mansion, two Mercedeses, a four-wheeler with chrome rims, and a Sea-Do. What do I need with an old man's two bits?"

I finished the beer, the rain still hitting the hood, and tucked the trash back in the sack. I reached into my glove compartment and pulled out the Polaroid I'd found of Bloom and Dahlia at the piano bar.

"You recognize them?"

Tavarius took the picture from my hand, bit his lower lip, and started to nod. "Yeah. Yeah."

"Her name is Dahlia."

"That's the man too," he said. "That's them. See that fucked-up ear?"

"Never can be too sure."

"What you gonna do now?"

"I'm workin' on some things," I said. "Don't want to scare anyone off yet."

"What these jokers got to do with Teddy's white boy?"

I shook my head. "That's the question, man."

He nodded. I grabbed my toolbox from the rear hatch and ALIAS and I ran for the doors. Annie stayed in the truck with the uneaten portion of my crawfish-and-Crystal po'boy.

In the little cove by the door, a curtain of rain fell close to my shoulder while I turned the key in the lock. The air in the bar popped inside from the vacuum.

ALIAS pulled at his shirt and loose water fell on his jeans and oversized jean jacket. "Shit."

The bar smelled of fresh paint and Sheetrock. I held open the door while ALIAS wandered inside. I followed, hearing my feet under me sound hollow and unfamiliar. Looking around. Confused. Our voices echoing from the emptiness of the place. I could almost hear the bass and rhythm guitar shaking the old bar despite the black walls and velvet drapes.

Whoever had owned the place had covered up the brick walls and dropped a ceiling from the new rafters. The mahogany bar, seasoned over years with whiskey and gin, had been completely destroyed in the fire and replaced with something black and plastic looking. A lot of mirrors and chrome.

I set the toolbox on the floor, found a light switch, and handed ALIAS a crowbar.

"Ready."

"For what?"

"C'mon," I said. "Let's tear it all out."

"All of it?"

I looked the bar up and down.

"All of it."

"Why you got a problem with it?"

"Because it makes me sick to think about this bar disgraced another second."

"You got a problem with things ain't to your likin'?"

"Yeah."

"Hard way to be."

I began to rip the Sheetrock away from the high walls. My shoulders ached and stretched and my breath labored. Rain fell outside, thunder cracked. About seven o'clock, I walked outside, where the rain had stopped and heat rose from the broken streets like a hundred phantoms. A greenish-yellow light leaked down from the Mississippi and all the air seemed darkly blue as if I wore tinted glasses.

The air smelled of ozone, cooked fish, and boiling meat from Lucky Dog carts ready to start the night. Friday night in the Quarter was about to begin. I checked on Annie as ALIAS carried out some of our mess to a Dumpster behind the bar.

I watched the street for JoJo.

I drank a warm beer while Annie did her business on some discarded handbills from the House of Blues and gave ALIAS five bucks to run down to the corner store to grab a Gatorade.

JoJo didn't come.

I was sitting on the stoop with Annie, the Manhattan sign broken at my feet, when Felix walked by. My friend and the greatest bartender in the Quarter ambled up to the steps and peered into the cave where I worked. "What's up, Nick?"

His bald head shone like a black bowling ball in the hard outside light.

He sniffed inside, wearing his white tuxedo shirt and tie, the Indian headdress in his hand. I got up, rubbed my blisters on my jeans, and followed.

Felix walked in the bar and looked down at the floors covered in broken Sheetrock. He ran his fingers over the old brick that had been blackened in the fire. "Y'all can't get this stuff off."

I nodded.

"We ain't gonna get arrested, are we?" Felix asked, suddenly pulling his hand back as if the walls were hot. "JoJo sold this place."

"I got it back."

He nodded with understanding and stood in the back of the room. "Too bad ole Rolande ain't around. He could wire the stage back up in about two seconds."

His words hung in the air, the thought of old Rolande and his scrunched Jack Daniel's hat. I kicked some of the Sheetrock into a pile and added my completed Dixie.

"I need some music in here while I work."

"I seen a jukebox for sale over at some place on Esplanade. Look like that ole one we had, only it loaded with stuff I never heard."

"I can replace the music."

Felix stood framed by the doorway, a wide swath of light from outside against his head. He stared up at the ceiling. "JoJo had a lot of friends might want to help."

"He's in New Orleans," I said. "But he doesn't want any part of this."

Felix looked at his watch and then added the Indian headdress to the trash heap. "Some little Italian man with one of those cell phones been tellin' me I work too slow. Pour the drinks too hard."

I smiled.

"You put me back on?"

I nodded. He didn't ask about his salary.

"I'll see you Monday morning," Felix said, and walked back into the street.

I found a cardboard box behind the bar and borrowed a pen from the dude at the used bookstore. I wrote in huge cap letters. JOJO'S BLUES BAR IS BACK. THE ORIGINAL WILL REOPEN SOON.

I hung the sign in the window and stood in the street admiring the work, my boots stuck in a big puddle of storm water. I even crudely drew some musical notes on each side of JoJo's name.

I smiled and stood back.

The rain began to fall again when I saw him. Just a blur of brown about a block away. His face just a blackened oval in some sort of hood. The night turned the sky purple and gray. A hard wind ripped down Conti smelling of the Mississippi River.

I walked toward the corner.

He turned.

Rain ran down his coat, sluicing from his body, as if made from oil. The man who'd broken into my warehouse.

He buried his head deep into the folds of the wet brown coat as if it made him invisible. He turned a corner.

I followed.

47

“WHAT YOU DOIN’, MAN?” ALIAS yelled to me.

“I’ll be right back.”

“No, you ain’t. What’s up?”

“Stay here.”

The man in the brown coat disappeared into a group of tourists walking down Chartres by the Fisheries building and across from the Napoleon House. Gold electric light leaked out of the glass doors from the bar as the man’s walk turned into a jog.

He was running, his brown hood tattered and worn, toward Jackson Square and St. Louis Cathedral. My boots clacked on the flagstone, most of the stores now closed. Antique weapons. Haitian art. High-dollar lingerie. Only two men running on an empty street. I could hear the breath inside my ears as he ran toward the steps of the great church and turned into Pirate’s Alley.

A few gas lamps burned in the narrow shot once used as an avenue for smugglers and thieves. The gap narrowed. He passed over Royal.

I hung back. Letting him run out.

I walked behind two women in yellow ponchos drinking Hurricanes.

When I looked again, he was gone.

I passed the women, running for a few blocks.

At Dauphine, I stopped in the middle of the street and turned in all directions. Dance music pulsed from the clubs on Bourbon. Crooked iron hitching posts with horse heads lined the now paved street. The dance music kept pumping.

I ran down St. Peter back toward the church, passing five college girls staggering in the street and holding a young girl up as her head lolled to the side.

I heard scraping.

I looked back down St. Peter toward Rampart.

I saw the hooded figure scaling an old broken drainpipe running along a brick wall. Moss and ferns grew wildly in cracks that he used for footholds.

He was almost to a fire escape that hung uselessly, headed nowhere.

I ran into the building, some kind of anonymous pool hall, and past a grizzled bartender slicing lemons. I moved toward a landing and ran up some beaten wooden stairs. The bartender yelled after me but I pushed through empty liquor boxes and crates of bottles to a door opening into an empty second floor. The dull light of a Falstaff beer sign out front lit half of the room.

I could hear the man's hands scraping the outside wall. Climbing.

I followed the sound, my eyes adjusting in the light, slowly walking to the window. The dark figure emerged on the landing. I could see his back turned to me.

I grabbed a stray Barq's bottle from the floor.

Someone ran after me from the steps below, yelling they were going to call the cops.

The yelling grew louder.

I squinted into the dark light.

The man in the hooded coat pressed his face to the glass.

I could not breathe.

His fingernails touched the dirty glass in sharp, long claws. Thick and hardened. His face was gray as a corpse, his eyes yellowed and narrow. Small broken teeth.

I stepped back, my breath caught halfway in my throat.

The face contorted into something someone might think was a smile as he pushed a foot against the sill and began to climb, almost arachnid in his movements. His legs disappeared upward by the time I tried the window, caked and frozen with paint.

I threw the bottle into the glass and kicked out the shards with my boot.

I found my way onto the landing and looking for a foothold to follow.

I heard sirens at the far edge of the Quarter. And when I reached another rusted ladder of a fire escape, I could see NOPD patrol cars stopping by the pool hall and the bartender pointing upstairs.

I climbed.

I pulled myself onto the sloped roof, the figure crawling over the peaked edge of the old metal. My hands shook and I felt with my knees and palms for something solid on the slant. Nothing but moss and mold and metal eaten with rust.

At the peak, I could see deep into Congo Square and the white-lighted marquee of Louis Armstrong Park. I lifted my leg over the peak and the wetness of the metal roof and slid on a steady slope toward the road below the three-story building.

I clawed at the wet metal, trying to stop, but only sliding more. A metal sheet dropped into the air, pinwheeling down.

I picked up speed, the ground below getting closer, and stopped just short of careening off the edge.

The heel of my boot caught in a groaning drainpipe. I held myself there, foot cocked into the mouth of the pipe, supporting all my weight. Three stories of air waited below.

Above me, the man in the coat turned back and then jumped over a narrow crevice onto another rooftop, maybe only three feet away.

More yelling from the broken window on the other side of the street.

Wind ruffled my hair and I smelled the tired beer and urine of Bourbon Street. My hands coated in rust and dirt.

I scrambled upward and made the jump.

A moon hung over the river, the peaks of the old district's rooftops shining silver in the early light of the summer. My T-shirt covered in rust and mud, sweat soaking my face.

I made two more jumps over narrow alleys.

Then the sound of his scattering feet stopped.

I edged onto my butt, taking a seat. I saw muddy shoe prints running off the roof.

I slid close to the edge and peered into a little banquette.

I turned to my stomach, feetfirst, and left my legs hanging until I dropped onto a second-floor wooden balcony overlooking a little garden. Red, blue, and yellow light scattered in a large open fountain and upon palm and banana trees. Thick asparagus ferns grew from clay pots.

I ran down a creaking wooden staircase and down through a little alley. At the end, a huge metal gate swung open.

Rampart Street. A couple of homeless men on the corner. A crack pusher running for me to make a deal.

"Hey, man. I bet you I know where you got them boots," he said.

I heard a horn honking from a car heading toward Canal, a hard thud on the other side of the grassless neutral ground, and saw the man I was following roll from the hood of a Buick.

I ran after him but he moved fast, dragging a leg behind him to the wall of the St. Louis Cemetery. He disappeared.

Two cop cars converged on me and shone lights into my face. I stopped.

One of them threw me on the asphalt and pushed a gun into my spine.

"I'm following—"

"Shut the fuck up!"

"Listen to me, man."

"Shut up before I kick you in the head."

I heard the handcuffs clamp hard onto my wrists as the two cops yanked me to my feet and pulled me to the back of a patrol car.

"Stop."

They did.

"What?" asked some twenty-something steroid freak as he gripped my arm tighter.

"That noise," I said. "Can't you hear it? He's hiding in one of those mausoleums. He's moving stones."

"Drugs," the cop said. "It'll fry your mind."

48

JAY MEDEAUX STOOD over me in the NOPD homicide bureau in a red-and-white softball uniform complete with cleats and scrunched cotton cap. He was popping a ball into his glove pocket and chomping on Big League Chew while he waited for me to finish my story. Two other detectives scribbled on reports in the pooled desk space, their heads down near banker's lights glowing green.

"You told two officers in the First District you'd seen a ghost," Jay said. "They thought you was juiced up."

Anytime Jay was mad he reverted back to his y'at Irish Channel accent, even though he'd graduated from Tulane with a 4.0. When we were roommates in college, he would rarely go beyond the Boot to drink beer because he was studying history and criminology. But when he was pissed, he went back home.

He tossed me the ball.

"You seen that movie *Lord of the Rings*?"

"Yeah."

"Sounds like you been chased by some of those goblins."

"I know what I saw."

Jay was a big guy with sandy-blond hair cut down to the millimeter. In the last couple of years, his linemen's gut flattened out and his face had grown more hardened.

"Nick, it's Friday night," he said. "Why'd you have to pick Friday freakin' night? We were winning. My wife was there showin' off her new tatas in this sweet tank top."

"New?"

"They were runnin' a sale in the paper. You believe that? Like they were selling used cars."

"Vroom. Vroom."

"You find JoJo?" he asked.

"Yeah, he picked up the kid."

"Come on."

Jay took me into a room where a large woman in blue uniform laid out some plastic binders filled with mug shots. I spent more than an hour flipping the sheets, looking at some wonderful freaks that could make only P. T. Barnum smile. But nothing matched the gray face with the yellow eyes in the window.

Jay walked me to a break room on the eighth floor, where he made some coffee and we sat near a window overlooking the tall Gothic-looking Dixie Brewery. Small mushroom patterns of crime lights shone for miles, seeming to spawn from the brightness of the parish jail. Everything in New Orleans worked from pockets of darkness.

"You really going to open the bar?"

"Why not?" I settled into my seat and used a napkin to clean the gutter grime off my boots.

"What about teaching?"

"I only teach two classes a year."

"What about all your research in Mississippi?"

"Do you want to be the devil's advocate or are you just trying to yank my chain?"

"Mainly yanking your chain," he said. "But I don't think you know what you're in for. Bills, loans, payroll. Out of your league."

"Maybe not," I said. "I have JoJo for advice. He knows a few things about running a bar."

"True," he said.

I looked over at Jay in his red-and-white baseball outfit and started to laugh.

"What?"

"You look like a big candy cane."

He didn't laugh.

"Nick?"

"Yeah."

"You'd tell me, right?"

"Yeah," I said. "It's all twisted and incestuous, man. Just give me a few days."

"It's not my case," he said. "I just hear things. They just took a bunch of files and shit from that record company in the Ninth Ward."

"What do they think?"

Jay shrugged.

"I understand," I said. "Any forensic stuff? DNA, fingerprints?"

"It's all being run," he said. "But right now, I don't see a lot of work being done."

"Why's that?"

"It's New Orleans, man," Jay said. "The dead need to wait in line."

Just as I began to stand, the officer who'd shown me the photopacks walked into the room and opened a binder to a new page.

"That him?"

I stood and flattened my hands on each side of the book. I began to nod slowly and didn't say anything. I looked at the dirt on my hands and wiped them on my leg.

"Who is he?" Jay asked.

"Some freak grave robber," she said. "Remember all those tombs in Metairie that got busted into a few years back? He stole old battle flags and Civil War uniforms. Guys in robbery been looking for him ever since."

"What's his name?" I asked.

"People call him Redbone. The name he gave when he was booked went back to some man he killed. Oh yeah, he kills people for money too. Sounds like a sweet man."

"Never convicted?"

"This guy in robbery suspects he kills people and lays them in old tombs. How we ever gonna find those bodies?"

Jay whistled low. "I got a couch," he said to me. "Stay a few."

"I've got the kid."

"Bring him too."

"That's okay," I said. "I'm used to looking out for myself."

"Listen, I know they're looking at this Cash guy hard," Jay said, exchanging looks with the officer and then back at me. "How 'bout we send a little warning to him?"

"It's not him."

"Right."

"Just give me a few days," I said.

"You still have that Browning?"

"I have a Glock I picked up in Memphis," I said. "Holds seventeen rounds. Very handy."

"Keep it close."

49

TREY BRILL WATCHED HIMSELF in a wall of mirrors, flexing his chest in his new green Abercrombie T and pushing his hair off his forehead. Christian finished out a set of incline presses behind him, his green eyes glowing light under his thick dark eyelashes. Trey watched his friend, so sleek, brown, and hard under the health-club lights. If he was a woman, he'd like Christian. Christian had style and knew how to whisper the right words into their ears at the bars. He knew how to order drinks and choose a cigar and how to talk anyone into doing anything. Trey would like to be Christian one day. He'd like to be that cool.

Trey traded places with his friend on the bench, smelling his Calvin cologne and feeling his sweat against his neck. He could only hit ten and Christian had done fifteen. But Trey knew he'd still be ripped for Belize this summer. They'd party down there with all those college girls until they couldn't freakin' move. Rum Runners and reggae and golf.

"Why you smiling?" Christian asked, wiping his brow with a white towel. Limp Bizkit playing over the PA system. *I did it all for the nookie.* Goddamn right.

"Thinking about fuckin' Belize, man," Trey said.

"Sweet," Christian said, and gave him a high five.

A couple of young girls in Nike workout tops and bare stomachs rolled by drinking pink smoothies. "That's nice," Christian said.

"Go work it."

"Na, I'm cool."

The men wandered by rows of mirrors, scattering their images all around them. Sometimes Trey couldn't tell who was who. Their images merging and changing and morphing into something else. Made him feel a little dizzy just thinking about it.

"What do you want me to do if that Travers dude comes by again?" Christian asked.

"Tell him to piss off," Trey said, sliding into the pec-dec machine and hammering out about eight quick ones. He grunted and slid off the seat as if coming down from a horse.

"He thinks you rolled ALIAS."

"He's an idiot."

Christian shook his head. "Fucking Malcolm Paris already took it for that and killing goddamn Dio. Why would a guy swing himself by a goddamn rope if he was lying?"

"Exactly," Trey said. "I'm not worried."

Christian looked at him, changing the weight on the machine to almost double Trey's. He gave Trey that scary look, the one where he stared into his freakin' mind with those weird green eyes. It was like he was psychic.

Christian began his set, not slamming the weight like Trey. He worked it slow and even.

"It's just," Trey started, "what if he finds out about Dio?"

"Fuck that shit," Christian said, finishing up. He leaned into Trey's ear and whispered—just like Trey had seen him do to women in the bars. Trey's neck pricked in gooseflesh. "Teddy will never let him expose those 'Lost Tape' CDs. Dead or alive, Dio is fucking Ninth Ward."

"Or ALIAS."

"ALIAS is a punk," Christian said.

"Teddy doesn't trust him, either."

"Would you?"

"Kid's smart," Trey said. "I'll give him that. He sure as shit has fooled stupid-ass Travers."

"Man thinks he's saving a poor little black kid's soul."

"But really he's playing with a demon."

They finished their workout in silence. Trey and Christian exchanging spots, complimenting each other on their set, and working together. Life unchanged since they were boys.

They were walking in the parking lot when Christian asked him, "If this guy doesn't stop harassing you, why don't you talk to Teddy?"

"Teddy's fucked in the head right now."

"How bad?"

"Far gone," Trey said. "He called me Malcolm the other day. Man, he misses that boy bad."

"Kind of like if one of us went before the other."

"We'll make it," Trey said, grabbing his friend's shoulder. "Just like we made out from that punch in Chalmette. No one's gonna fuck with the boys' business."

As they climbed into Trey's BMW, the color seemed to shift in Christian's eyes. A coolness spread across his face and his lips parted.

He stared at Trey as if seeing him for the first time.

They didn't talk all the way back to Metairie.

50

"I CAN'T FIGURE THAT BOY OUT," JoJo said, drinking his 9 A.M. café au lait from the end of the bar as if he'd never left New Orleans. "He wasn't a bad worker. Got up in the morning, fed the cows, took the work to heart. Listen to me. You understand?"

I nodded. "When did he take the money?"

"Notice it two days ago," he said. "Ask him about it and he said to me, 'So what if I did take your money?' What makes a child like that?"

I was finished up whitewashing the brick that had been blackened in the fire. I liked the way the paint covered and sealed the grooves, the unevenness of the old pattern of mortar. By the back loading dock, Curtis Lee screwed down ten-inch pine planks into the subfloor. His little cassette recorder shaking with some Little Walter I'd given him to replace the Whitesnake.

Curtis, with a long cigarette trailing from his lips, laid out the floor in a yellow pine jigsaw puzzle and pieced it together with his drill. The cigarette's ash hung at least an inch long as the sound of the drill almost worked in time with Walter's music.

"That song take you back, don't it?" JoJo asked his buddy Bronco, who worked his brush on the opposite wall.

"I guess."

Bronco wore a long-sleeved blue work shirt and dark jeans. I had yet to see him splatter a drop.

"You don't like Walter?" I asked.

Bronco shook his head. A long scar on his forearm looked smooth and pink in the morning light.

JoJo sipped on his coffee and returned to the *Picayune*.

"We knew him," JoJo said.

"Best harp player I ever heard," I said. "I don't think anyone can even touch his licks."

"You're right," JoJo said. "But that doesn't mean Walter wasn't a evil motherfucker."

Bronco kept painting.

"Tell me about it," I said.

"Nope," JoJo said to me, but looking over at Bronco. "Some things are meant to stay up in Chicago."

When JoJo wanted to keep a secret, he could keep it for decades. You didn't try.

"Y'all mind watching Tavarius?" I asked. "I've got to talk to some folks."

"On Teddy's business?" JoJo asked.

"Have to pay my debt."

"Don't be goin' and payin' it in full," JoJo said. "All animals lay with their own kind."

"What's that supposed to mean?"

"It means Teddy's music brings on hate," he said. "Rap doesn't elevate us. It makes children turn to violence to buy things they don't need. Money, money, money. Trashy women. That's not music. Glorifies people being ignorant. Blues is music."

"So what happened with Walter in Chicago?" I asked.

Bronco shot JoJo a mean stare and JoJo just shook his head at me.

"Maybe ALIAS just doesn't know how to ask," I said. "Maybe he needed the money."

"For what?" JoJo asked. "Two hundred dollars would buy half of Clarksdale. Besides, he didn't want for nothin' at my house. He got a room. Loretta cooked and he worked. What else he need?"

"I don't know," I said. "I'm sorry."

I reached into my wallet to see how much cash I had on me to pay him back. He caught the wallet between his rough hands.

"Don't embarrass me."

"Did I tell you about his mother?"

JoJo turned to listen. Bronco shook out a long Kool cigarette from a pack and excused himself outside.

"His mother overdosed a few years back," I said. "Tavarius was thirteen. They were living in Calliope and he didn't tell anyone about it."

JoJo watched my face, his jaw dropping slack. His eyes softened.

"He didn't want anyone to take her away," I said. "Teddy said he'd heard ALIAS thought he'd go to jail if anyone found out."

"Lord," JoJo said.

Curtis had finished half the floor while we talked. The puzzle pieces taking shape into the soft, yellow wood.

"Rap's just dreams," I said. "People in that world just want something to wish for."

JoJo nodded. "I heard one time Muddy and old Wolf got into an argument up in Chicago. They kept lighting hundred-dollar bills to see which one would turn chicken. Bought a harp the next day."

Tavarius walked into the bar, carrying a box of rollers and paintbrushes and some high-gloss black paint for our new front door.

"Old School," he said, nodding over at me.

He handed JoJo the change, his hands pretend-shaking as if he were a beggar. "It's all there."

JoJo counted it out into his hand. "You got a receipt?"

"In the box."

Tavarius tore open a bag of Doritos and wandered back to where Curtis had unfolded a *Playboy* he'd found in the trash.

JoJo went to the front door, his feet finding bare spaces in Curtis's pattern. I watched JoJo, framed in the white afternoon light, laugh with

Bronco. Bronco cupped the cigarette tight to his face, squinted up his eyes, and bellowed smoke deep from his body.

Behind me, Tavarius walked forward into the bar.

I could not help but notice the imprint of his sneakers on the fresh wood.

51

DAHLIA'S CARRIAGE HOUSE off Napoleon was empty. I peered through a window at the top of a wooden landing and saw a bare bulb shining over an empty room. Packing crates, tape, and discarded magazines lay on the blue carpet. The summer light shone gold and hard through the edges of the oaks and the wetness from last night's rain scattered down on the uneven sidewalks. I asked around but no one seemed to know her, so I walked back to my truck and scanned through the sheet that a bail bondsman I knew in Memphis had faxed me. I located her two most recent addresses, places where she'd received paychecks or credit cards, and headed out to the Hollygrove neighborhood by the riverbend only to find another vacant place. Nothing.

I soon turned back the way I came, into the Irish Channel near the Parasol Bar. An old white-boarded drinking hole that served Wednesday specials on Guinness.

The Irish Channel is a mostly black neighborhood squeezed between St. Charles Avenue and the river. Shotgun shacks and little bungalows. Postwar working-class houses with chain-link fences and mean-ass dogs. It was Saturday and folks hung out on porches and on the stoops of their houses, smoking and playing with children with ragged toys.

I matched the address with a narrow little shotgun so small that it looked like a doll's house, and walked up a creaking paint-flaked porch. Someone was frying bacon in the back kitchen and playing some T.L.C. "Don't go chasin' waterfalls."

A woman sang in the back, and when I knocked on the warped screen porch, she popped her head out and pushed the hair from her eyes. About halfway through the long shot of hall, I knew it was Dahlia.

She wiped her brown hands on a white towel and walked toward me.

Long-limbed with straight black hair and soft almond-shaped eyes, she wore a tan halter top tied at the neck and tight blue jeans. No shoes. A casual smoothness about her walk, a relaxed but confident sexuality.

I swallowed. The Polaroid shot. Only better.

She inched open the door and tugged a smile into the corner of her mouth. Her eyes were so huge and brown that she sort of swallowed you with them. Her teeth white and perfect, lips sensual.

"I work with Trey Brill."

"No, you don't," she said. "Your name is Nick and you think Trey ripped off one of your boys."

I smiled.

The halter top didn't quite stretch to the edge of the jeans and I noticed how flat and hard her stomach muscles were. I was conscious of her breathing.

"You mind if we talk out here?"

"Come inside."

I didn't want to but followed as she returned to the kitchen. I waited in the parlor.

She had a television stranded on a rickety metal-and-faux-wood cart on the right wall as you walked into the room. On the opposite side sat a yellow-and-black couch, a beanbag, and a cheap rocking chair filled with a small back pillow reading LOVE. Small hearts and a couple of angels had been embroidered on the material.

A silent air-conditioning unit sat in a far window. The room's air was heavy and moist and felt even more humid than it had underneath the thick oak trees outside.

I heard water hissing onto a blackened skillet. She walked back in the room from the kitchen. When I sat down on the couch, she fell in beside me, her arm brushing against mine.

"I'm surprised I found you," I said. "I'm surprised you know who I am. About the only thing I can do is offer you some money to tell me about you and Trey."

She leaned back in the pillows and stretched her arms over her head, yawning, her breasts swelling in her shirt. Her chest moist with sweat.

"I'll also tell the detectives that you were just a player. It was Marion who worked the con, hired by Brill. Right?"

She dropped her chin, put the flat of her palm across my cheek, and crawled into my lap, her legs straddling me. I froze.

Her fingers looped around the back of my neck. She pursed her lips, closed her eyes, and kissed me on the mouth.

I did not kiss her back, but I didn't knock her off me either. I could not breathe.

"What?" I asked. My voice was not raised but instead had dropped to almost a whisper.

"That was a job," she said. "I'm through."

She smelled like vanilla and ripe flowers and I gently pushed her to the side and stood. She rolled onto the side of her butt and propped herself up with one arm, dark hair spilling over one eye. She drew some imaginary lines in the material of the old sofa. She sighed.

"Trey's just a boy," she said. "You playin' with his mind."

"And that made you want me?"

"Maybe," she said, sticking the back of her thumb into her mouth. "Maybe I just wanted to fuck with you."

"Get in line."

"People always like to fuck with you?"

I nodded.

"Poor baby," she said, withdrawing the thumb from her lips.

She picked up the remote and switched the channels, the high-pitched laughter of a sitcom filling the room. *Three's Company*. She changed the channel again, soft music. A love scene. And then again, two people fighting. WWF pro wrestling.

"*Rockford Files* comes on at six."

Her eyes tilted up and met mine.

"Tell me how it worked."

"He hates you a lot."

"What do you want?"

She tugged at her thumb again with her strong lips and wet them with her tongue.

"I'm tired," she said. "Either play with me or leave."

"Trey had Malcolm killed."

"Who's Malcolm?"

"Come on."

"How much?" she asked.

"Depends on what you have to say."

"Listen, Trey didn't know about the job on the kid."

"So, you and Marion just stumbled upon a mark who just happened to work with a man you fucked."

"I met ALIAS at a club with Trey," she said. "A kid. A kid that is a millionaire. Marion wanted to use him. This wasn't about Trey."

"Where's the money?"

"Marion took it."

"Where is he?"

"Fuck off."

"Why are you still in this shit hole?" I asked. "He left you. Didn't he?"

"Yeah, he's gone," she said. "Way gone."

I started to laugh.

Her jaw tightened and her nostrils flared.

She reached out to claw my face.

I grabbed her wrist and pushed her back into the couch. I held both of her arms over her head and placed a knee between her legs. "Trey hired some street freak to kill Malcolm and me. Right? You heard of a man called Redbone?"

She spit in my face. I let her go, my breath rushing from my mouth.

"I don't know Malcolm. I tole you me and Marion's thing got nothing to do with Trey. Tell him. I don't care."

I heard feet on the boards of her porch and moved close to the door. I steadied my breath and looked down at her. She tossed her hair over her shoulder and reached down on a glass-and-chrome table filled with copies of *TV Guide* and *Star* for a pack of cigarettes and a lighter.

The screen door opened and a large black man walked inside. In his fifties with a short black beard. Greasy white T, hard dark jeans, and fucked-up Wolverine work boots. "Dataria? Who the fuck is this? What y'all doin' in my house?"

She lit the cigarette and blew smoke up at a cheap fan rocking in the sagging ceiling.

"Oh, just a boy, Daddy," she said. "He came over and tried to save my soul. Ain't that right?"

He moved toward me, his hands clenching around the handle of an old lunch pail.

I headed out to the porch and walked to my truck.

I heard him yelling more, a slap, and then a high-pitched scream from inside the tiny house.

I thought about the scream and then kept smelling her on my shirt the whole way down St. Charles.

52

I REMEMBERED JIMMY RIGGINS as the white boy from Nebraska who carried defensive linemen on his back like children as he shot through blocking holes and scrapped for five to ten yards almost every time he touched the ball. He wore black reflective paint under his eyes like some leather-helmeted wonder from another era and after games often wore fur coats he'd made from animals he killed himself. Wildcats and Kodiaks from Alaska. He bragged once of making love to three women simultaneously and of outrunning a deer that he'd startled in a backwoods creek in rural Louisiana. He'd been on three *Sports Illustrated* covers, cut a locally produced country-western album, and made All-Pro for four years as if the NFC's fullback was a position he owned.

But after a string of eight DUIs, even fans and front-office types in New Orleans became a little worn with his personality. And then five years ago, when he was photographed sunbathing nude with a sixteen-year-old singer who'd made a name for herself on a nationwide shopping mall music tour, the ride was over.

He was traded to the Cardinals, the worst of all pro football franchises, and soon disappeared. Replaced by a stable of fresh new runners with better knees and media-savvy personalities.

I never knew Riggins that well. After all, he'd been an offensive player, and even on the same team, folks tend to stick to their own kind. But through the *Picayune* stories I found yesterday, I learned of a lawsuit he'd filed against Trey Brill three years ago. And after calling around to some old teammates on Sunday, I found Riggins's address—a rural route in Slidell, only about fifteen minutes out from the city.

The country road wound around a small creek and through a cattle pasture where fattened red-and-white cows chomped down grass. I followed my coffee-stained map through three or four country roads until I found the house.

The place was colorless, eroded clear of paint from decades of rain, with a ripped screen door hanging off a lower hinge. Behind the old house and under a live oak draped in Spanish moss sat a little squat trailer, the towing hitch held vertical by a pile of concrete blocks.

A yellow "No Hunting" sign had been nailed to a dying tree.

Two Big Wheels, a rusted-out Fiero, and an early-nineties F-150 with K-C lights had been parked in a muddy, grassland ground.

I knocked on the door and then hung back off his stoop beside some piles of two-by-fours and bricks. I listened to the crickets hanging into the woods of pine and large oak. In the deep woods, I heard feet shuffle.

Near the edge of the woods, a man giggled.

Then a shot.

I ran fast around my old truck, where Annie yelped to me from the passenger seat, and through a scattered patch of trees.

I squatted down into a ditch by the edge of the small forest. Pines, palmettos, and knotted old oaks surrounded me. Vines and broken branches and decaying stumps covered the forest floor. A thick black snake twisted out from a hole in a toppled tree and sauntered away. Overhead, only small pricks of yellow light broke through the leafy ceiling.

A flash of a plaid shirt showed deep in the woods.

Another giggle.

"Riggins," I shouted. "It's Nick Travers."

My voice echoed as I crouched forward and moved out of the ditch and into the trees.

Another shot cracked farther away and I saw the driver's side mirror of my truck explode. I moved slow, still bending at the waist, watching.

I only heard crickets. Soft feet crunched.

A woodpecker returned to a dead oak tree and a couple of squirrels scattered in the leaves and needles.

More feet ran and then slowed.

The woodpecker stopped.

Then returned.

Dry heated air ran through the woods. A small creek oozed through the uneven splice of a narrow muddy bank.

I crept over the water, several hundred yards from the trailer.

I thought I could come back on whoever was out there.

I was a silent Indian creeping through the land. I could not be heard. I imagined sneaking up behind this peckerwood and catching him. Maybe not.

I tripped over some fishing line tied to a bunch of beer cans, cutting into my palms, and fell to the ground.

A long bowie-knife blade found my throat and I heard a voice I remembered from a decade ago say, "When y'all gonna realize this is the U.S.A., not the U.S.S.R.? I don't owe shit."

I looked back. "Hello, Riggins," I said.

"Travers?"

53

RIGGINS TOOK ME and Polk Salad Annie to a small camp he'd built in the woods. Nothing more than a child's play fort made of plywood, furnished with large spindles that once held telephone wires and big tree stumps for seats. I found a stump and sat down by a little ring of rocks filled with charred wood. Riggins poked at the wood with a stick he'd found and belched into his fist.

Annie licked his face.

"You didn't come out here to bring me a fuckin' fruit basket or build me a goddamned house," Riggins said. "Because some of those dickbrains came out last spring and said I need better shelter."

Riggins had kept the crew cut but decided at some point to grow the whole Grizzly Adams beard. His once thick biceps had grown fat and meaty and it looked as if his stomach had doubled in size. He'd cut his flannel shirt at the armpits and I noticed the Saints tattoo still running down his shoulder. A COUNTRY BOY CAN SURVIVE printed on a Rebel flag flew on the opposite side.

"Some guy that sells RVs out in town knew where I was livin' and because he's some mucho jock sniffer, decided I need some shit called 'a hand up.' I said that sounded like a hand job and to take both of his hands to spread his ass real wide to make room for his fuckin' head."

"I need to talk to you about Trey Brill," I said. I had to squint into the sunlight shooting through the oak leaves and vines just to watch his face.

The branch in Riggins's hand snapped and he brushed at his beard with his fingers. He nodded for a while and spit into the dead fire.

"You seen my wife?" he asked.

"Didn't know you were married."

"When Brill cleaned me out, she left me for my next-door neighbor," he said, his muscles tightening under the bristled cheeks. "A guy who made fuckin' watches for a living. Watches out of jewels and faces of old movie stars. Guy had this hair transplant that looked like the goddamn head on a little girl's doll. Goddamn. I stole his Jet Ski, rode it down to St. Charles Parish, and then set the motherfucker on fire."

I nodded.

"You knew about me and Brill, right?" he asked. "You're not thinking of having him run your money. God, I thought everybody knew how he fucked me like a monkey on a football."

"Tell me about it," I said. "The money. Not the monkey. I saw that you filed suit for mismanagement."

"Yeah, my lawyer was a cocksucker," he said. "You know that little weight coach we had? The one who drank protein shakes and wore bikers' pants? He told me this guy was the best in New Orleans. All he did was clean out the rest of my bank account and have his secretary send me a 'sorry for fuckin' up your life' card on my goddamned birthday."

I picked up a couple of stones on the ground and whizzed them into the woods. The afternoon sun had flushed blood and heat into my face. "What did he do, Riggins?"

"You're gonna think I'm the biggest dumb-ass you ever heard," he said. "Almost don't want to tell you."

"Trey's fucking over Teddy Paris."

"Fat Teddy?"

I nodded.

"Remember when I sent that fucking whore to meet Teddy after we got back from San Francisco?"

"Yeah," I said, my face unchanging. "Hilarious."

"Man, that was funny as shit."

He laughed for a few minutes, really chuckling to himself, until he dropped his big head into his hands and his back began to shake.

"What did Trey do?"

"He sold me my own property."

"Come again?"

He snorted and pulled out some Copenhagen from a tin. "I know that sounds crazy. But a few years back, he had me invest in this condo project out in Gretna," he said, tucking a pinch into his lip. "Well, a year after I retired, I didn't get dick. I get this lawyer and he has some accountant check things out. Turns out, I'd already put in for a hundred grand on the place. He'd sold it back to me for fucking three. Shit, I didn't know one of these deals from another."

"I guess Matlock wasn't your lawyer," I said.

"The police and my lawyer couldn't prove shit," he said. "He's got these little corporations set up all over. More hidden names than assholes in China."

"He run over anyone else?"

He nodded. "Tim Z. Bone. DuBois."

"You know how to find them?"

"No," he said. "But they were all in the same deal. Tim Z. wanted to grease Trey's ass with STP and run a rabid squirrel into his cornhole with some PVC pipe. He got put in jail just for tellin' Trey about it on the phone. He's got one of those restraining-order things on him now. But in the end, we all decided he'd wallow in his own sin. You know, that's back when I was all into the Fellowship of Christian Athletes shit. I thought the world was gonna end in 2000. That's when I built the bunker."

"Never can be too careful."

"I got enough cans of beans to make the whole nation fart on cue."

"What made you trust this guy so much?"

"He'd keep your mind on other things," he said. "Like this one time, he had this woman come over when I had the gym. To sign contracts and shit.

She looked just like Barbie. Had big fake tits and blond hair and the IQ of a squirrel."

"Smart as the one who would run into the PVC pipe?"

"What?"

"Never mind."

"Well, anyway, we ended up doin' it in a three-way mirror after the gym had closed."

"So there were six of you?" I asked.

"Yeah," he said. "That's funnier than shit. Would you quit fuckin' with me and let me tell the damned story? That's what you wanted, right?"

He didn't smile.

I did.

"I found out when we were about to go to court that she didn't even work for Brill," he said. "She was a damn stripper at that place on Bourbon called the Maiden Voyage. You know, where they used to brag they had the Best Chest in the West?"

We walked back to the trailer, Annie by my side, Riggins leading the way. He strategically spit as we walked, and pointed out different markers that signified boundaries of his land.

"I guess you getting ready for training camp," Riggins said, his eyes wide.

"Jimmy, I haven't played for ten years."

"Really?" he asked, squinting into the sun.

"No lie."

"Been chopping a lot of wood," he said. "I'm gonna call the suits tomorrow. Tell them I'll take a little less for this season."

"See you out there, brother."

From my rearview mirror, I watched Jimmy wave from the middle of his long dirt road. I noticed a wall he'd made from small logs that seemed to go on forever. Before I turned a corner, I saw him grab his ax and start on another tall pine.

54

SUMMER HEAT BAKED oil puddles in the eight-story garage where I sat on the hood of Trey's new silver BMW with a rusty crowbar in my hand. I'd taken Annie back to the warehouse and spent my last hour counting people walking off the elevator, checking out trucks in the garage, and noticing all the oil spots that reminded me of presidents' heads. I thought about Maggie and her farm, Polk Salad Annie taking a crap on my sofa yesterday, and ALIAS stealing from JoJo. I tried to remember what JoJo had told me about the liquor-license changeover and a bouncer he knew we could trust.

With restocking the booze, booking the bands, and making schedules for the waitresses we'd have to hire, I hoped I'd still have time to teach. I just wanted to keep the bar running half as smooth as it had under JoJo. I wanted to keep everything the same.

A small bell rang and the doors opened. Footsteps echoed through the concrete cavern and I heard laughing and a woman's voice playfully telling someone to "shut up."

"I'm fuckin' starved," Brill said as he punched his key chain and the BMW's horn honked and lights winked. I didn't move.

Trey caught my eye. I shifted the crowbar into my right hand.

He began to walk faster, leaving the woman in his wake. She tilted her head, looking toward me, sitting hard on her friend's car. She was in her midtwenties and blond. Boy-short hair and pixie face. A tight white top, Capri pants, and a pink sweater tied around her shoulders.

"What the fuck?" Trey asked.

The woman ran, her arms flouncing on each side of her body, heels wobbling beneath her tanned calves. "Trey, don't. Trey."

He reached for his cell phone and I assumed called 911.

No light crept into the floor of the parking garage from the windowless walls. The air smelled like carbon monoxide and garbage.

Brill gave his directions and the little blonde hung on his arm.

"Where's Dahlia?" I asked.

"Fuck you."

"Let's talk."

"About what?"

"How you stole from Jimmy Riggins and raped a drunk little girl. Or how you were grabbing the ass of the woman who conned ALIAS the other night at Whiskey Blue."

He began to walk away.

I popped three hard ones with the crowbar into the hood.

"Shit!" Trey screamed.

"Malcolm was a good guy," I said. "He knew about you siphoning off money from Teddy. Right?"

He shook his head and ground his back teeth together. His face was red and blotched. He wore a blue dress shirt and loose tie. Khakis and big brown New York designer shoes.

"How much did you pay Dahlia?"

"Who's Dahlia?" the blonde asked.

"Shut up," Brill said.

A red Toyota truck circled up the curving drive of the parking deck, light casting over me, Trey, and the girl. The car kept rolling, tires squealing, as it headed upward. Trey stood still. "Fuck you," he said. "Fuck you. Beat my car. I don't give a shit."

He turned to walk away. I felt a surge inside me, my hands shaking at my sides, and I ran toward him, the crowbar clanging to the ground. I grabbed him by the back of his shirt and threw him against a dirty minivan. It knocked the wind from him and he dropped to his knees as the woman screamed.

The minivan's alarm began to sound with the impact.

I gripped the front of his shirt, lifting him to his feet.

He was crying now and trying to catch a breath. His lower lip twitched and he babbled some obscenities at me.

With one hand, I banged him against the van again.

"Listen, you spoiled little shit," I said. "I know what you are. You wipe your ass with people like that little girl. I know you left Christian holding the bag while you ran games on Jimmy Riggins and some of my teammates. I know Dahlia was the girl who conned ALIAS along with Marion Bloom. She told me. But I bet this was the first time you ever had someone killed. I don't care who strung Malcolm up in that tree or what kind of shit you planted in his house. You called it. And you had that same street freak you hired come for me."

I tightened my grip on his oxford cloth. "Malcolm worked for what he had. He wasn't a twisted little fuck like you."

When I stood back, I noticed that part of his shirt had come off in my hands.

The girl kneeled, weeping, and holding out her hand. Her fingers stretched out to Trey, who was getting to his feet and pointing at me.

Trey moved inches from my face. I could smell coffee on his breath as he yelled hard. "Don't you see? Don't you fucking see?"

The girl screamed, "No. No." She tugged at his arm, pulling him away. "He's going to kill you."

"It's ALIAS," he said. "Ask Teddy. There was no con. Teddy knows. Did you ask Dahlia about ALIAS? She's been with him for months. They took the money together. He lied and told Teddy he'd been conned. Did you ever ask Teddy about the charges he filed against ALIAS last year and the ten thousand ALIAS stole? Or when he caught Dahlia giving ALIAS head in the back of his Bentley?"

"ALIAS doesn't know Dahlia," I said. "She was with you at Whiskey Blue."

"She's just some ass, man," he said. "She's fucked everybody at Ninth Ward. She was there because that's where the rappers go. Man, I was drunk when she came over to me. Have you seen her? What would you do?"

The girl behind him began to sob harder. I noticed a gold sorority insignia around her neck.

"Bullshit," I said.

"Why would I fucking kill Malcolm?" Trey yelled, grasping his hair in his hands. "He ran the whole company. The only thing Teddy can do is fuck it up. Malcolm was my friend too. I miss him."

I stepped back, his words flying into me with blood and foam from his mouth. The woman pulling him away, the alarm on the car still blaring into my ears.

"That kid is evil, man," he said. "Ask Teddy if I'm lying."

I watched him.

"You hate me because I have money," he said. "All guys like you and Riggins want to be my friend and then hate me for what I am. Fuck you. Fuck all of you."

I gritted my teeth and stood by the car, watching Brill and the girl slip into the BMW, back up, and spin away. The car fishtailed, nearly striking a Cadillac, before disappearing down into the parking deck.

55

TEARS RAN DOWN Teddy's big cheeks while he answered the question from the BET VJ for *106th and Park.* A camera and sound guy cornered him in his big leather sectional while the feed went out live. A few groupies lounged in Teddy's pool in bikinis with margaritas, watching the sun set into a nice blender of oranges and reds. Louisiana Caribbean. I leaned against a wall by the open kitchen and drank a Coke. There were cheeses and wine, little quiches, fancy toast, and big bowls of caviar on his marble counter.

I didn't like watching Teddy blasted with all those white-hot lights. I knew the showman in him had made him get back to work too soon after the death of his brother.

Has times been tough? Is the talk of the end of the Ninth Ward label true? Is there any truth that Malcolm's suicide came out of some debt to a rapper from East St. Louis?

"Silkie," Teddy said to the young bald man dressed in a baggy Fat Albert sweatshirt and stocking cap. "I think people talk about greatness. And my brother was great. It's just hard for people to get over that he's gone."

What about what folks are saying about Malcolm's relationship with the late, great Diabolical? That their relationship had been seein' some dark days before Dio went missin'?

Teddy twisted a fat diamond ring on his finger and nodded. "Let people talk. Let 'em talk. I'm here to tell people that Ninth Ward is keepin' on top. We goin' out to represent all New Orleans like my brother's dream. Ninth Ward, Sixth Ward. Calliope. Magnolia. We keep on rollin'."

What about the feud with you and Cash?

Teddy shook his head and smiled. "Never was no feud," he said. "People like to talk and divide us. People like to break us apart. But we all the Dirty South."

Dirty, dirty. Now let's send it back to New York with a new one from a New-Orleans-boy-made-good-in-Beverly-Hills, Master P.

The VJ shook Teddy's hand and apologized if the questions got too personal. Teddy shook his hand back, clasping it long and firm, and then shoved the VJ in the chest with the flat of his hand.

"Get out of my house, you goddamn punk-ass nigga."

"Hey, man," the VJ said. "Fuck you."

Teddy lunged for him.

I ran behind Teddy and pushed his swinging arms to his side. He stormed outside and slammed the French doors behind him. Outside, he smiled, leaned down to the pool, and flirted with a couple of women.

After the crew packed up and left, the VJ talking shit about a lawsuit, I took a seat in the leather sectional. Teddy came back and turned on a DVD of *Goodfellas*.

It was the scene where Pesci and De Niro were burying the body and laughed about the body parts being thrown around. Teddy laughed with them, his eyes glued into the TV world.

"Teddy?"

"What's up?"

"We need to talk."

"Wait till you see this," Teddy said. "They go back to his mamma's house for more spaghetti. Ain't that some shit? Do you like spaghetti? Man, I could eat the shit out of Italian. You know, lasagna and fettuccini. Man, I had some eggplant with Parmesan that would knock your dick in the dirt."

"Yeah," I said. I stood and walked back to the table of food.

"Hey, man? Grab me a candy bar up there."

"There aren't any."

"What?" Teddy said, leaping out of his seat. He stood over the table and frowned as if someone had served several helpings of dog shit. "Not even a goddamn Snickers. Shit. Sometimes I wonder what I pay people for. You know I got all these people round me on my payroll and they ain't doin' shit. Man, I should open my own goddamn catering business and have it done right. We'd have candy bars and shit and Pepsi and shit. Real food."

"I'd skimp on the shit," I said. "Want some caviar?"

"That shit got class, but man, it tastes just like fish."

I smiled.

"Let's ride," he said, grabbing his keys and running for the door. I couldn't even catch a breath.

Two minutes later, we were riding in the Bentley, top down and new beats cranked. He drove about eighty in a forty.

"That's the one we cut the other night," he said, sweat beading down his puffy jowls as he talked. "You remember. 'Project Girl.' *Shiit.* Man, that's what it's all about. It's all about the ass. Can't you see that 'Project Girl' pop that ass? You got to make them pop their ass. That's what Malcolm used to say. Shit, pop it. *Pop it.* Can't you see it?"

He let go of the steering wheel and pretended he was gripping two mounds of muscular butt. "Malcolm was a magician. Malcolm could make the crowd slow down, speed up. Pick up the whole world at the projects in Desire and have them roll with his beats. Man, I'm gonna miss those beats. Those crazy NOLA beats. Hard and representin'."

"Where we headed?"

"Get me a goddamned Snickers."

"Teddy, you ever have any problems with ALIAS?"

"What you mean?"

"He ever steal from you?"

Teddy turned down his stereo, the heated salty air rushing through the car. The clouds over Pontchartrain growing fat and pink in the soft evening, almost raw like a new wound. The air smelled like fresh-cut grass and mint. Sprinklers misted over the trimmed grass.

He lit a cigar from his pocket.

"Yeah," he said, thick smoke flying from his mouth. "Kid took two of my credit cards last year. Bought some things."

"What?"

"Man, I didn't want to talk about this shit. ALIAS is my boy. You know how he get to your heart, all that shit he been through."

"What did he buy?"

"Aw, man. Who tole you about that?"

"Just tell me."

Teddy sighed.

"Everything," he said. "He worked those Visa cards hard."

"Like what?"

"I'm talking like twenty thousand? Yeah, some shit like that. Crazy shit. Like bikes from Toys 'R' Us and five thousand worth of Air Jordans."

"You think maybe he worked this con on himself to get it out of the trust fund?"

"Came to me a few times."

"You ever think about mentioning it to me?"

"I don't know," he said. "How you gonna ever know?"

"You ever see ALIAS with a girl named Dahlia?"

"The stripper?" he asked. "I don't know her."

"What about Dataria?" I asked, pulling out the Polaroid with her and Bloom.

"Yeah, you showed me that shit."

He stole a glance while driving, then pulled the car to the side of the road. Cars whizzed past us, honking, and Teddy lifted up his sunglasses to get a closer look.

"I ain't neva seen that bitch," he said. "But man, she could make a dead man's pecker twist into a pretzel."

"She has a way."

He nodded, pulling out, and cruising down the road with two fingers. Driving slow. He turned into a space at the BP and killed the engine. A couple of teenage boys hung back and pointed at the Bentley parked away from the gas pumps. They knew him.

"Come on," he said. "You want a Snickers?"

"I'm cool."

"Zagnut?"

"I'll take a Whatchamacallit."

"A what?"

"Teddy."

He laughed. "Man, I'll be right back. Be cool."

I sank into the rabbit-fur seats and watched Teddy bound into a Canal convenience store in his $2,000 Armani. He held the cigar in his right hand and clutched a dozen candy bars to his stomach with the other.

I watched him pay the cashier with a $100 bill from his diamond-crusted money clip.

He ate and drove, the cigar now smoldering in the ashtray. The Snickers taking the place of the Cuban.

"I heard you caught ALIAS with a woman in the back of your car one night."

"Oh yeah," Teddy said. "He was gettin' him some. He's old enough. Didn't think much of it."

"Could it have been Dahlia?"

He shook his head. "Man, I don't know. I know some of my boys were talkin' about it the next day. Said the woman was lots older."

"Like Janet Jackson older? Or Eartha Kitt older?"

"Who's Eartha Kitt?"

"Catwoman."

"About double his age."

I buried my head into my fingers, my elbow propped into his door. I didn't want to see any of the road ahead.

"ALIAS says she was the one who conned him," I said. "He says he didn't know her."

"Man, I don't know what to think," Teddy said. "Yesterday, he come over to see me and gets to talkin' about y'all's trip to Clarksdale. He said you wanted half of his money if you get it back."

"I never said that."

"For real?"

"Man, come on."

"Kid's workin' our crank, ain't he?"

"Looks that way."

"Goddamn. Goddamn."

The sky twisted into dark patterns forming a black-and-peach quilt over the lake. I couldn't see the shore on the other side. Pontchartrain seemed to be an endless sea.

56

IT WAS NIGHT now and I drove for about an hour, down to the bar, then back home, where I called JoJo. I finally found him and Bronco at the Spotted Cat in the Marigny watching a guy I knew named Washboard Chaz and some twenty-year-old Italian kid who I'd heard could play Robert Johnson note for note. They were drinking Dixies and laughing with Chaz, his beaten washboard propped in his hands, when I walked into the dark little bar off Frenchman. The place was a narrow shot of bar with a small wood stage by the door and a grouping of mismatched chairs by a plate-glass window. Candles in glass bowls flickered from small tables and on top of the bar.

I bought a Dixie from the bartender, said hello to Chaz while exchanging places with him, and took a seat.

"Think he'd do nicely for a Wednesday night," JoJo said.

"How's the kid?"

"Note for note," JoJo said.

"No shit?"

"No, sir," he said. "And Eye-talian to boot. How 'bout that?"

Bronco clicked open his stainless Zippo and lit a Kool. He nodded at me, his cheekbones and red-black face something out of a history book. Men clearing the Delta with mules.

I walked outside where I'd left Annie next to a hitching post and let her drink the last few sips of my beer. I went back in and settled back in my seat so I could see where she was tied.

"You still gonna do a red-beans-and-rice on Monday?"

"Be a fool not to," I said.

"When did that stop you?" JoJo said, his eyes watching mine. No grin forming on his face.

"Where's the kid?" I asked.

He shrugged. "Left with some hoodlums in some kind of pimped-out truck."

"How long?"

"Couple hours," he said. "I ain't got time."

"Bronco?" I asked. He turned. "You enjoyin' the sights?"

He turned to watch a young girl in a red silk dress make herself thin, sliding through the crowd at the bar. He nodded, smoke coming out his nose. "Mighty fine."

I FOUND ALIAS alone at his mansion. The door was open, the rooms cavernous without any furniture. I followed the lights and ended up out on his back patio, where he lay reclined in a lounger staring up at the night sky. He had a forty by his side and his tan lug-soled boots crossed at the ankles. He looked over at me and then looked back up at the stars.

"What's up?"

Annie trotted over to him and started licking his mouth.

"Damn, dog," he said, kind of laughing like he was twelve.

I looked away. "I talked to Teddy," I said.

"He say anything about givin' me my damned dogs back?"

"He told me about you taking his credit cards last year."

He didn't turn, pushing Annie away with the back of his hand.

"No one likes to be lied to," I said.

"What you talking about?" he said. "I never said shit about that."

"So you admit taking his cards," I said.

"We was just funnin'."

"That's called theft."

"Man, get that pole out your ass," he said. "Teddy spends more money on toilet paper."

"Stand up," I said.

He mumbled something.

"Stand up," I repeated. The sound of my voice made Annie's ears wilt. She walked away.

ALIAS slid his feet to the ground, stood in his sloppy Saints jersey, and groggily looked up at me. The black sky and stars seemed like a dome above our heads. The moon huge and split in half like a paper prop on a small stage.

"I know about Dahlia," I said. "Don't much blame you; she has plenty of heat."

"That bitch? Man, you trippin'. What's wrong with you, Nick?"

"You told Teddy I wanted to keep half the money I find."

"Bullshit."

"I've known Teddy for twelve years," I said. "I've known you two weeks."

I looked away from him at the hard concrete surrounding his pool. Stray boxes and packing tape littered on the ground. I could feel the summer beginning to move in, ready to harden, before that final heat of August when it leaves us.

The sudden thought made me think of family trips to the beach and the way everything faded.

"Go, then," he said. "Ain't got time for you."

"I let you in," I said. "JoJo and Loretta took you in like they did for me."

"Go!" he yelled. "Get out of here."

"You've lost it."

"What?"

"My trust."

"Fuck you, man. Fuck you and your trust and your goddamn ways."

I turned with Annie, feeling her wet snout against my hand as I walked back through the empty white rooms.

In my rearview, I saw him watch me as I drove away, the red glow of my taillights cast over his face.

57

GHOSTS WAKE YOU SOMETIMES. *You seen your mamma at the end of your bed once, smokin' a cigarette and cryin'. Tears made out of blood. You seen your kid friend, Touchee, lyin' on his bloody stomach like when y'all was at the block party and he walked through glass. You close your eyes tight and don't like to cut off the light in your closet. Even when it's empty like tonight. All your clothes, CDs, DVDs, and stereos taken over to Teddy's place. Man tellin' you he got to cut back till that next record out. You lay awake tonight in your old kingdom, watching that bare bulb in your closet. Nothin' but miles of empty shoeboxes.*

You cross your arm over your eyes, hear the wind cut off the lake. Tomorrow you got to be out. Tomorrow you got to come up with more rhymes. Aggression. Repression. Depression.

Yeah, you know all those words. They seem to come right out of the air into your head. Almost seem like you got someone whisperin' things you don't know into your ear. You tell Teddy about that one time, right when he got you out of Calliope, and he say it ain't nothin' but inspiration.

You wonder where that been lately.

Eyes shut tight, you sleep. Seem like hours before you feel the hot breath in your ear and feel cold fingers wrap your face.

"Open your mouth, my l'il nigga, and you get cut," man says.

You wide awake. You breathe hard through your nose. Sheets wet from sweatin' all night without no AC.

"You betta calm the fuck down, boy," the voice say. "You hear me? Ain't no secrets. Ain't nobody rip your ass off. You ain't nothin' but a liar. Lie to yourself. Lie in your mind."

The hand ease off. You bite at the fingers but they gone like air.

You get tangled in the sheets and fight—seemin' like with yourself—until you fall hard on the floor. You can feel. Not see. It's 3. It's 4. Ain't no dawn in sight.

"Whay you at? Come on." You swing into blindness, black night.

You still smell that funk-ass breath. You feel heat and sourness in your face.

The closet door still cracked to keep out those monsters and ghosts and shit like when you was a kid.

A flash of platinum. Your symbol. Your Superman S on the ground.

You kneel down in that long yellow sliver of closet light that cuts real narrow when it crosses your hands. You holdin' the platinum.

"That's mine, kid," the voice say. "It too heavy for your neck."

And into the cut of light, you see him.

You can't breathe. You feel suspended in water, like when you in a pool and you don't weigh nothin'. Your fingers and legs tingle. You got to hold yourself 'cause you feel you about to piss.

It's the face from the bus. It's God.

"Yeah, you right, my nigga," he say. "Dio back."

Your hand stretches from you, like you ain't got no control, and offers that piece of jewelry to Dio, chain twisted up in your fingers. You just want him to go, take what's his. He's dead.

Sweat runs cold 'cross your neck.

"Malcolm kept pushin' too," Dio say. "Don't be a hero."

You close your eyes tight and open them to nothin'.

You hear footsteps runnin' down that wide marble staircase. Hard feet.

You run to the top, look down, moon flowin' like spilled milk onto your floors black and white and onto the bald head of a dead man.

Another man waitin' for Dio.

He got a brown coat that seems to rot off him. Gray skin and yellow eyes.

You can't move.

Your legs give out. Breath all tight, hands on the cold marble ground. You fight for that cool air, trying to find it. Needing that bubble.

When you get to your feet, they're gone.

You wonder if you right in the head.

But that funk smell stays.

58

A KNOCK ON THE WAREHOUSE DOOR before 10 A.M. better mean something important. People have their summer rituals and for me it was about 9, a big bowl of Cap'n Crunch, and then maybe a *Josie and the Pussycats* marathon or some reruns of the *Banana Splits*. I knew someone had to be kidding by breaking the sacred tradition. I yawned, punched the intercom at the street, and politely asked, "It's cartoon time. What?"

"Old School, let me up."

I held the button there for a moment, trying to think of something to say and not coming up with shit. I buzzed him up anyway and flicked on the bank of industrial switches lighting up the warehouse.

The power brought to life my stereo, caught on WWOZ, and some late-morning zydeco. Good ole Boozoo Chavis.

Annie padded her way into the kitchen and bit at my hand.

She yawned, thrusting out her long boxer legs and her butt in the air. I scratched her ears and tugged my way into some 501s and a white T.

ALIAS bounded into the warehouse, holding a box of Krispy Kreme donuts and a gallon of milk. "Come on," he said. "Eat up. We got work to do."

I started to make coffee, doubling the dose of chicory into the old blue speckled pot and laying it onto the burner.

"Oh, yeah," I said. "What's that?"

"Had a visitor last night."

I yawned.

"Mmm-hmm."

"That man you chased down from JoJo's bar."

Big fat ceramic Christmas lights burned red, green, and blue over a little tin overhang that ran from my far wall over my stove and old GE refrigerator. The warehouse felt safe and solid.

"You never saw him."

"Ain't that many people with yellow eyes. Had that raggedy-ass brown coat too. Just like you said."

The coffee began to hiss a little, still not perking. I reached under the sink and pulled out a bag of trash, tying it tight. I hooked Annie on her leash with one hand and grabbed the trash in the other, making my way down to the street.

I left the trash on my stoop and kept on walking barefoot down Julia Street.

ALIAS followed. Annie sniffed the ground.

I heard him still talking behind me.

The morning light was clean and bright. A light blue sky, small wispy clouds. I thought about heading down to the restaurant supply place with JoJo. And we needed a new neon sign. We needed that bad before we opened. Blue cursive letters.

"Ain't you listenin', jackass?"

I turned. Annie squatted on moss growing on some old bricks.

I stared at him.

He smiled a gold smile. I kept staring.

"He wasn't alone, neither," he said.

"Fred Flintstone was riding shotgun."

"Hey, man. Fuck you."

I shook my head. "I don't have time for this."

I walked Annie across the road, fishing into my jeans for a pack of cigarettes and lit one, walking slow back to the warehouse. Some asshole had smashed a blue bottle of vodka on the street and I wished I'd worn shoes.

He stood by my small blue door. His hands crossed over his chest while he leaned back into the old red brick. A red baseball hat with a Japanese character for an insignia. The streetcar clanged way down on St. Charles. I looked at my watch.

ALIAS's eyes narrowed, his face falling into the shadow of the street. He would not look me in the eye.

"Come get your donuts," I said. "I'll take you back. How'd you get here anyway?"

Annie tugged at my leash and I let her run on through the door and up the steps.

"Took a cab," he said. "You eat 'em, Travers."

"Hey, you don't have to be like that."

"Do what you like."

He turned away.

I smiled at the ground. "Who was it?"

He got maybe ten yards down the street and turned back, staring into the sun. His feet pigeon-toed. "What?"

"Who was with freak?"

His mouth grew crooked. "Does it matter?"

"Who?"

"Dio."

"He's dead, you know."

He nodded, still squinting at me. "Yeah."

"Go home, ALIAS," I said.

59

JOJO AND FELIX MOVED small tables around the hardwood floor trying to arrange the place like it used to be. They were doing a pretty good job, because for a second when I walked in, I was a little startled that maybe the bar never closed at all. The front door was open, four iron ceiling fans working hard with a straight shot to the rear exit. JoJo had scrounged up some old juke posters from Magic Bus Records Shop and that company from Slidell had finally delivered the jukebox. She wasn't as pretty as that old sixties classic that had melted in the fire, but she was thick and chrome and stocked with all the great old blues. Bobby Blue to Z. Z. Hill.

"I got this old cooler from that zydeco bar on Bourbon," JoJo said, pointing to a long refrigerator with a Jax Beer logo on the side. He slid open a top door to show the galvanized steel interior loaded down with Dixies. Regulars, Blackened Voodoo, and the Crimson Ale. "Don't be a dumb-ass like that man. Keep it simple. Buy from places shuttin' down."

"How much I owe you?" I asked.

"A million dollars," JoJo said.

Felix dropped a mop into a sudsy bucket filled with hot water and

Murphy's Oil Soap and began to wash down the wooden plank floors. I missed the old scarred hardwoods but these were thick and long and would soon become as beaten as an Old West saloon.

"How'd you do that?" I asked, nodding to some blackened grooves already worn by the back door.

JoJo walked over to the bar, where he pulled out a long section of chains. "I whupped the shit out 'em."

Felt right and good to have JoJo break the place in. He walked around taking in every little curve and pocket, his mind workin' on the way it should be.

I grabbed a beer from the old cooler, feeling good on the bar stools I'd bought earlier.

JoJo punched up "Mannish Boy" on the jukebox. The version Muddy did with Johnny Winter on the *Hard Again* album back in the seventies. The album, all bullshit and academic rhetoric aside, is by far the most enjoyable blues record ever made.

"If you don't like that," JoJo said, "you got nothin' between your legs."

Muddy sang he was a man. Johnny Winter howled and screamed, backing him up.

Felix moved his hips a bit as he mopped.

JoJo slid behind the bar and opened a cold Dixie with a bottle opener he'd installed under the flat top. "You got four bottle openers all down the line. Don't want to be foolin' with nothin' you got to look for."

I nodded. He sat beside me, taking a sip.

"Come back, JoJo."

"No, sir," he said. "Not yet."

He smiled. He looked around the dim light of the bar, Muddy alive again on Conti Street. "Besides, if I come back now, how are we gonna see what you gonna do?"

I sipped the beer. It was two o'clock. I didn't care.

"You want to get a muffuletta down at Central?" JoJo asked.

"Yeah, let me get it," I said.

JoJo smiled. "I'll let you."

"When you headed back?"

"After I eat my muff."

"Come on, JoJo."

"It's all you, son," he said. He patted me on the back. "How's it feel?"

"What's that?"

"To be grown."

I smiled, the beer was cold in my hand, and I understood.

Felix kept mopping. The blues played on. Old rhythms returned.

"ALIAS has lost his mind," I said, and told him about my run-in with Trey Brill and what I learned from Teddy. "This morning, before I picked up the tables and chairs, he told me a dead man had come to visit him in the night."

"Maybe it happened."

"Hell no," I said. "I'm done. Teddy can deal with him the way he wants."

"Look deeper," JoJo said.

"Oh, come on, JoJo," I said. "That kid conned you and me and Loretta. I'm sorry I wasted your time."

He looked at me. His brown eyes looked heavy with the creased skin around them. "I don't waste time," he said. "There's more to Tavarius. That kid is all right."

"Maybe he killed Malcolm too," I said. "He made up a damned good lie about folks ripping him off. He's so smart, JoJo. I mean, that kid can lie."

"Easy when you do that," JoJo said, standing from the bar. "Ain't it?"

"What's that?" I said, enjoying the beer and watching Felix mop.

"Handin' off your troubles."

"Why are you on his side?" I said. "You were through with him too."

JoJo settled into his seat, the jukebox cutting on to a new record. He watched the blank row of old brick as he used to when a mirror hung there. He took a sip of beer.

"I was wrong."

"Come on."

He opened his wallet and folded down two hundred-dollar bills on the table before me.

"Found it in my jacket last night," he said. "Tavarius was tellin' the truth and I shut him out."

JoJo left me there to think with the folded bills.

And I did for a long time.

60

AT SUNSET, I RAN down St. Charles, turned onto Canal past all the camera shops and jewelry stores, and wound my way to the Aquarium, where I followed the Riverwalk downriver. I passed the vagrants sleeping on rocks still warm from the sun and watched rats skittering through overflowing trash cans. I almost tripped on one as it ran back with a hot dog in its mouth and headed into the rocks along the Mississippi. My Tulane football shirt was soaked in sweat. I tried to slow my breathing and pick up my pace as I stopped at the Governor Nichols Street Wharf. I put my hands on top of my head and noticed everything turn a murky gold and red. The brick and stucco of the old buildings of the Quarter softening.

I decided to cut back through the old district, before the streets became flooded with cars and tourists. I jogged my way down Royal Street, looking up at the scrolled ironwork on JoJo and Loretta's old apartment, and wound my way around a street musician who used his dog to pick up tips with its mouth.

I wondered if Annie could do that.

She'd probably take the cash and then piss on their foot.

I slowed, made a couple of cuts, and found myself at the old Woolworth's and a blank stretch of Bourbon. Where Bourbon met Canal, I heard a brass band of teenagers running through the standard "Somebody Is Taking My Place."

Trombones and trumpets. A skinny kid with an overpowering dented tuba.

All of them were black and wearing T-shirts and shorts.

A little girl, about four, walked around with a shoebox filled with loose coins.

I stopped. Caught my breath.

In the fading light of the day, all gold and dark blue, in this unremarkable little stretch of the Quarter, a half-dozen kids entertained about twenty people. They rolled through "Saints" and took a big finish with some really wonderful solos.

Just when you grew to hate New Orleans with all its dark places and overwhelming violence, you saw something like a bunch of ragtag kids making some spectacular music. I wondered about the violence and the art and how it all fit together.

I felt bad when the little girl walked past me and I didn't have change in my jogging shorts. I showed her my empty palms and shrugged. She scowled and turned her back to me.

Suddenly the band broke into a song I knew. A heavy funk with the tuba working the hell out of the beat.

I started tapping my foot, the light fading to black all around us.

My smile stopped. My face flushed.

They were playing ALIAS.

61

I SPENT THE NEXT MORNING at the New Orleans Police Department flipping through the missing persons file of Calvin Antoine Jacobs, aka Dio. In the empty office of a desk sergeant who was friends with Jay, I made notes onto a yellow legal pad. I read through interviews with Teddy and Malcolm, other rappers who knew Dio, and a couple that saw him taken away outside Atlanta Nites by two men in ski masks. One reported he heard a muffled pop from inside a black van. I read back through the interview with Malcolm. He talked about the man's talent and some folks in Calliope he feared. The name Cash was mentioned several times. But Malcolm was their suspect.

Still nothing. Not what I'd hoped to find.

Jay popped his head in and asked if I wanted to go to lunch at Central Grocery.

I declined.

"You must be sick," he said. "Life is a bag of Zapp's."

"This report doesn't make any sense," I said. "It just kind of drops."

"When someone goes missing, not a lot you can do, bra. You know how many people just disappear in New Orleans every year?"

"You know how many should?"

"You heard from that street freak that was harassing you?"

I shook my head.

"Look out for yourself," he said.

I peered down at my legal pad and some notes I'd made. About thirty minutes later, I found a vending machine and drank a Barq's. I ate some Oreos. I walked down a linoleum hall and let myself back into the records room.

What bothered me was that no family members had been interviewed about this guy. When I researched someone, often that was the first place I'd go. Who knows someone best but his own people?

I asked the sergeant—a burly white-haired man who kept a screen saver of George W. Bush on his computer—for an explanation. He stood, his back to the thin walls of pressed wood, where he'd hung photos of himself with three German shepherds sitting at his feet.

"Was he a transient?" he asked.

"No."

"Who'd we find?"

"People he worked with."

He nodded.

"He has an address that shows a place on Lakeshore Drive," I said. "But I know he'd been in prison. Why isn't there anything about that in the record?"

"You need to call the Department of Corrections for that," he said. He flipped through a Rolodex, squinted at the tiny card, and read off a name and number. "She'll get you what you need. Tell her I told you to call."

I shook the desk sergeant's hand.

"Good when you can do something," he said.

"Did you work the street for long?"

"Long enough to piss someone off and end up here."

The contact from the Louisiana Department of Corrections was a pleasant woman named Lisa. She sounded completely foreign to the Lisa I'd lived with when I played ball. She sounded as if she had a heart. A brain too. I told her the sergeant's name and that I was researching for a buddy of mine and she told me to give her a few hours.

"Some inmate at Angola escaped this morning," she said. "Those freakin' reporters won't leave us alone."

I drove back to the warehouse and walked Annie down to Louisiana Products for a po'boy. I made coffee.

At 3, she called back.

"I have two Calvin Antoine Jacobses," she said. "The first has a DOB March 3, 1974?"

"Let me double-check that birthday."

"Is he currently incarcerated?" she asked.

"No."

"Then that's not him. The only other Calvin Antoine Jacobs I have in the system died two years ago."

"This guy I need is missing," I said. "No one ever found him. I didn't think he was ruled dead."

She paused for a second. "This guy died in Angola. Let me see . . . he was from New Orleans. Lived at 2538 Constance. He was convicted of two counts of manslaughter and one count of car theft in 2000."

"Wait."

"What?"

"I think I love you."

"Excuse me?"

"Read back that address."

She did. I smiled.

I promised her free drinks at JoJo's next time she was in New Orleans. Anything she wanted. My children. My dog. She could be bald with a harelip and I would've kissed her at that moment.

"What else can you tell me about Mr. Jacobs?"

"A lot," she said. "What do you need to know?"

62

I WAS DOWN ON CONSTANCE an hour later passing a little neighborhood grocery, Parasol's Irish bar, and rows of old shotguns until I found the one where Dahlia lived. I parked a block down the street, slid on The Club, and walked down the skinny broken sidewalk and under shady oaks to her door. I knocked. No one answered. I found a place to sit on her small porch, the deck wooden and uneven. I sat for a while, wilting in the heat. I walked back to my truck, stopped, and went back to the house. A warped gate closed the way to the back of the shotgun. It was locked.

I looked down the street and then back the other way.

I hopped the fence and followed a stone path covered in pink bougainvillea that grew over a fence and rotted awning. On the shaded back patio, white and purple impatiens hung from large baskets. In the deep shade, I recognized some yellow jasmine growing from iron grillwork. The air smelled of musky sweetness that enveloped me.

"My mother loved them," she said.

Dahlia smiled at me, hands covered in white gloves and mashing potting soil into a terra-cotta pot. She wore a boy's white tank top covered in mud. The cotton hugged the perfect shape of her breasts and tiny waist. She ran her forearm over her brow.

Her dark hair had grown curly in the heat and her large eyes watched me, her jaw loose. Lips parted.

"You want to tell me about your brother?" I asked.

"Jesus," she said. Smiling. "You don't stop."

"I think I have it all figured out, but why don't you tell me."

She tilted her head and wrapped her long brown hair into a ponytail. Her hair seemed moist and rich. I could smell her scent. She smelled like coconut oil and warm skin.

"How'd your brother know Christian?"

She held her stare. "My daddy doesn't like you too much."

"He thinks I'm trying to save your soul."

"Too far gone for that." She pushed out her lower lip with mock sadness.

"Calvin was the real thing."

"Calvin was a genius," she said. "He was tested when we was kids and he was off the charts. My daddy tole me they put him in a room with a bunch of toys to figure things out. You know triangle to triangle? Circle to circle? He did all right till he clocked some poor child in the head with a block."

"Couldn't stay straight?"

"Hell, no," she said. She looked at me, suddenly reminded of who I was and backed off. "Oh no. That's enough. Take what you got and leave."

"Let me come inside."

"That just leads to bad things."

"Not for me."

"Don't you like women?" she asked, brushing my chin with her index fingers.

"I like 'em too much," I said. "They get me in trouble."

"You got a woman now?"

"Yep."

"Where she at?"

"She's waiting on me," I said. "I can't leave till I find out what happened with Dio."

"Dio," she said. "Shit. Calvin wouldn't ever taken no name like that. That was *his* invention."

"When did you find out?" I asked, leading her into an area I didn't know myself.

"Last year," she said. "When he was dead."

"Dio?"

"The one they called Dio."

"They used him and killed him."

She smiled and patted my face. "Right."

She walked up some concrete blocks and into her house. I followed. She had her back turned to me leaning over her cast-iron sink. Her blue-jean shorts hugged her rounded thighs and her shoulder blades stretched under her brown skin. I was drawn to her neck, the beads of moisture collecting right among the tiny, soft hairs.

"They pay you to be quiet?"

"When I heard those rhymes, I knew," she said. "Calvin had been workin' on them since he was twelve. He had notebooks full of 'em. He wrote in them all the time. Made hand copies and sent them to me, even in jail. The ones that came out. The ones about Uptown life and all that? That was him. They didn't change a word. His heart lived in those old ragged notebooks. We may have moved on, but his soul was still in Calliope where we was raised."

"What happened?"

"A guard scrambled his brains," she said, turning her back to me. She was crying. She tilted her head into her hands. Sunlight skimmed through the oaks and broke apart in strobe flashes across her face. Her back door kept slamming open and shut in the summer wind.

I could still smell the jasmine. So sweet and rich.

"I heard he filled the guard's water bottle with horse shit," she said. "The guard later said Calvin had tried to kill him with a broken piece of glass."

I nodded, leaning against the back wall of the tiny kitchen. The ragged wallpaper made soft rubbing sounds.

"So his cellmate was Christian Chase," I said.

She nodded.

"He pay you for keeping quiet?"

"Trey Brill did," she said. "I came to them quick and asked for a cut. They let me in. They took me to dinner and later out to clubs with them."

"And whose idea was it to work ALIAS?"

She shook her head.

"Come on," I said. "You've come this far."

"They fucked me," she said. "Both of them."

"I'm sorry."

"They played with me for ten months," she said. "I came to them whenever they wanted me. They put me on video and would make me sit there while I watched it with their friends. But they didn't know who I was inside. It was my goddamn idea to run the kid. Marion and I got the idea when he came into the club that night. Kid was fifteen with millions. He had time to make it back. Besides, that was money built on my brother's soul. Without Calvin, you wouldn't have no ALIAS."

"Come with me," I said. "I need you to tell this to a friend of mine."

"I'm not talking to the police."

"Shit," I said, grabbing her hand. "Come on."

She twisted her head back and forth like a child. "No."

"Did you know this guy, Dio? The one who used your brother's lyrics?"

"Yeah," she said. "Of course."

Her eyes narrowed. I was losing her.

"They killed him and Malcolm."

"They didn't kill him," she said.

I looked at her. The door kept slamming shut and she walked over and latched it, the wind still blowing through the screen.

She grabbed my hand. "Come lie down with me."

"I think you're sick, Dahlia," I said. "You need to find comfort in yourself."

"Just lie down," she said.

"What did Trey and Christian pay you?"

"Seven thousand to keep quiet," she said. "Trey said he knew a man who could make me disappear. He said the man liked to be paid in soiled money left on top of folks' graves."

"What about ALIAS's money?"

She stared at me and shook her head. "Trey got it," she said. "He said he could double my money if he put it all in stocks. I tried to get it back the other night when I seen him out. I ain't ever seein' that money. Yeah, he knew about ALIAS."

"Talk to my friend," I said. "He's a good man. We need to know who killed Malcolm and Dio."

"Listen to me," she said. "Dio ain't dead. What you think happen to a boy in prison over six years? You think he might change a bit? Maybe get his teeth knocked out. Get branded. Maybe if he grow a beard and sport some jewelry and earrings, that even his own folks don't know who he is."

I couldn't breathe.

I was afraid she would stop.

"That Christian Chase don't have a soul," she said. "I told him I loved him once. He told me I was just loving my own brother 'cause that's who he'd become."

63

TREY WAS SOMETIMES AMAZED by his own intelligence. He'd have a few glasses of good red wine or a few Amstel Lights and sit back and smile at how it all had played out. He grew the business from one player in the NFL to ten pro players, four rappers, an entire label, and eighteen high-level Uptown clients, including a city councilman and the heir to a hot-pepper-sauce franchise. He stared out from his window in the CBD down at a billboard on Canal for Cartier watches and another for a new line from Victoria's Secret, the woman's stomach as flat as a plate, her hips expansive. The night was purple, fluorescent lights flickering on the wide boulevard.

He opened his humidor on his desk and clipped off the end of a cigar. He thought ole Chase might want to hit Cobalt tonight. Molly was out of town and he'd line up a couple of dates from a score he'd made at Lucy's last week.

He checked his properly mussed hair in the mirror and lost the tie.

"Hey, dog," Trey said as Christian crossed the room in a black sleeveless T and tight khakis with sandals. He'd cut his hair so close that he was starting to look like that rat from Angola Trey had picked up at the bus station two years ago.

"He knows," Christian said. "He fucking got to Dahlia. I told you, you stupid fuck, we should have axed her ass two months ago."

"She was your punch," Trey said. "He doesn't know shit."

"That was my dad on the phone," Christian said. "Told me not to come home ever again. Said two detectives just showed up at his office asking about my relationship with Calvin Jacobs. What the fuck, man? What the fuck did you do?"

"Calm down," Trey said, pouring himself a few fingers of Knob Creek. "It'll work out."

"What!" Christian screamed. "Are you goddamn crazy?"

"All right, let's think. How do you even know this had something to do with Dahlia?"

"Who else could lead them to us?" he said. "It's all your fault. It's all your fucking fault. We had goddamn everything we wanted and you had to go in with that cunt to take ALIAS."

"She wanted a cut of something."

"Then give her some of your money."

"I wanted her to get dirty, too," Trey said. "You know how that works."

"Like we all get dirty?" Christian asked. "Like how you had Redbone make that con man from the strip club disappear after you took ALIAS. Sometimes it doesn't play out like that."

"What?" Trey said, mussing his hair in the mirror again. "You getting all street on me again. Don't confuse yourself. You know where you come from. Don't start actin' like some stupid nigger."

Christian balled his hands at his side and ran for Trey. He stood so close that their noses touched. The foulness in Christian's breath and the fear that poured from his own skin made Trey's heart race.

He tried to calm himself. "Just chill out."

"Some of us don't have our daddy to hold our hands."

"Hey, man," Trey said. "Fuck off."

He turned his back to Christian. He didn't mean anything by it, but as soon as he pivoted, he knew he'd made a mistake.

"I'm not going back to Angola," Christian said. "Not for you."

Christian's hands darted from his chest and took Trey by the throat. He threw his friend onto his back on the glass desk. Trey felt a heavy split down the middle, cracking like an ice pond from their weight.

Trey's head rhythmically beat onto the glass.

Trey heard more cracking and tried to yell and scream for help. But he could only think it, his mind unable to control anything. He couldn't move or speak, only feel the saliva pool on his lips and feel the blood and wetness pour from his mouth and eyes.

"This ain't your game, dog," Christian said.

64

MY CELL PHONE RANG as I headed back from NOPD, where I'd left Dahlia still talking with Jay. I answered, driving with one hand, passing Medina's on Canal and crossing under I-10. I'd planned to meet JoJo down at Acme for a plate of jambalaya and some oysters. This was their last night in New Orleans. He and Bronco had finished up packing the apartment.

"He's with me," the voice said. Cell-phone static crackled over the line.

"Good for you," I said. "Who is this?"

"Let's play," he said. "I have ALIAS, you fucking dumb-ass. I have my goddamn gun screwed in his ear right now. You fucking do one more thing and I'll drop his ass in the sewer. You fucking hear me?"

"Slow down, Christian."

"Fuck you," he said. "Meet me down in the Ninth Ward on Piety. There is a house at—"

"I meet you where I say," I said. "Fuck no. I'm not meeting you."

The connection died.

I didn't breathe for about a minute.

The cell rang again.

A better connection. He didn't say anything.

"I'll meet you at your folks' house," I said. "In Metairie."

"No," he said. "This isn't about them."

His voice was strained. The words hard but almost forced from his mouth in a quiet yell.

"That's it. I'm headed to Old Metairie right now. You can decide on a place. Wait, okay. Yep. Just turned. Headed down I-10. I'll be there in fifteen."

I hung up and made a quick phone call.

The cell phone rang as I ran my truck about eighty, skirting the edge of the Metairie Cemetery. High up on the interstate, the mausoleums looked like a small city. Endless rows of crypts.

I answered the phone.

"Where?" he asked.

"You know the country day school?"

He didn't answer.

"You know, where you and Trey got to be friends?"

"You say my friend's name again and I'll kill this little boy with you on the phone."

METAIRIE COUNTRY DAY sat at the end of a neighborhood cul-de-sac in a large whitewashed brick house with green shutters. Huge magnolias and oaks stood in bright spotlights in the darkness. Behind the main house, classrooms stretched under two porticos separated by a commons. I heard my feet on the brick walk passing the classrooms as the wind scattered in the oak leaves and branches. Newsletters fluttered on a school bulletin board advertising ski trips to Switzerland and on-line shopping for Eddie Bauer, Lands' End, and L.L. Bean. Elephant ears and monkey grass grew strong in freshly tilled soil.

I was far from JFK High.

I walked to the end of the portico and the last classroom. It was 10 and I didn't hear anyone.

I looked into a darkened playground at the still swing sets and empty slides and then back at the long open walkway.

I heard a car door slam behind the school and playground and saw the chugging exhaust of an old car's tailpipe in the brake lights. I reached for the gun tucked in my belt but left it there.

I walked back toward the front of the school and the main house. I stared over a railing at the little cul-de-sac and the houses lining the street. My truck was parked into a little curve under a light.

I looked at my watch and decided to make one more sweep.

I turned on my heel.

A tremendous force whopped my skull.

I tumbled to my knees, trying to gain my balance, but only finding my palms for support.

Everything was black. I could feel the heat of the blood from my skinned hands.

The air smelled of garbage and decaying skin. My eyes rolled and my vision faded from brown to black. I felt wire around my throat and tore at the hands that choked me.

65

I COULD NOT BREATHE, the air snuffed from inside, my face filling with blood. My gun fell to the ground.

I jabbed my elbow back into the freak's chest and leaned forward, pulling him off his feet. I pressed my thumb into his wrists and felt his hands open. Bone and gristle snapping. I bent back his hands and butted him in the head.

He staggered back, facedown, slowly getting to his feet. He raised his head. Grayed skin wrinkled and decayed as a dead leaf across his skull. He reached into his coat and pulled out a little revolver.

He smiled with rotten, uneven teeth that looked like a brown picket fence.

I heard the crack of a gun; I closed my eyes.

The freak doubled over and sprinted down under the dark colonnades. I grabbed my Glock and followed a trail of thin, dark blood.

I'd heard the same car running by the playground and practice fields.

I turned the corner and Bronco joined me at my side. He kept pace, a mesh Caterpillar hat scrunched down in his eyes. I was damned glad I'd called them.

"JoJo's got cover from the back," he said. Grinning with the hunt. "You want me to drop that man from here?"

The freak was only about ten yards away, running past the darkened shapes of metal ponies and swing sets. His right hand grasping his left arm and staggering.

JoJo crossed before him, a thick shotgun sighted across the freak's eyes.

Bronco stopped running and held his Colt in his right hand.

We slowed to a walk.

The man wheezed as if broken inside, sputters of air coming from him. His yellow eyes squinted, face twisted into a feral look of an animal cornered. His lips quivered over his broken teeth and he moved his hand to his pocket.

"Where's the boy?" JoJo asked, pumping the gun.

The man kept wheezing.

Bronco came up fast behind him and slammed a boot into his lower back with a hard steel toe, knocking him to the ground.

He kept his boot there, breathing hard, and shook out a cigarette from a pack, placing it dry into his mouth. "Me and JoJo used to run deer up and down Clarksdale when we was kids. I got to be pretty good. 'Cept JoJo won't admit it."

"Bullshit," JoJo said, dropping the shotgun and sauntering over to the old car.

"Well, hello, Tavarius," he said so we could all hear.

I followed and found the boy tied with laundry line across his ankles and wrists. A torn piece of brown cloth gouged deep into his mouth. He tore at it with his teeth and tried to break free when he saw JoJo.

JoJo untied him.

I dialed 911.

"What you doin'?" Bronco asked.

"Calling the police."

"Not on this," he said, grinding his steel toe into the small of the man's back. "He's out of the game."

He kicked at the man's head, so quick and violent that I had to turn away.

Bronco picked up the man, as if he was recently found roadkill, and dragged him to the old car. The heels of the killer's old brogan shoes scuffing behind him. The muscles and veins in Bronco's huge forearms bulging with his years of strength.

"Get the keys."

I did, turning off the ignition of the old Pontiac, painted a light gold. Vinyl seats covered in duct tape.

"Pop the trunk," he said.

I did.

"See you back at the bar," Bronco said.

"Wait."

"Come on, Nick," JoJo said. "Let's get this kid safe."

Tavarius was rubbing his wrists. He refused to look me in the face.

"I'm sorry," I said. "I know about Dio."

He shook his head and walked away.

JoJo winked at me and followed.

66

I HEADED STRAIGHT for the Ninth Ward, driving along Claiborne under the interstate, past the old Victorians boarded up and left rotting, their third-story windows only feet from concrete and steel and speeding cars. I passed little community groceries that sold beer from iced trash cans and offered health care through a backroom doctor. Kids on bicycles circled me at street corners. Lazy-eyed crackheads tried to sell me fruit that had been cut and locked into Ziploc bags, and soft-faced women with protruding bellies wandered shoeless out on Elysian Fields. Under the nearby oaks, the ground had been worn as soft as talcum powder in the yards of the rotting antebellum homes.

I crossed over the channel on a short bridge. Cheap little billboards advertised discount cigarettes and beer, a free AIDS hot line. Barges hugged the edge of the docks and mammoth warehouses sat in rusting humps.

I took a turn onto Desire and wound through the little red, blue, and yellow shotguns. Ninth Ward Records sat behind its wrought-iron fence topped with decorative fleur-de-lis in a big squat concrete building of black and gold. Teddy had his electric-blue Bentley parked by the main glass door.

I walked inside and headed straight back to his office.

He was rearranging his CDs when I walked in. Must have been thousands of them in little piles all over the carpet. He had on a black suit with a red shirt and fedora. I noticed he hadn't shaved in a while and his eyes looked rheumy.

"We need to talk."

He nodded, moving like he was a hundred back to his big white sofa. He took off his jacket and stretched out his huge arms across its back.

I stood and crossed my arms over my shirt.

I looked down at my boots.

He was silent.

"ALIAS was conned," I said. "And so were you."

He moved forward, a big bear finding his place, and rubbed his hands together. "What happened?"

"Dio wasn't real," I said. "One of Trey's buddies just acted it out. He'd stolen this guy's rhymes when he was in Angola."

"What the fuck?" Teddy asked, suddenly awake. "Man, what are you talking about, Dio wasn't real?"

"The real Dio was a guy named Calvin Jacobs. He was killed in prison."

Teddy shook his head. "I knew that boy. That boy made my company. I was with him when he got jacked by those men at the club."

"You knew Christian Chase," I said. "Trey Brill's buddy? The real Dio's sister is Dahlia, man. She got in with Brill 'cause she knew the truth. It was her idea to work the con on ALIAS. ALIAS wasn't lying, man. She roped him in with Trey's blessing."

"Slow down," Teddy said, standing now and pacing. "This don't make no goddamn sense. Trey Brill set all this up. Did all this to me? Why? He don't need money. Why he taken me out? And Malcolm. Jesus."

Teddy started to cry and I made an awkward move for him, patting him a couple times on his back. "Trey got Malcolm killed," he said, sobbing. "Didn't he? Malcolm knew about Dio. Malcolm knew."

"Only thing I can figure."

"Lord, Lord. He killed my brother." Teddy ran to his desk and I watched him. Manic and angry. Three hundred pounds of crying grief. Wringing his hands, face crunched tight in sorrow.

"You made this all happen, Nick," Teddy said. "You got everybody to come to Jesus. Thank you, Nick. Thank you, Nick. Thank you, Nick. Malcolm knew you'd do right."

He hugged me awkwardly again. "Brill is dead," Teddy said.

"It's okay," I said. "The cops are looking for him. Dahlia turned on Trey and Christian."

"She what?" Teddy asked.

"They messed up her mind," I said. "Her soul is gone. They used her up, man."

"Jesus. Jesus," Teddy said. "Malcolm said you'd set it straight. I didn't believe him. That day when we come to you, I told him he's bein' foolish. But that boy knew you'd set it straight. He always look up to you. Even when he was a kid."

I smiled. I patted Teddy on the back. "Come on, let's go."

He fell to his knees. He dragged all the papers off his desk and toppled hundreds of CDs. He tried to stand, bounding like a trapped elephant, scattering plastic everywhere.

"Malcolm," he screamed. "Malcolm. Lord God. Help me."

He found his feet and gained his composure, wiping his face with the tail of his red silk shirt. He mopped his face, exposing his massive hairless stomach.

I watched him as he reached into the drawer of his desk and pulled out a handgun.

"Jesus, no," I said. "The police will get his ass."

"Trey couldn't get enough. He had to bring in the kid."

I looked at him and tilted my head.

Before I could speak, Teddy leveled the gun at me and fired off three quick rounds, dropping me onto his white carpet. I had to bite into my arm to stop the heat and pain.

"We wouldn't never found out about Trey and Dahlia wasn't for you," Teddy said. "We appreciate that."

Hard shoes kicked into me and rolled me on my back with the toe.

I stared up into the green eyes of Christian Chase.

67

YOU CAN'T SLEEP. *It's 4 A.M. and the old man snorin' in Nick's bed, his friend Bronco watching a black-and-white movie from the Old West. Bronco doesn't care much for the man in the mask but he sure like that Indian that ride with him. Every time some shit goes down, Bronco give you a nudge in the ribs and say wake up and listen.*

The warehouse seem like a big cave to you, some kind of place where you keep an airplane. Big fans work up the tin ceiling and the smooth wood on the floor feels soft on your bare feet. But you ain't got no comfort. Neither does the dog. She knows something wrong. The way she just hang by the door, making some whimperin' sounds.

The old man shootin' up out of bed in his nightshirt, silver hair on his chest. "Nick?"

"It ain't him," you say. "He ain't back."

"What time is it?"

"Four."

He sighs real tight. "Let's go."

"Where?" you ask. "I called Teddy fifty times."

"Show me," JoJo said, snaking his belt through his britches and buttonin' up his shirt.

Bronco watches him, stands, cuts off the TV, and straps the shoulders onto his country-ass overalls. His eyes are real hard as he reaches for his cigarettes and some shotgun he bought that he call "Sweet Sixteen."

"Smells," JoJo said.

You nod. Things are wrong. Feel wrong in your head.

You stand and walk over to the sink, pourin' cold water into your hands and watching the sink fill up while you wash your face. As you bend into the water, you watch the Superman symbol Dio touched sink into the clear water like an anchor.

"I know," you say. You wipe your hands on a dry towel, feelin' funny and dry in the mind 'cause of the time. Your mind awake; body want to sleep. "Let's roll."

Don't take no time when you down at Ninth Ward. You remember the first time Teddy drove you here and you thinkin' that the roof was really made out of gold. But it just look like painted tin tonight in the shine of them crime lights. Bugs gatherin' all around them.

You bang on the window and one of Teddy's cousins, this boy y'all call Poochie, come to the door. He smile and wave when he see you. Poochie ain't but like two years older than you and he look like he playin' dress-up with his cornrows and skinny head in that blue uniform.

"Nigga, you even got a gun," you say, givin' him the pound.

The old man whack you in the back of the head. "Where's Teddy?" JoJo ask.

Ole Poochie shake his head and say he don't know. But the way he won't meet you in the eye mean he lyin'.

"Poochie, don't pull my dick, you seen him down here with my boy Nick."

Poochie nod.

"So where he at?"

"They left, man. Don't go ridin' me about this shit."

"Somethin' happen?"

JoJo shake his head. Bronco already headin' down the hall.

"Hey," Poochie yell. "Hey."

But Bronco and JoJo already lookin' inside of rooms and offices and wanderin' round the studio where you supposed to cut a record tomorrow.

"JoJo!" Bronco yells. The old man go and you follow.

Poochie try to grab your arm but you already inside Teddy's office and see Bronco down on one knee, just like that Indian scout in the movie, sniffin' and trailin' animals and shit. Only this time, don't take much.

A big ole pool of red blood mixed in that high, white carpet.

"What up, man?" you yell at Poochie. You get in his face. "What up?"

"They gone, man," he say. "That's all."

"Where?"

Poochie shake his head again. "I don't know."

"Where's Teddy?"

Then you see the gold hook, the one laden down with keys to the two Bentleys and three Escalades, and that big Scarab sport boat. The big ole fish key chain ain't on the hook.

"Where's Nick?"

"I seen him come in," Poochie say. "But only Teddy and some dude left."

"Who?"

"I don't know," he said. "Some punk nigga."

"Was he branded?" you ask.

"I don't know."

"What he look like?"

"He had eyes like him," he said, pointing to Bronco.

JoJo look at you and y'all know.

"How long they been gone?"

"They was yellin' in here and shit for a while and then they left 'bout an hour ago."

"I know where they at," you say. "But he gone."

JoJo look at you.

"He got his boat out in the lake. Man, we ain't ever gonna find him. That boat run."

"We need a faster boat, kid," he says. "What you got hidden with all your toys?"

"Na," you say. You reach into your wallet and find a platinum card, raised lettering. "But I got someone who can hook us up."

The C-phone already caught in your hand callin' on Cash.

68

I PRESSED MY PALM to the wet bloody mess below my rib cage. My fingers trembled and my breath slowed. All I could smell was new car in the trunk of Teddy's Bentley and something ripe and sour. My head bounced against a tire iron every time he slowed, my feet crinkling on some shopping bags where they'd placed me. I don't know if they thought I was dead, or cared. I'd passed out right until I'd been carried out. Everything seemed dulled. My head throbbed from where I fell and hit the edge of Teddy's desk. I was in shock. My mind unclear.

I kept my palm to the wound, trying to stop the blood. Apply pressure, that's what you did. Right? I tried to breathe. I wanted to kick at the side of the car. I wanted to try and rip out of the trunk. But I was shut inside, didn't have the energy, and knew any sound would just draw them to shoot me again.

I breathed. And swallowed.

I felt as if someone had carved into my flesh with a hot knife and kept twisting the blade inside me. *Jesus. Jesus.*

I closed my eyes and prayed.

Teddy. My mind wasn't right. Teddy.

We hit a bump and a solid, fleshy mass lolled against me. In the dim glow of the taillights, flickering on and off in a red strobe, I turned my head and saw Trey Brill staring at me with glassy blue eyes. His face gray and covered in dried blood.

"Goddamn," I yelled. I couldn't breathe. I couldn't move in the trunk. I felt as if my body had been wired together and shut inside a coffin.

I kicked hard, denting in the side of the car. I gritted my teeth.

The car slowed.

I heard muffled voices.

I closed my eyes, slowed my breathing even more. I turned my head away from Trey and the smell of his body releasing all of its fluids.

Outside, hands beat on the trunk

"Calm down," Christian said.

"It'll be okay," Teddy said.

"Cool."

"Okay, Malcolm," Teddy said.

"Man, chill."

"Malcolm?"

"I'm not fuckin' Malcolm," Christian yelled. "Now open the goddamn trunk and let's get this shit done."

I kept my eyes shut, felt Teddy's meaty hands lift under me like a spatula and cradle me into his huge arms. I let all my muscles go slack. No breathing. I held my breath.

"I'm sorry. I'm so sorry. Lord God Jesus. Jesus my savior."

"Teddy, shut the fuck up," Christian said.

Their feet crunched on gravel.

Feet shifted upon wooden planks and I heard the slap of water against pilings. I opened my eyelids just a crack. Still dark. The glow of security lights over dozens of boats parked in narrow little slips.

His feet stopped and he dropped me onto the deck right on my hurt side. I bit so hard into my lip that I could taste blood, an electric current of pain lighting up my body. But I didn't scream.

In my mind, I saw clear blue water leaking from my eyes and a black shroud covering my face in a tight mask. I took in air slow.

With a thud, Trey's body dropped onto the deck beside me like a freshly caught fish onto ice. I smelled his odor and heard a ticking sound. When I opened my eyes, I saw nothing but his large Rolex's second hand sweeping across the black face. His wrists turning purple and light gray.

Teddy cried, almost as if he'd become a child again. Sniffling, wailing.

An engine started and puttered.

Christian used my back as a springboard to pop back up to the slip and untie the lines. Seconds later, we moved out.

In the dim blue-black light of the false dawn, I prayed some more.

I thought of my body resting as I bled. I thought about my energy storing up. I'd just lie still for a while. Try and keep conscious. I bit my hurt lip to feel more pain. Keep alert.

My face flush to the ground, brown water running into my purposely open mouth, I saw a revolver on Christian's hip.

"Stop, cryin', boy," he said. "Hard part's over."

I heard the radio tune around the dial.

He found a rap station playing a song that kept on with a steady beat. "Oohhhwee." More beats. More rhymes. "Ooohhhweee."

Christian rapped along as he steered.

Teddy moved beside him, silk shirt bloody and untucked.

I could only see his back and fat neck stretched tight as he looked down into the water. "Where we goin', Malcolm?"

"You my dog, Teddy," Christian said. "You right. We brothers now."

69

THAT DOCK WHERE TEDDY *keep that Scarab is empty as hell. Light just comin' over the edge of the lake while you and JoJo and Bronco look out from the marina at all the places where they could've gone out in that black water. JoJo's old truck parked next to Teddy's Bentley, right by the edge of all those boats, all faded blue and dented. JoJo looks across Pontchartrain and then over at Bronco, who shakes his head.*

"Ain't no way," Bronco says. "That's the biggest thing I ever seen."

"Where that friend you promise?" JoJo asks.

"He comin'. "

"What's he to you?"

"He owes me."

"For what?"

"Whatever he want."

"Words are nothin' to a thug," he says. "This boy don't sound no different than an animal."

Just as he say that, his old truck gets swallowed up by five white Escalades and a bright yellow Ferrari where you see Cash float out shirtless with leather pants. He wears sunglasses and got a toothpick cocked out the side of his mouth.

JoJo look over at you and shake his head.

"He got a boat," you say. "Fast as hell."

He looks over at Bronco. Bronco nods.

"Have no fear," Cash say.

You ain't got no time for no introductions and no time for a lot of words.

"Travers out on the lake," you say.

"What?" he ask. "You want me to take out my sweet little boat for his ass?"

"Listen, goddammit," JoJo say, gettin' in Cash's face and seein' Cash ain't used to that. "You either help us get out on that lake and look for my boy or get back to shinin' your sissy-ass chains."

Cash smiles platinum and grunts. "Who you, old man?"

"The man been kickin' ass before your granddaddy even got his dick wet."

Twelve of Cash's Angola crew moan and laugh. Cash look at them, givin' that mean eye, lettin' them know to shut that mouth.

"Why you want to help that white boy?" he ask.

JoJo turns. "Come on, Tavarius."

"Tavarius?" Cash asks, laughin'. "Man, now that's funny. That your name, ALIAS?"

You look at him, cockin' that head and lookin' up into his eyes. "Yeah, that's my name."

Y'all walk through the crowd, bumpin' shoulders with some of those do-rag niggas, when Cash yell: "You wit' me now?"

You turn and nod.

"Well, let's get in the goddamn boats. Ain't never too early for no ride."

JoJo look back, cuttin' his eyes straight down the narrow little dock. "What you got?"

Cash flicks his forefinger out—almost makin' it out like a gun—and point to one of them Cigarette racin' boats you seen when you down in Miami. Man, you heard them things could run you all the way down to the Bahamas before the hour through.

But this boat don't look nothin' like that shit in Miami. This one ghetto hard all the way. It's purple and gold and got the words BALLIN' III *painted in shiny looped letters at the back and the cartoon head of a pit bull in a dia-*

mond collar snarlin' up front of that sleek, long boat. Look like some kind of rocket ship.

"Y'all take the other two," he yell to some of his boys.

Down the dock, you see Cash got two more boats that look like the same.

"I designed them myself," Cash says as y'all walk back. "Only limitation is that imagination."

"Lord God, help the world," JoJo said. "Your ghetto ass know how to steer?"

"Sit down, ole man, and strap your ass in, 'cause we headed to the goddamn moon."

The engine start with a chug, chug, chug *and y'all is rollin' out hard as that edge of the lake, where it look like black glass, is turnin' all purple with the sky.*

Y'all is flyin', skippin' over tiny little waves listenin' to Mystikal tellin' the world to get out his way. Salty mist hittin' your eyes. Tastin' the lake on your lips.

JoJo holds on tight.

Bronco finds himself standin' right by Cash, lookin' into the wind.

You see that old man's smile match the thug's.

70

"WE NEED SOME WEIGHT," Christian yelled to Teddy. "Teddy? You listenin', man? I said, we got some weight?"

"You're right, Malcolm. It's all right. We get the weight. Sweet Jesus. We got that weight."

Christian started laughing. "Stone-cold crazy. Stone-cold. Malcolm. Yeah, boy."

The speedboat cut hard and picked up speed. I felt the water beating hard on the hull and slapping us up and down with the chop. I kept my eyes closed, growing nauseous.

Christian kept rapping along with the radio station in his khakis and sandals. I peeked back at Teddy standing by his side. I looked over at Trey and the way his head bobbed, his body slapping down with the hull every few seconds.

I felt bile rise in my throat.

I got to my feet. Everything shaking. My balance teetering, head swimming in long Olympic strokes. I held on to the rail and, without any great stealth, made my way, trying to get the revolver Christian wore tucked in his belt.

I was within a few feet when he spiked the throttle and threw me onto my back with a thud. He laughed. Teddy peered down at me—but it wasn't Teddy in his eyes—and he looked away. Dumb and mute.

Christian slowed the boat. A constant chugging from the motor.

He stood over me and kicked me hard in the head.

He kicked me again.

I curled into a ball and then rolled to my hands and knees.

I used the rail and got to my feet, puking all over my shirt.

Everything felt like it was spinning and turning.

"Teddy," I said. "Come on, man. What happened? It's still you. It's still you."

He slowly twisted his head from side to side. "No."

"Come on, man."

Christian leveled the gun at my head, the biggest wicked grin forming on his lips. Green eyes slanting. A pink, blue dawn sliding over the black water, framing his body.

He jumped and fell.

On the deck, Trey's hands wrapped around Christian's ankles. Blood poured from his mouth and he made a gurgling, croaking sound.

Christian fired off three rounds into Trey's head, sending misting blood across the white fiberglass of the hull.

I leapt for him, grabbed his throat, and head-butted him. I plunged my thumbs into his voice box and he made a muted shriek as it cracked in my hands. The gun clattered to the ground.

Teddy never moved as Christian fell. I picked up the gun.

Without hesitation, I aimed it at Christian's head and pulled the trigger.

Click.

I pulled it again.

Click.

I heard another click and turned.

Teddy was back. Or some part of him.

He had the hammer thumbed back on his .357 Magnum. His eyes and face were dead. No light, no feeling. His black skin slick with sweat. He aimed the barrel toward me and said in his deep voice, "Sit your ass down till we find a good and dark place to kill you."

71

CASH HUGS THAT COAST *of Pontchartrain, that mean ole humpbacked levee running for miles out onshore. Look like the spiny back of a dragon blockin' you from seein' anything off the lake. The sky is so pink and gray. These big-ass long clouds that crack and stretch like broken slabs of concrete in the early day. The sun just a slice of orange over that long, green levee, colorin' these old fishin' shacks on tall crooked wooden legs that stretch out long and crippled. Some of them is just legs now, weather and time and shit bleachin' all that wood away.*

Cash slow his purple boat, his right hand on that wheel that look like a racecar. He open up his C-phone and start talkin'. He yellin' into it, tellin' them to "Work 'em. Work 'em."

He flick it shut and turn to JoJo. "My boys seen 'em. They was right down by the causeway and must've got scared. They's runnin' 'em back toward us. Both my boats like two pit bulls."

JoJo smiled. "Hot damn," he said. But then he stopped smilin' when Cash turn the boat toward the bridges headin' out of the city. "They see Nick?"

Cash shook his head. "Just Teddy and some other brother."

"That brother is Dio," you say.

"What?" Cash says, wealth flashin' in his mouth. He starts to laugh.

"Dio ain't dead," you say. "Some rich motherfuckers over in Metairie made him up. He ain't neva real."

"What you mean, not real?" Cash asks, lookin' back. Real concerned now.

"I said that nigga weren't eva real," you say. "This boy Christian just actin' thugged up. They weren't his rhymes, man. He stole them off a dead man he knew in Angola and then made his own self disappear. They schemed all them lost records and shit."

Cash shook his head. "That the boy on the boat?"

"Yeah."

"He got to win the Academy Award," he say. "I even heard folks out in Calliope say they his people."

Bronco reach into a duffel bag and hands JoJo a long, black pistol.

"Teddy know about this?" Cash ask.

You say he did.

"Lord help 'em both," Cash say. "You gonna kill 'em, old man?"

"I kill anyone gets in my way."

"You with him, Tavarius?" Cash ask.

"All the way."

"Y'all just thugs and don't even know it."

Cash lay down the throttle and that long green levee break behind you. Y'all runnin' down a long old railroad bridge crossin' the water.

"The Trestle," JoJo says, to no one in particular.

CHRISTIAN STEERED the boat while Teddy tied Trey's body with thick white rope and wrapped the cord of a ship radio around his neck, letting the heavy transmitter fall to his chest. He duct-taped a big red fire extinguisher to his dead body and pulled the cover of a black pillowcase over his head.

"Goddamn, he wouldn't quit lookin' at me," Teddy said. "You like that, Malcolm?" He started to laugh. "You like that?"

"Yeah, Teddy," Christian said. "Good boy."

I held my place on a backseat, rolling and rocking with the boat. My entire body smeared with my own blood and vomit. Dark maroon stains across my palms.

"Teddy, you remember that time you won the Atlanta game? You scooped up the ball and ran in for a touchdown. We went down to that bar in the Quarter and later on you danced on a table with that midget. You remember that? Man, we had a good time."

I smiled up at him.

He tilted his head at me. His eyes narrowing. "You ain't nothin'."

"I'm your friend. It's Nick."

"Nick?"

He smiled for a moment, eyes softening.

His shape darkened as we headed for the long train bridge—Christian squeezing through the narrow opening—sewing our way under two more long bridges of the old highway and then the interstate twisting north. He smiled as the day softened all pink and gold all the way to the Gulf. Christian running us close to the shore and cursing God for only finding marsh.

We slowed to a chug as he looked for solid ground.

I held out my hand to Teddy.

The smile shut off.

"It's all gone too far," he said.

We were on the far edge of Orleans Parish, the edge of the Bayou Sauvage.

I could smell the foulness of the bayou rot as we moved away from the lake and deeper into the high grass. I'd hunted around here sometime back with JoJo, a place called Blind Lagoon.

I heard the scream of a nutria in the slate-gray-and-pink morning. The swamp rat's bloated body swimming in the high grass, slabs of yellow and brown teeth like a prehistoric animal. Red eyes watching us in the fresh light.

Dawn was here.

Dead cypress silhouetted the landscape like amputated appendages.

As Christian slowly moved into the marsh, engine revving and stopping, revving and stopping, I saw an eagle turn in the sky and hang there for a moment, just riding in the wind that moved him.

72

"AIN'T NOBODY GOING *to get through that mess," JoJo say, lookin' into that smelly-ass swamp. Cash keep the boat back a ways from where Teddy stand on the Scarab. You once wanted that boat but now you want to drill holes in it and watch it sink way down deep into all that brown-green ooze you passin' through.*

You hear the crack of a gun. A bullet spiderwebs the window on Cash's boat.

JoJo pushes you down. Cash yells.

"He's dead," he says. "I should've killed that fat son of a bitch when I got the chance. Goddamn. Shootin' my boat. Man."

He reaches for a big-ass .44 he got kept in a little cover by the steering wheel. "Yeah, that's right." He revs the motor and drifts closer. "Come on, motherfucker. Cash here to play."

Bronco inches down on the side of the boat, his gun aimin' right toward the Scarab.

Y'all drift.

The sound of the cars on the bridges fade away. All you see now is high grass and these tall things that look like bamboo. Ducks. Big funny-lookin' pelicans and shit. The high grass parts and you see an alligator.

You fall down on your face tryin' to get to a corner. It's green and scaly with a knotty back swimmin' away from the boat.

JoJo look at you and kind of laugh. "Bronco? Guess Tavarius don't like gators any better than you."

"I make that motherfucker into a pair of boots."

Cash squeeze off a couple shots and you hear Teddy's boat shoot out, engine revvin' real hard. Cash slam down that throttle and y'all ride, beatin' through the tall grass and sendin' up muck, like some kind of green-ass milk shake, splatterin' behind you.

"Got him," Cash say, laughing. "We got him."

Teddy's boat revving real hard. Smoke shootin' from the engine, whining almost like a scream, but not moving.

CHRISTIAN TRIED to reverse the boat and then run her forward. But nothing would get him untangled from the high grass and mud that clogged the propellers of the engine. I looked back and saw JoJo with Cash in this big, purple Cigarette boat and then Bronco and ALIAS. My eyes wavered and I bent at the waist for a few more dry heaves.

Christian turned to me, seeing the smile form on my face, and plodded back, knocking me in the chest with his fist. I tumbled back into the water, twirling in the bayou, feet sucking deep into the muck, and finally finding the way to air. I swallowed in light and oxygen, brushing reeds away from my face.

He looked down at me. "Push, goddammit. Push us out of this shit."

I moved to the side of the boat, found my fists on the hull loosening, handprints painting brown patterns on the white paint, and pretended to move the boat from the reeds.

Christian revved her motor again and foul-smelling bubbles of marsh gases erupted from deep in the bottom.

Teddy stood over me, his arm extended with his gun. He squeezed off a few in the direction of Cash.

Still, I heard the steady, constant motor of Cash's boat. Chugging. Ready to pounce.

I pretended to push more. My weight not moving a feather.

Teddy disappeared from the stern.

I walked backward in the thick water. The water level coming up to my neck.

I saw a water moccasin glide and curve sideways from the middle of the little lagoon.

Cash hit the engine hard and the long torpedo of boat shot forward hard and fast.

Teddy fired, the glass windshield exploding from Cash's boat.

The boat whooshed by me and collided hard with Teddy's Scarab. A cracking thunderous crash.

I heard two splashes and saw Teddy scrambling into the water, paddling his way to a shore that barely existed. Deeper into the reeds and grasses.

Silence. The engines died.

Yelling.

JoJo jumped in and high-stepped his way to me.

I felt my eyes roll back in my head and I tumbled backward.

He caught me and dragged me to a long flat of mud. My face flush into the gray muck, seeing scattering animals' footprints. The early-morning heat rising in odorous waves from the pile.

I collected myself. Wavered to my feet.

I heard a few more shots.

Two other big purple Cigarette boats ran close to the line of tall grasses. Some of Cash's boys getting up to their waists, guns held high over the water, slogging through. I saw a couple up to their ankles in marsh. Each step taking a grimace from the men, mud and decaying earth sucking them down.

I heard rustling. Grasses shifted near where I stood.

I wandered forward, the heat and sun and loss of blood wrapping the whole earth in a halo.

JoJo yelled for me.

I fell to my knees, sinking up to my elbows and thighs through it all, water and mud covering my face. Losing a boot and pulling off the other one, crawling for the sound through a tunnel of broken reeds, where cloven feet scattered in a labyrinth of high grass.

I tumbled out about thirty yards on the other side.

I stood on a muddy little bank, the bayou holding me up to my knees.

Teddy was stuck, frozen. Birds trilling all around us.

He turned to me. His red shirt muddy and torn. Dirt and mud caked over his face and into his hair. He looked almost comical.

But he wasn't laughing.

His gun hung loose in his hand.

TWO *of Cash's boys haul Dio's ass out of the damned bayou, pulling him out by his neck. Cash stand like some kind of general, shirtless and scarred, on our boat waiting to meet him. He reach down into the water, grab him by his arms, and pull him on board with all of us. Ain't no real sound comin' from nowhere. Just animal sounds and water slapping real low from beneath them bridges. You don't say a word.*

You just walk over with Cash and look down at the man you thought was God.

He look the same but don't seem the same.

He look at you, recognize you know he ain't shit, and then see his eyes jump down to your Superman platinum.

He reach for it and you knock his hand away.

"You just takin' my place," Dio says. "You just like me."

Cash says, "Shut the hell up." He knock him across the mouth with the butt of his gun. Then you hear him cock the motherfucker and hand it to you.

It feel strong and warm in your hand and don't take you but two seconds to aim that bitch right at Dio's heart.

"What's your name?" you say.

"What?"

"What's your name?"

JoJo behind him now and he got his hand out. He got his palm out, waiting for you to lay that steel in his hand.

"Shoot him!" Cash yell. "Shoot. Shoot."

JoJo shake his head on the other side.

"My name is Christian," he says. "Christian Chase." His eyes are green but loose and heavy. He don't show nothin'.

You thumb back the hammer and let it down loose.

You hand that gun to JoJo.

He take it.

Just as you step back, Christian turn and come at Cash with a knife in his hand. He gets that blade right at his face.

But Bronco steps from beside you, grab him at his wrist, and you see the punk drop to his knees and start cryin' like a bitch. The knife fallin' out of his hand.

Cash pick up the knife, look at it, and toss it in the water.

He nod at Bronco.

Bronco nod back at him, their shapes gettin' thrown down on the tops of water in a silver mirror.

A boat pull up beside you and Cash pulls Christian from his feet and throw him in with some of his boys.

"Welcome to the Dirty South, Christian Chase."

Cash smile at y'all from the other boat, throwing you the keys.

They float off and turn, breaking hard in the middle of the bayou and headin' back out into Pontchartrain.

JoJo's hand feel good on your shoulder.

I LOOKED at Teddy frozen in the mud. We didn't exchange words. His eyes watched something beyond my shoulder, maybe a sound he heard, and wavered deep into the marsh that held him.

"Come on."

He stretched the gun out from his arm. His eyes reflected a person I'd never met.

"We all go back to mud," Teddy said, the fat shaking under his chin. Contorting with the emotion in his voice. "My preacher used to tell me and Malcolm that. Told us to be like the mud. That's what we came from. What we all gonna be."

I breathed, smelling the putrid smell of animals and plant life rotting around us in a big compost pile. Bile rose in my throat.

I heard boats buzzing and scattering away out in the bayou.

He pulled the gun back into him. An eagle swooped down and then caught a wave of rising air, shooting quickly back up into the blue sky.

Teddy Paris smiled. "Always knew you could take a joke, Travers."

He slid the gun into his mouth and pulled the trigger.

The hard cracking sound brought a scattering of birds and insects floating off the marsh in a black stream and pinpointed dots that covered the white sun.

I dropped my head, turned, fighting the marsh, and made it halfway back through the grassy tunnel carved by a wild animal.

I crawled to get away from the place I'd seen Teddy slowly disappear into the bayou.

73

THE WORD CAME DOWN *two weeks later that Ninth Ward Records was no more. You thought you was headed right back to Calliope, slidin' right back in with your grandmamma and workin' block parties to feed yourself. But right when you think you broke, you find yourself in New York City. You and Cash got a mack deal with a record company that been around for a hundred years. You see pictures of all them folks that come before you down this long white hall at these tight offices. Jazz women and blues daddies like the old man and Nick listen to. And that's all cool, 'cause you know someday you just gonna be down that same line.*

That new joint you're workin' in New York keepin' you away from the Dirty South. You like seein' your face off buses and bein' thug-lipped over Times Square and it's cool and all meetin' Diddy and LL at some party in the middle of a big park made out of green grass. But somehow you feel like you losin' you. Your rhymes not comin' out the way you feel. The beats you hear sound like someone openin' up a tin can.

You make a call. You on a plane.

You ride onto Canal, cruise uptown, pick up that little honey you'd met at this club with Malcolm Paris back when, and roll down to the Quarter in a white Escalade limo. See how Old School makin' out. You don't need to know. You just wonderin'.

You pay some big man in a straw hat five dollars at the door and see Loretta howlin' a big mess onstage. Man, you ain't never known that woman could sing like that. She got a storm inside her that always seem quiet to you.

Nick behind the bar with some bald black man. JoJo hangin' in the back, leanin' against the wall by the door. He smilin', watchin' his wife and Nick. Kind of takin' it all in. You smile at that, shrug off your mink coat, and order a bottle of Cristal from some little honey waitress. Little Miss you with punch you in the ribs and you laugh till they ask you for ID and say champagne ain't on the menu. And that shit ain't cool.

Loretta keep singin', all wrapped up in some fine-ass green satin. Face all painted up, silk hankie in her hand. "Don't ask me no questions, and I won't tell you no lies."

The music is old. You don't like it. But you can't help but move your feet. 'Cause you been to where it come from and some way you knowin' more about yourself.

Nick come by and say hello to you and your girl in between sets, but a few seconds later, he get called back to the bar to give a mess of folks some more beer. He seems to like poppin' the tops of those Dixies and you thinkin' about grabbin' some while he ain't lookin'.

Your date not hangin' with the scene and disappears back into the bathroom. You tell her to hang. But she want to move on now. She got some girlfriends down at some club that you used to know. Everything in New Orleans change. But still the same.

The old man and you talk about New York and he ask you about some clubs in Harlem that you know ain't even real. He make fun of your mink and them boots you paid a thousand bucks for and you laugh at that. 'Cause that teasin' ain't no disrespect. That ole man like you.

Nick still won't pour you no alcohol and you knock hard on the bathroom tryin' to find the girl. You hear her laughin' inside and you push open the door, findin' her snortin' up off the top of a towel rack with some little white dude.

She don't see you. But you leave her there and walk the Quarter. You got

$2,000 in your pocket, a room at the Monteleone, and a record in the gate just jumpin' for number one.

You sit down at Jackson Square, where you used to make money shinin' shoes, and down past the mall, where you was thrown out for hustlin'. Your mind race over these months. Teddy's ride. Malcolm and you hangin' at the clubs. All the champagne and the way Malcolm treated you. He tellin' you it's family. But he just treatin' you like he treat himself.

Time on your Cartier say you left the bar two hours ago. You thinkin' about the girl, you guess. Ain't no way you thinkin' about Nick and the old man. But they all there. Them doors on Conti closed, houselights on in the bar, and JoJo and him just clearin' up beer bottles into a trash can.

JoJo singin' along to the jukebox.

You knock on the glass.

And Loretta lets you in.

Everyone stops for a while. No money bein' counted. No beer bein' drunk.

Just all y'all sittin' at this little table. Loretta and JoJo. You and Old School. And you laughin' about things that been and some things that JoJo think gonna happen.

That jukebox slows after the last song. Neon and chrome real bright.

Another record slips onto the turntable and finds its groove.

That beat, man. It's old but strong.

You're home.

Epilogue

I STILL TRAVEL the Delta when I find myself lost. I like the feel of the wide expanse of flat brown earth, the clapboard bars with cold beer and greasy pork sandwiches, the tiny white Baptist churches that shake and pulse with religion on Sundays, the barren plantations and forgotten towns where ghosts still live. JoJo and I would meet halfway during our exchanges, most of the time along Interstate 55 down in Vaiden for a chicken-fried steak meal. It was early fall and even just off the interstate, I could smell the leaves burning from the little houses and trailers off the road.

I had a seat in a booth when JoJo walked in and hung up his Carhartt farm coat on a spindly hanger by the door. He slid into the seat, scanned the menu, and tossed it in the center of the table.

"ALIAS didn't care much for this place," I said. "Ordered a cheeseburger."

He laughed. "Maybe he knows something we don't."

"Yeah," I said. "Why wouldn't that surprise me?"

"You seen that new video he got out?" JoJo asked.

"He's doing fine in L.A.," I said. "Asked me to come out and see him."

"You going to?"

"Can you see me in L.A.?"

"He may need you to," he said. "This ain't over. You understand?"

"I do."

"When you side with a man, you keep on."

"Yes, sir."

"If not, you ain't no better than Teddy."

I looked out at the trucks lining up to hit the interstate. On the side of a trailer, someone had painted the image of three cowboys running cattle in a wide open prairie. The fall sun struck the painting as it turned and elevated up on the high road heading north.

"What made him sick in the mind?" JoJo asked.

"I don't want to talk about it."

"You're mad at yourself, but you always knew it," he said.

I nodded. We ate the chicken-fried steak and drank coffee, talking more about ALIAS, two new hands JoJo had hired on the farm, the team I helped coach at JFK, and the possibility of getting Buddy Guy to play a small show during Jazzfest.

"Meet you back here in ten days," he said. "Same time."

I nodded.

"You quit teaching," he said. "Didn't you?"

"Tulane hired a Harvard professor to replace Randy," I said. "He wanted me to expand upon theories of the blues and intercultural dimensions of the framework of the South."

"That's a lot of thought about blues."

"Tell me about it," I said. "I can do what I do on my own. And the bar is working right now."

JoJo laughed. "Blues ain't nothin' but a botheration on your mind."

"I've heard that."

We shook hands and I watched his old truck stop before heading south to New Orleans. I thought I heard some pounding bass work and bounce coming from his cab. I tried to listen harder but JoJo pulled out onto the road and the music followed.

I shook my head.

I drove as far as Batesville. If I turned west, I'd head to Clarksdale, where Willie T. Dean wanted to meet. He said he had the most unbelievable lead on the best bluesman I never heard of. True Willie T. Always the next adventure.

I stopped at Highway 6 and instead headed east. The sun sank down behind me, swallowing the road and disappearing into the Delta.

I took a shortcut off 6 and wound down through a cypress swamp where men in small boats drank beer and fished with cane poles, the misty blue-and-yellow light filling the cab of my truck, where Annie slept on the rear seat. A bone tucked under her paw.

The fall sky was slate blue and gray when I arrived at the dented silver mailbox and turned along a long gravel road. The small white clapboard house waited, draped in big ceramic Christmas lights. Maggie's truck parked sideways by a propane tank. Her cotton shirts, faded blue jeans, and her son's jerseys riffled in the wind.

I parked alongside of her truck. The red, green, and yellow lights warming up the chill.

Annie and I followed a stone path as the door opened, an old screen door slamming shut from a rusted spring.

Maggie tucked her hands into her jeans and shrugged her shoulders in a tight black T-shirt. The summer tan still coloring her face and long arms. Wind sifting her black hair across her eyes.

She reached down a hand and pulled me up onto the porch.

The crossroads were far behind me.